Deeply Examined
A Dark Medical Romance

Lexi Davis

The story, all names, characters, and incidents portrayed in this production are fictitious. No identification with actual persons (living or deceased), places, buildings, and products is intended or should be inferred.

Book Covers by Hayley Gallant, The Author Buddy, 100 Covers.

Character art by: Lorena@Chocological.art, Hungrydamy (ETSY), and Irdeinfierno

Copyediting by Dymond and Associates

Copyright © 2025 by Lexi Davis

All rights reserved. No part of this publication may be reproduced, distributed, or transmitted in any form or by any means, including photocopying, recording, or other electronic or mechanical methods, without the prior written permission of the author, except for the use of brief quotations in articles or book reviews and as permitted by U.S. copyright law.

ISBN (eBook) Book One 979-8-9903958-8-6

ISBN (eBook) Book Two 979-8-9903958-9-3

ISBN (eBook) Book Three 979-8-9925298-0-7

ISBN (eBook) Book Completed 979-8-9925298-1-4

ISBN (Paperback photo cover) Book Completed 979-8-9925298-2-1

ISBN (Paperback discrete cover) Book Completed 979-8-9925298-3-8

Contents

Foreword	1
Dedication/Playlist	2
1. Chapter 1	5
2. Chapter 2	15
3. Chapter 3	22
4. Chapter 4	29
5. Chapter 5	37
6. Chapter 6	51
7. Chapter 7	54
8. Chapter 8	62
9. Chapter 9	73
10. Chapter 10	84
11. Chapter 11	96
12. Chapter 12	117
13. Chapter 13	125
14. Chapter 14	139
15. Chapter 15	145

16.	Chapter 16	154
17.	Chapter 17	171
18.	Chapter 18	184
19.	Chapter 19	186
20.	Chapter 20	204
21.	Acknowledgments	215

Foreword

TRIGGER WARNINGS/AUTHOR NOTE (CONTAINS SPOILERS)

Please check trigger warnings. Your mental health is important to me. Please understand this is a work of FICTION. In real life, I would NEVER EVER condone a person in a position of authority, such as a doctor, engaging in a sexual relationship with their patient. If you have medical trauma, especially from OB/GYN events/experiences, please don't read this book as it may be triggering. It's never my intention to make a reader feel uncomfortable. One of the reasons I love writing romance is because it gives readers a safe way of exploring taboo topics and of pushing boundaries. It's totally okay if this is not for you. XOXO, Lexi

Explicit language, child abuse recounted (happened in the past), explicit sexual content, violence (beating), bondage, dubious consent (DubCon), dominance, manipulation/coercion, stalking, public sex, foreign object penetration, medical play kink.

Dedication/Playlist

Dedication: For all the women who love a sexy villain with—or without—a redemption arc.

***

"Darling, I'm a nightmare dressed like a daydream."
–Taylor Alison Swift

***

CONNECT ON SOCIAL MEDIA—LET'S BE FRIENDS
Instagram, TikTok, Facebook: @authorlexidavis

***

Playlist

<u>Deeply Examined playlist available on Spotify</u>

Fall for me-Sleep Token
Healing-Kygo and Jonas brothers
Milk in the morning-Powfu, Jomie & Zaini
Don't you give up on me yet- Jonah kagen
Gateway drug-Daniel Seavey
American girl-Nessa Barrett
Panoramic View-AWOLNATION
Where's my love-SYML
Deep Blue-the midnight
Wolves- Selena Gomez and Marshmello
Someone to love-Christian French
If I killed someone for you – Alec Benjamin
Heaven- Julia Michaels

Remember that night-Sara Kays

Don't blame me-Taylor Swift

Up at night- Stephen Dawes

Cigarette- Alfie Jukes

Constellations-Jade LeMac

Die First - Nessa Barrett

https://open.spotify.com/playlist/11rmN2pPmCK1sBnEPbuzm0?si=IkwKHAwGQJSBgt6IG_M1dA

Chapter One

Jessica

I'm naked the first time I meet him. Wearing only a flimsy paper gown, I shiver under the relentless blast of air conditioning. He walks in, broad-shouldered, effortlessly confident, the most handsome man I've ever seen.

At first, his back is to me as he closes the door with a soft, deliberate click. All I can see is thick, midnight-dark hair, catching the fluorescent light like strands of polished ink. Then he turns, and a jolt shoots through me, sharp and startling, like static electricity crackling across my skin. My breath stutters. My stomach tightens, a reaction I can't control.

He's over six feet tall, slightly older than me but not yet gray-haired or wrinkled. A sharp, square jaw with a divot in the chin—one that would make Superman jealous. Full lips, smooth and unchapped. And his eyes...

Flat. Cool. The color of storm clouds. Looking into them, I see nothing but the reflection of myself.

When those mirror-ball eyes meet mine, he freezes, just for a fraction of a second, so short I must have imagined it.

Adam

One second, it's just another patient chart. The next, I'm staring at my past.

It starts when I walk into exam room six and see her.

Jessica Jones.

My high school crush. Or, let's be honest, my obsession.

I used to watch her from across the lunchroom, in the hallways, by her locker, which was six down from mine. I'd memorized her schedule, carefully adjusting my route to be close to her. Back then, I studied the way she moved, every flick of her hair, every soft laugh that curled around my ribcage and stayed there. I'd been so focused, hellbent on getting into the university of my dreams. Nothing could distract me from my goals.

Except *her*.

Almost fifteen years have passed, and she hasn't changed a bit. Same gorgeous face, long honey-blonde hair, big green eyes, and slender body. I remember how she was always laughing with her friends, oblivious to the guy who watched from the shadows, wanting her so badly it ached. The last time I saw her, she was wearing her cheerleader uniform with its short ruffled skirt that showed off the rounded flesh of her ass when she bent over.

Late at night, I used to jerk off to the thought of that sight.

Shit. Sometimes I still do.

I freeze for a split second, waiting. Wondering if she'll recognize me the same way I recognize her.

But of course she doesn't.

I might have been a senior and she was a freshman, but it didn't matter. I was a loser nerd in secondhand clothing, invisible unless someone needed test answers. And she was *the* popular girl. We lived in different worlds.

Things have changed now. With the rigor of medical training, I had no time to eat, so I lost weight, shed twenty pounds of fat and replaced it with twenty pounds of pure lean muscle.

Now women chase *me*. Beg for *me*. Worship *me*.

I give her another moment to look me over, to see if she remembers.

Nothing.

Jessica stares without a flicker of recognition. No hesitation. No tilt of her head, searching for my name. It's like I'm a stranger.

A sharp pang hits my chest, unexpected and unwelcome.

I bury it instantly.

She doesn't recognize me?

Good.

Let's keep it that way.

Praying she won't remember the name, I introduce myself.

Jessica

"I'm Dr. West," he intones, his voice deep and rich, like whiskey poured over ice.

"What can I do for you today, Ms. Jones?" He's looking at my chart now, long tapered fingers flip slowly through the pages.

"Oh, er." I command my brain to stop its wild scrambling, but I'm so overwhelmed by the man that it takes a long minute to answer. "My physical," I say finally. "I'm here for my annual exam."

"Is that so?" he asks.

"Yes. That's it. Just a routine exam," I confirm with a nod.

"Hmm." A noncommittal hum from him. The sound reverberates through my body.

He stalks closer, and I swallow nervously. Before, I was freezing, but now I'm suddenly hot. The warmth starts low in my stomach and spreads until it reaches my fingertips and toes.

Cold eyes flick over the thin paper gown that I clutch closed against my chest. They move down to my bare thighs, which are crossed one over the other.

"Spread your legs."

"Ex-excuse me?" I stammer, taken back by his abruptness.

"I said, spread your legs," he enunciates slowly. "I have to get out the stirrups." He gestures to where I sit, to the stirrups folded into their designated slots in the exam table under me.

"Oh! Yes, of course." I lift my legs and hold them out to each side.

Great, now he thinks I'm stupid.

Dr. West bends low to pull out the stirrups and unfold them. Small pieces of white fabric are on each end, where my feet will go, almost like the stirrups are wearing socks. I stare at the scraps of fabric, perplexed.

He follows my gaze. "To protect your feet from the cold metal."

"That's thoughtful. Thanks." I place my bare feet with their sparkly red painted toes into each side and scoot closer to the edge.

"Your comfort is my utmost concern," he drawls. I think he's teasing, but I'm not sure.

"Lean back."

I slide down until I'm lying flat on cool paper that crinkles beneath me.

He looms at the end of the table and stares at me, his expression unreadable.

"Good," he declares after a pause. He disappears, and there's the squeaking of rolling wheels. Earlier, I'd noticed a small white stool in the corner of the room. I assume he's moving that over to me now. I expect him to sit, but he doesn't.

Instead, there's the sound of splashing water and the ripping of paper towels. I crane my head to see his back to me as he washes his hands. He wears a long white lab coat over dark blue scrubs. Even through all that material I can see the powerful muscles of his shoulders ripple with every motion.

God, he's hot, I think, followed quickly by, *why does he have to be so hot? That just makes this even more uncomfortable.*

The truth is, I *hate* getting my annual exam. I should have done it months ago, but I'd put it off, dreading the indignity and discomfort of it. I hate how you have to get completely naked. I hate how invaded I feel afterward.

Calm down, I tell myself. *You have to do this.* The last thing I want is to miss some terrible diagnosis because I was too chicken to go to the doctors. Between my low salary as a high school teacher and the medical bills from when my parents died, there's not much left in my bank account. If I got sick and had to take time off, I'm not sure I could cover my rent.

Lost in these thoughts, I jump, startled, when Dr. West reappears next to me. Without a word, he peels back the front of my gown, releasing my naked breasts. My hands fly up to cover my nipples, which are peaked from the cold air washing over them and maybe also from the handsome doctor.

He pulls my hands away and lays them down along my sides.

"Breast exam," he says gruffly.

Oh.

Now I feel like such a dummy. Of course that's why he's looking at my chest with those strange eyes.

His hands are slightly wet when they clamp around my right breast, the one closest to him. Slowly, with both hands, he kneads the tissue in a clockwise direction, and it feels good, like a massage. The rhythm relaxes my body until I sink fully into the upholstered tabletop. I let out a sigh allowing my head to loll. Once he's done on the right, he crosses over to my left side and repeats the motion of palpating my breast slowly and thoroughly. I watch through my lashes as his eyes follow the path of fingers. He's concentrating, a small furrow in his brow.

"Do you do this?" he asks, without looking up. "Touch yourself?"

My eyes fly open. "What?"

"Do a self-exam? Have you noticed any lumps? Anything out of the ordinary?"

"Oh." I relax back onto the table and answer his question. "No. I mean, yes, I do self-exams, but no, I haven't felt anything abnormal."

"Where do you do it?"

"Do what? The self-exam?"

He nods, his warm hands moving over my skin.

"Usually in the shower, when I'm washing." His fingers move closer to my nipples, lightly brushing them with each rotation. My breath catches, sputters. That feels a little too good. It feels...arousing. I clear my throat and try to distract myself. "Is that okay? To do it in the shower? I thought I read that somewhere."

"It's fine," he answers and pinches my nipple, hard.

I yelp, rocketing into a half-sitting position, with my upper body supported on bent elbows.

Dr. West puts a large hand on my shoulder and forces me down. "I have to examine your nipples to eliminate any subareolar masses."

"Of course." My cheeks heat with a blush.

Why did I overreact?

"I'm sorry. I was surprised, that's all."

He doesn't answer. He rolls my nipple between his thumb and index finger, watching as he does it. There must be a nerve in my breast that communicates directly with my vagina because every time he squeezes my nipple it sets off an ache between my legs.

Crap. I'm getting turned on. This is so embarrassing.

He places one hand on each breast and cups them, gathering and lifting the rounded globes. Then he drags his palms across from bottom to top. Every time he touches my erect and sensitive nipples, it feels good, exquisite actually. Each brush of his skin against mine heightens a needy emptiness between my legs. I struggle to control my breathing, which has sped up, coming in short soft bursts. When Dr. West flicks the tip of my nipple with his fingernail, I can't contain my gasp. My eyes fly up to him, and I open my mouth to apologize. To explain away my unprofessional response—but maybe he didn't notice it because he appears unfazed. His expression is cool and calm.

"Your breasts look good. I don't feel anything worrisome," he says.

"That's a relief," I answer, watching as he pulls bright-green latex gloves out of a box on the counter. He puts them on and straightens each one.

My phone buzzes next to me, where I left it. I glance over at it and grimace when I see the name "Brad" flashing on the screen. A quick tap silences the noise.

Dr. West is staring at me with one eyebrow raised and his foot impatiently tapping.

"Sorry," I mumble. Warmth climbs my cheeks. He must think I'm so rude.

Without responding, he takes a seat on the stool and presses the back of his hands against my inner knees to open my legs wide. I stare at the ceiling, mortified. I got wet down there when he was touching my breasts, and I'm sure he can see it.

Should I say something? Is he going to say something?

Dr West drags a silver, long-necked lamp to him and turns on the light. He adjusts it until it's directly pointed at my exposed core. I close my eyes against the glare. Warmth from the lamp washes over my inner thighs and across my pelvis.

"You're going to feel my touch now," Dr. West warns in his low baritone.

I feel his finger run along my seam from the back to the front, bumping up against my clitoris at the end of the stroke. I suck in a breath at the fireworks that result. He repeats the motion, and I open to him like a flower. I swear I hear an appreciative murmur, but I must have imagined it, because when I open my eyes to peer down Dr. West's face remains an expressionless mask.

He separates me with another back-and-forth motion, rubbing his finger deeper into me. Now he's breached my inner folds. He brushes across the opening of my vagina and then uses the tip of his finger to slowly circle that inner ring. It feels amazing. I'm already wet so his touch glides effortlessly. He runs along the rim several more times as I resist the urge to push down toward him. I want more of this sensation. I want his fingers inside of me. I want his dick inside of me—*wait*! What am I thinking? This is my *doctor*. I shouldn't be having these ideas about him.

If only he weren't so attractive.

As if he heard my inner turmoil, Dr. West fulfills my secret desire. He slips into my opening, just an inch, and then withdraws it.

I whimper. I can't help it. The sound just comes out of me, but it's quiet and I hope he didn't hear. My next whimper is louder when, in one smooth thrust, Dr West shoves all the way in. He holds it there, rotating it around.

"I'm palpating the back wall of your vagina," he says.

"Mmm-hmm," is all I can manage.

He moves his finger, pulling it almost all the way out before pushing it back in.

I try to hold still, but it's hard not to lift my pelvis toward his touch. My heart rate picks up, along with my breathing. I curl my hands into fists by my sides and bite back the moan that climbs my throat.

A second finger joins the first, stretching me. He swirls his fingers around and then pushes even deeper than before. My pelvis rises to meet him. I can't control it. His other hand comes to rest on my pubic bone. With his palm he pushes down, holding me in place. His fingers dangle, brushing against my clit, which is swollen with desire. In this position, he holds me prisoner. One hand stimulates my clit while the other pumps into me, over and over again.

My muscles tense as an orgasm builds slowly in my center. I bite my lip and attempt to take my mind off what he's doing by counting the ceiling tiles. This is so humiliating. I can't orgasm on my doctor's fingers.

That's not who I am.

I'm a good girl.

The regular kind.

Not the hot, sexy kind.

My effort to distract myself fails when he applies his thumb to a grinding circle on my clit. My back arches off the table, and I groan. I've been examined before, but never like this. It feels *so* good. Better than anything my previous boyfriends have done. Maybe it's because he understands anatomy that Dr. West seems to know exactly the right amount of pressure and where to apply it.

My hips buck against the weight of his hand. He adds a third finger, filling me up in the most delicious way. His hands coordinate, one pushing into my drenched pussy and the other rubbing hard against my clit.

"Oh, my god," I wheeze in a whisper. I lift my head to see that he's staring at my core, his features smooth as if he doesn't notice the way I'm responding to his touch.

He picks up the pace, and my orgasm builds until my entire body is trembling. I try to hold it back, but the sensation is overwhelming. My nerve endings sizzle. My muscles pull taut. My mouth drops open as I gasp for air.

He cocks a finger inside me, and I orgasm, my back bowing off the table. Waves of pleasure bathe me, running from my head to my toes. I bite my lip so hard to keep from crying out that I taste the sharp tang of blood.

Dr. West rides the orgasm out, still moving his fingers in a way that's almost painful with how overstimulated I am down there. The motion extends my orgasm even longer. Finally, he slows and then pulls his hands away. I slump, boneless and trembling, against the hard table.

My eyes track him as he walks over to the trash can and pulls off his gloves, which glisten with my arousal. He steps on the foot pedal, and the lid pops open. With a flick of his wrist, the gloves go flying into the can.

Adam

I shove my hands into the pockets of my white lab coat so she can't see how they tremble.

My god.

It happened. I just got off Jessica Jones using nothing more than my hands. Teenage me is doing cartwheels. Talk about a bucket list item I never thought I'd get to complete. I'll always remember the hushed sound of her moans, the pink on her cheeks, the way she rolled her head from side to side as she orgasmed. I'm going to be jerking off to this for the rest of my mother-fucking life.

She wasn't the first patient to get turned on when I examined them. It's a normal physiological response. Sure, maybe it's more common in my patients since I'm decent looking, but it's not unheard of for any doctor. Usually when a patient acts that way, I try a different technique or end the exam early. With patients who repeatedly have that response to me, I transfer their care to another doctor. I take my responsibility, my position of power as a physician, seriously. I never lose control of the situation. *Never*.

But this was different. *She* was different. That single little whimper told me she wasn't just tolerating my exam—she was enjoying it. That sound had lit a fire in my veins. I wanted to hear it again. I wanted to push her, see how far I could get her to go. I never thought it would be all the way. Never thought she'd actually come.

This is a dangerous game I'm playing. Reckless. My job is the one thing I care about in my entire godforsaken life, the only thing I feel good about. I can't risk it, even for her. The medical board wouldn't look too kindly on that little interaction that just occurred. I can only imagine how awkward my deposition will be when she sues me for sexual misconduct.

Lawyer: Dr. West, were you aware the patient was becoming aroused?
Me: Yes, I was.
Lawyer: What did you do to stop it?
Me: Deliberately stroked her clit because for the past decade I've been dying to know what Jessica Jones sounds like when she comes.

Yeah, no thanks. As much as I might like the well-equipped gyms they have in prison, orange isn't my color.

Right before I leave the room, angling my body so she can't see the bulge in my pants, a nasty thought occurs to me. What if she's doing this with other men? Back in the day, she had a constant stream of guys after her. Who wouldn't want to date someone as pretty as she is?

The flash of possessiveness I experience is so strong that I have a sudden urge to take her home and chain her up. I could turn on the alarm system. Lock all the doors and keep the key so she could never get out. Keep her as my little pet forever.

What a strange thought.

I have many lovers, most of whom enjoy the same proclivities I do, but I have a rule to never see the same woman more than twice. I don't do relationships. Just the word makes me shudder.

Jessica eyes me warily, probably wondering if I'm going to mention what just happened.

I won't, though. Too awkward for both her and for me.

Refusing to meet her eyes, I look down and scribble nonsense in her chart to buy myself time to think. It's a good thing she won't be back for another year, I decide. By that time, it won't seem odd that a different doctor has been assigned to her. Not me. As fun as this trip down memory lane has been, it's better for us both if I never see Jessica Jones again.

I turn back to her with my most bland, most professional smile. "The nurse will call you with your blood work results within two weeks. It was a pleasure to meet you, Ms. Jones. Have a good life."

Have a good life, really? Way to make things weird.

A single flash of her baffled expression before I close the door behind me, sealing her out.

Forever.

Chapter Two

Jessica

The next week passes in a blur. My dreams are full of gray eyes and warm hands. Twice I give in to temptation and masturbate to the thought of him, once in the shower using my hand-held sprayer set on high and once under the sheets with my pink vibrator. Both times, I call out his name when I come. It's ridiculous. I don't even know his first name, so I scream, "Dr. West. Yes! Oh, my god, Dr. West," as I orgasm.

Maybe I am sick, but sick in the mind rather than the body.

When my phone rings on Saturday morning with the name of his office on the screen, I have to check twice to make sure I'm not hallucinating.

Is he calling me?

My knee jiggles with nervous excitement as I accept the call.

It's not him—of course it's not.

"Ms. Jones," his secretary says, her voice rushed and shaky. "We're so sorry, but we made a mistake when we booked your appointment—*I* made a mistake, actually. I should have put you down for an annual exam with pap smear, but I left off the pap. I checked and your last one was three years ago. You're overdue."

"Oh, I had no idea."

"Dr. West has a last-minute cancellation today at noon. I know that doesn't give you a lot of time. Can you make it?"

Pretty sure I'm the only woman in the world who heard they needed a pap smear and responded with a shiver that's more excitement than anxiety. The doctor-patient relationship is supposed to be professional, sterile, detached. And yet, here I am not dreading this visit. I'm *eager*. I tell myself it's for my health, but the sick truth is I'm secretly hoping it's for more than that.

"Yes," I agree immediately. "I'll be there."

This is it. I'm going to see him again.

By the time my appointment arrives, I'm a bundle of nerves and anticipation. Inside the exam room, I strip quickly and pull on the scratchy paper gown. My movements are so jerky that I rip a small hole in the paper, right over my breast.

Why am I so clumsy?

My phone jangles next to me, ringing its chime that means I've gotten a text message. Hoping it's not Brad harassing me again, I peer down at it.

Sarah: Did you hear back yet?

Jessica: Lol. Chill. I just put in my application yesterday.

Sarah: So that's a no??

Jessica: No. Not yet.

Sarah: I'm just excited. Once you get to NYC, we can hang all the time. Go on double dates. Finally meet our Mr. Rights.

Jessica: I know. I can't wait.

Sarah: You won't miss Chicago?

Jessica: Hate to leave my students, but that's about it. Nothing else is keeping me here.

Sarah: Assistant Principal Jessica Jones sounds pretty great.

Jessica: It really does. Hey, I'm at the doctor's. I'll call you later?

Sarah: Okay! Love you.

Jessica: You too.

I'm smiling as I place the phone back on the table, next to my thigh. Sarah's my cousin, but we grew up more like sisters. Both only children, we lived blocks away from each other until eighth grade, when her family moved to New York. Even with the distance between us, we've stayed close, talking regularly and visiting a couple times a year.

Ever since my parents died when I was in high school, she's begged me to move out to her, but I've said no, hesitant to leave Chicago, the only place I've ever known. The place that still holds so many memories of my mom and dad. I thought I'd live here all my life. That I'd find the right guy, settle down, and raise a family, just like my parents did, but the years have flown by and, although I've had lots of boyfriends, none of them have stuck. Now, I'm in my late twenties, surrounded by friends with children of their own. The truth is that it's been hard watching everyone move ahead without me, embracing their adult lives, while I've been left standing out in the cold. At this point, I'm losing hope that my soulmate will ever show up.

The door swings open, and my head snaps toward it, expecting to see *him* walk in. I'm disappointed to find it's not Dr. West but his super-attractive nurse. She's blonde and curvy and does the top three buttons of her shirt really need to be unbuttoned? Jealousy claws at my stomach.

Stop it, I admonish myself. Dr. West isn't mine. I'm not even sure what went on the last time I was here, but it definitely didn't mean anything. So what if he'd given me the best orgasm of my life without even taking off his clothing? That didn't make us boyfriend and girlfriend. I had no right to be envious of his nurse.

But still, I wonder what exactly *is* their relationship? Is he using those magic fingers on her too?

She smiles brightly and says, "I'm here to get your vital signs, Ms. Jones." Her shirt rustles as she moves to my side and pulls a blood-pressure cuff off the wall. I read the name tag clipped to her sheer blouse. *Nurse T. Jensen,* it reads. While I'm staring at the tag, it's impossible not to notice how the buttons of her shirt strain against her enormous chest. She must be a double-D bra.

I glance down at my own unimpressive B-cups and feel depressed. Why would Dr. West want someone like me when he works next to *her* all day long?

She attaches the blood-pressure cuff high on my arm and sets her stethoscope in her ears. When she inflates the cuff, it squeezes my arm painfully. I suck in a hiss of pain, wondering if she's doing it on purpose. Is it possible that she's as threatened by me as I am by her? That can't be it, right?

I'm going crazy. The strange encounter with Dr. West last time has officially driven me insane.

After she finishes with the blood pressure, Nurse Jensen takes my temperature and attaches a clip to my finger to make sure I'm getting enough oxygen.

Once that's done, she tells me, "The doctor will be in shortly." Her hips swish as she exits the room.

I'm left alone, shivering on the hard table, because, once again, the air conditioning is turned on high. I lay back and wrap my arms over my chest to shield myself from the blast of Arctic air.

Time stretches out. I hear voices in the hallway, but they fade away. Footsteps pause outside the door, but no one comes in. A phone rings faintly, probably in the lobby at the front desk. This is taking forever. The longer I wait, the more I begin to worry.

What if Dr. West had to leave for an emergency and they've assigned a different doctor?
What if he's cold to me and barely touches me?
What if he's disgusted by me and how I acted last time?

Adam

It's my lunch break. I should eat but instead I'm staring at a photo.

Black and white, grainy with age.

It's from my high-school yearbook. I searched through box after box in the back of my closet after the visit from *her*, Jessica. For a minute I'd had a rising sense of panic. I'd been worried I threw the damn thing out. It would make sense, really—I hated that yearbook and all the memories it contained. Luckily, I was lazy and never bothered to get rid of it. I found it finally in an old moth-eaten suitcase I'd bought from a thrift store when I was a broke-ass college kid.

The spine cracked with a loud *snap* when I opened the dusty book. I'd flipped through it, confirming what I'd remembered—that Jessica Jones was on practically every page. There she was leading the freshman welcome rally. There she was, class treasurer, posing with the Student Council. She was feeding the homeless, teaching kids to read, walking rescue dogs during after-school outreach programs.

So shiny I can't look away from her.

Like the obsessive asshole that I am, I brought the yearbook with me to work today, so I can page through it during this time off. The same way I'd looked at it every night since that odd appointment with Jessica. The one where she—*nope*. Not thinking about that, a promise I've broken every day so far with my dick in my hand.

There's a knock on my door. I blow out an annoyed sigh, exhaling sharply through my nose. My staff knows not to bother me during this rare thirty minutes of alone time.

I bark out a harsh, "Come in."

Hayley, the new front office assistant, creeps in like she's walking into a minefield.

Another burst of irritation. My staff respect me, some even like me, but they're also scared of me. I'm strict, rigidly professional, and quite frankly, never any fun.

Dr. Benedict, one of my partners, gives each staff member a ribbon-topped mason jar of homemade snack mix for Christmas. She hand writes thank you notes, with personal details inside. I give them each a crisp one-hundred-dollar bill. My gift cost at least eighty dollars more than hers, but they always clasp the jars and notes like they're cherished heirlooms versus the stiff nods and forced smiles I got in return for the cold, hard cash. I don't get it. Do they not understand basic economics?

No matter. I'm not in the market for friends.

Just an efficiently run medical office.

"What is it?" I ask Hayley with a scowl.

She wrings her hands like they're wet dishcloths, and she needs to squeeze them dry, "I—I'm so sorry, Dr West. I made a mistake."

"What?"

"There was a patient…I should have scheduled her for an annual with pap, but I only put her down as an annual. You saw her earlier this week."

Foreboding stirs. My stomach does a nauseating flip flop. "Which patient?"

"Ms. Jones, sir."

I hate it when she calls me sir. I'm in my early thirties, hardly a relic.

"Doctor." I correct automatically.

Her face burns red, "Sorry…doctor."

I return to staring at Jessica's photo. Distracted by long blond hair in a high ponytail, I absently tell Hayley, "Reschedule Ms. Jones with Dr. Benedict whenever her first available appointment is. It's okay if it's a few weeks from now." I don't look up, assuming she hears the dismissal in my tone.

"Um…I can't sir—doctor."

Running out of patience, I slam the yearbook closed and spit out, "why not?"

"Because she's in exam room six. You had a cancellation, so I put her in the spot."

The air shifts, grows thick, suffocating. My grip tightens around the yearbook, the brittle spine cracking beneath my fingers. My pulse hammers at the base of my throat.

She's here.

My expression must be thunderous because Hayley squeaks out a quick, "I'm sorry! Did I do the wrong thing? I figured you'd want her back as soon as possible."

I open my mouth to yell at her, so she never makes such a stupid mistake again when her words hit me.

Want her back.

Fuck. She's right.

I *do* want Jessica to come back so I can see her. Not this unsatisfying black-and-white image. No, I want the full color real life woman, warm and soft and moaning.

This is the worst idea I've ever had.

"I'll be there in a minute," I mutter, reopening the yearbook. It automatically flips to Jessica's class picture. I've looked at it so often, the spine at that page is bent into submission.

I can do this. I can see her without losing my shit.

If only I could convince myself I don't like Jessica. That I hate her. That I resent her. But hate shouldn't feel like this. Hate shouldn't make my skin burn at the thought of her body under mine. Hate shouldn't have me gripping the edge of my desk, trying to breathe through the memory of how soft she looked that day in my office.

Come on. Hate her.

I take another look at the yearbook. Twenty-three pages she's on.

Jessica, always Jessica.

Smiling. Perfect. Untouched by the world.

And then there's me. A single, forgettable square on one lonely page. No clubs. No teams. No adoring captions. A nonentity in the background of her shining, golden existence.

I don't remember my classmates. But I remember her.

I tell myself it's resentment that churns in my gut. That it's injustice, not obsession, twisting my grip around the worn leather cover. That it's the discrepancy—the overwhelming presence of *her* and the absence of *me*—that makes my jaw tighten.

That's the only reason I keep that penny in my nightstand drawer.

The one she dropped in the parking lot back in high school. The one I picked up. The one I've packed and unpacked through college, medical school, residency, bringing it along with me every time I've moved like some pathetic memento of a past I should have burned a long time ago.

I should throw it away.

I should throw *her* away.

But first, I need to strip her of the illusion of perfection. Of everything that made her special. Everything that made her so much better than me.

I need to see her the way I saw her last week—unraveled, helpless. At *my* mercy.

Yes. That's the new reality. The new status quo.

This time, I'm in control.

This time, she'll see me. She'll feel me. And this time—when I've taken everything she once held above me—maybe then, finally, I'll get her out of my system. I'll be free.

A knock pulls me from these dark thoughts.

Nurse Jensen, my partner's wife, steps in with paperwork for me to sign. "What do you have going on tonight, West?"

"The usual. Work out. Trade stocks. Read. Go to bed," I say truthfully.

She rolls her eyes, well aware of my routine. She's been trying to set me up with her single friends for years. "You need a wife, or at least a girlfriend," she scolds, crossing her arms over her ample bosom.

A flashback to high school, the bathroom by the gym. My face pushed into the toilet. How the girls snickered when I walked out with my hair dripping wet, covered in shit. I could've fought back, but I didn't. By that time, I'd realized I couldn't get kicked out of any more schools. I needed to bend if I wanted to achieve my goals. Still, it lingered to this day. The gleeful sound of them laughing at me. "I don't need a wife or anyone else."

She shakes her head, looking at me with something close to pity. "Everyone needs someone, and those little fuck bunnies you spend one night with don't count."

I shrug, tired of this conversation. We've discussed this topic many times before. "I have needs, and my needs are met. Now, if you'll excuse me, I have a patient to see."

I stand, straightening my coat. Time to put an end to this.

To her hold over me.

To my fucking weakness.

I push open the door and go to exam room six.

Chapter Three

Jessica

By the time he finally enters, I'm a mess of anxiety and insecurity.

"Ms. Jones." He gives me a nod, his expression unreadable.

Uh-oh. Is he angry, upset, or, worst of all, doesn't care?

He looks over my vital signs the nurse wrote down.

"Have you been continuing your self-exams at home?" he asks.

An image of me screaming into my pillow with my vibrator between my legs flashes through my mind.

"Yes, doctor," I answer.

"Good," he says, and I feel a twinge of pride. I'm not sure why, but I want his approval.

He moves toward me and explains, "Today we're going to do a speculum exam so I can get your pap smear done. Do you know what that is?" He gestures to a metal tray that's been pulled up to the side of my table. A long sheet of paper towels are draped over the top of it, so I haven't been able to see what the tray contains. With an efficient movement, he whips it off, revealing a variety of jars, Q-tips, and swabs. A large silver speculum sits on the tray. It's bigger than any I've seen before, with its long neck secured by screws.

Dr. West picks it up and holds it out before me. The overhead lights reflect off its shiny surface.

"Yes, I've had that done before," I answer.

He frowns at that, the expression fleeting. "I doubt you've been examined as deeply as I'm going to do. I need to take a good look today."

I shouldn't feel excited by those words. It's so wrong, yet somehow I am. "Okay," I agree breathlessly.

Dr. West unfolds the stirrups, and I place my heels into them. Without warning, he grasps my hips and drags me down to him. He pulls me so that my butt almost hangs off the table. Like the last time, he turns on the bright light and directs its beam at the space between my legs. The wheels squeak when he takes a seat on the rolling stool.

"Let's see what we have going on here," he says. I watch him apply a thin layer of lubricant to the speculum.

"Drop your knees to the sides," he commands.

I do as he asks, letting my legs fall open. A wave of lamp-warmed air hits my core, which is already damp. Moisture has been pooling there ever since he walked into the room.

This time, when his fingers separate me, I can feel the warmth of his skin through his gloves. It's surprising, so I jump slightly.

"Hold still," he admonishes.

"I'm sorry, doctor."

His fingers have moved deeper. They are probing, sliding along my folds, searching for my opening. It feels divine to have him touch me again. My head drops back with a sigh.

He gives a small grunt of satisfaction when he finds what he wants. He slips a finger inside of me and works it around, stretching me out. It's wrong to enjoy his touch like this. I try to ignore how it turns me on. I try not to moan, but it's impossible.

He's a lightning rod, and I'm the lightning. I can't help being attracted to him.

Suddenly his finger is gone.

I want to cry from the loss of it.

"I'm putting in the speculum now. You're going to have a sensation of fullness."

Surprisingly gently, Dr. West eases the cold metal into my channel. It's so big, it's uncomfortable. I tense against it, my muscles going rigid.

"Relax. Let me in," he says, his voice stern.

There's a clicking sound as he opens the speculum even wider. I do my best to hold still, but it's unpleasant. The stretching sensation is bordering on painful. Just when I think I can't take it, he cranks the device open even farther.

"Ow," I complain.

Dr. West looks up. "Does it hurt?"

I don't want him to think I'm weak, so I lie and say, "Only a little." The truth is, I feel like I'm about to be split in two.

He tsks, a disappointed sound. "I need you to hold still. I have to get a good look." He focuses those stormy eyes on me.

I nod, eager to please. "I will. I promise."

Lifting my head off the table, I peer down at him.

Dr. West wears a frown of concentration as he looks through the speculum. "I'll gather samples to send to the lab for your pap," he tells me. He picks up a bristle tipped swab from the tray. There's a pinch when he puts it in and spins it around. Then it's out and he drops it into a tube, sealing it away. Next, he selects something that looks like a Q-tip, but huge, like a giant would use. He sticks it into me, and I can feel it rolling along my inner walls. It's pleasant, and the pain from the speculum fades, replaced by this new sensation.

After a minute, he pulls the swab out and holds it up to the light to look it over. The tip glistens with moisture.

"I'm going to get a clitoral sample now," he says. "Did you know the clitoris has a hood on it?"

I shake my head no.

"It does. A small piece of skin that protects it, almost like how a sleeve covers your arm."

He reaches up above where the speculum protrudes. "If I pull back the hood, your clitoris is exposed and is more easily stimulated." He pushes the skin back, and a blast of air hits the sensitive area. Dr. West takes the damp swab and rolls it over my clit in a smooth, firm motion. My head drops back on the table, and I sigh out a moan. Whatever he just did felt amazing. I'm instantly turned on. Then he taps the swab against my clit which has begun to swell. Tap. Tap. My knees jerk involuntarily at the contact. I can feel arousal pooling around the speculum. He circles the swab over my clit, around and around.

I'm panting. An ache grows between my legs.

"Good," Dr. West says, sounding pleased, but I can't look at him to see his expression. My eyes are squeezed shut, focused on what he's doing to me.

"I'm going to palpate your insides and check for any masses or irregularities," he says. Still stimulating my clit, he sticks his fingers into the opening of the speculum. "I can reach much deeper now that I have this holding you open." I can feel him in there, stroking me. My hips rock to the motion.

"I have three fingers inside of you now, Ms. Jones," he says in his deep, gravely voice. "Can you feel them?"

"Oh, yes," I breathe out.

He pushes into me even more. The speculum digs in, but all I feel is his touch. Electricity is building in me, zinging along my spine and heading straight to my core.

Dr. West moves the swab more rapidly now, and my body moves with it, vibrating under his careful ministrations. He bends his finger slightly, and it increases the pressure against the sensitive skin down there. I whimper, rocking my hips to his rhythm. I'm so wet now that there are moist slapping sounds every time his fingers bottom out in me. There's an orgasm growing inside me, just the tease of it but getting bigger every second.

"I want you to touch your breasts now," he says. "I need to see if you're doing your self-exam correctly."

I hadn't noticed before, but the jerking of my body as it moves in time to his fingers has knocked my gown open. My chest is on full display, tits bouncing as my hips roll. Without hesitation I bring a hand to each breast and knead the soft flesh.

"Like this?" I ask tentatively, not completely sure what he wants from me.

"No. Harder. To do a proper self-exam, you must be firm."

I peek down and quake at the scowl on his face.

To appease him, I press my fingers with more force into my breasts.

"Don't forget the nipples," he tells me. "Remember what I told you about how there can be masses hiding behind them. Palpate that area. Don't neglect it."

I move my hand to my nipples and give them each a sharp tweak, which sets off a pleasurable twinge between my legs. A low moan slips out of my lips.

"Am I—am I doing it right?"

"Yes. Much better. Please continue."

I smile at the approval I hear in his tone.

His hands move faster as I pinch and roll each nipple between my fingers. My nerve endings trade signals between my nipples and core. I've never come without direct stimulation of my clit before, but I'm so turned on by this drag of his fingers in my pussy with the teasing of my breasts that my legs begin to tremble as a climax rises in me.

Thrust, pinch, stroke, roll, rub, flick. Everything merges together, and it all feels so good that I'm panting, my chest heaving, my hips slamming against the table. The pleasure and fullness and friction make me grind against him. The orgasm rips through me. I buck wildly, one foot slipping off the stirrup in the process. It goes on for a long time, the most intense orgasm of my life.

Finally, Dr. West slows down. He removes his hand and picks up a plastic bottle with my name on it from the tray. He rubs the fingers of his glove along the inside of the bottle, leaving behind a smear of my wetness. After he's screwed the cap back on, he holds the bottle up to the light and peers at it.

"That should be enough sample for the lab."

The high I was riding from the orgasm comes crashing down. Of course, he was just collecting body fluid to send to pathology. For a moment I had been delusional and I had thought he liked pleasuring me, but that's silly. A schoolgirl's fantasy. He's a doctor doing his job. I'm just another patient. The thought that he's doing this with other patients makes me jealous. How many women has he finger-fucked in the name of science today?

No. No. I shouldn't think of it that way. He's a professional doing his job. That's all this is between us. Nothing more. I can't even be mad about it. It's not like he's ever promised me more. I pull the paper gown tight over my now-chafed breasts.

Dr. West sees that I'm struggling to sit up. He comes over and puts his hand on my shoulder to help me into an upright position.

"You did well today," He tells me. Even though I know it's wrong because he's my doctor, happiness expands its wings in my chest.

Adam

God. That felt good.

Watching her fall apart on my fingers. How the tremors rolled through her as she lost herself in the pleasure *I* gave. It was intoxicating. Addictive.

I'd been so determined to hurt her. To remind her who held the power now. But then she'd whimpered, just a single, soft, fragile sound. The speculum had been too wide.

My resolve had faltered.

I want to make her feel. Pain, yes, but only the kind that lingers, that melts into pleasure until she doesn't know the difference. Today, I'd read her and been slow when she needed slow. Fast when she needed fast. Jessica was so…transparent. Her desires were right there, written across her pretty face.

There for *me* alone to read.

That realization unsettles something in me. I've had women before. Many. Some begged for me. Chased me. They offered themselves freely, eager to be conquered. I've taken them all, and I've enjoyed them. But none of them—*none*—have ever been like this.

I've never been this sure of someone.

Never known exactly what would shatter them.

Never wanted to break them just to see how they'd come undone.

But with Jessica?

I *know* her.

I know how she writhes and how she burns. I know the way her pleasure coils into something desperate, how her lips part when she's on the edge, right before she falls.

I should leave her alone—but fuck—I want more.

I'm not done with her yet. Not even close.

My pretty prom princess.

She used to be untouchable.

Not anymore.

Jessica

Dr. West stands close to the door with his head bent as he makes a note in my chart. Our appointment is about to end. The reality of it leaves me hollow, the empty ache of having lost something.

"Did you know I make house calls?" he asks.

I perk up at that. *Is he suggesting we see each other outside of the office? Does he want to take this further?*

"Oh?" My voice is cautious, but my pulse betrays me, kicking up a notch. I must be imagining this, right? It seems too much to ask, that *he* could be interested in *me*.

He nods, amusement dancing in his expression. This is the most animated I've seen him so far, and it feels like a gift, to get this glimpse of the man behind the white coat. He settles back into his usual cool façade. He pulls a small white notebook and ballpoint pen from his pocket. It only takes a few seconds for him to scribble some numbers on a piece of paper.

"This is my cell phone." He holds the paper out to me, seven digits neatly printed. No messy doctor handwriting. "Text me your address later. I'll come to your place on Friday at 7:00 p.m."

I take the paper and stare down at it, cocking my head. "Don't you have my address in your files?"

"I do." He sets his jaw and says no more.

Puzzled, I chew on the inside of my cheek. It takes a long minute before I understand. This is his way of giving me the option to reject him. To have control of the situation for once. If I don't want to let him know where I live, he'll respect that. He won't look it up.

Mostly, I've viewed him with lust. For the first time, a slow flush of affection works its way through my system.

I beam at him, which makes him blink in a way that's almost comical.

"Okay!"

"Okay," Dr. West repeats slowly, then says words that send my heart soaring. "It's a date."

Chapter Four

Jessica

That night, when I get home, I give in and call my best friend, Monica. I haven't told her anything about Dr. West yet. It had all been so strange and almost humiliating, but now that he's coming to my place, I can't hold back. With rushing words that tumble over each other, I spill all my secrets. All the weird, dirty, and *very* inappropriate things that happened in the doctor's office. Monica is appropriately shocked and impressed. She gasps, says "no way" approximately twenty times, and then makes me rewind and tell her everything all over again.

"I don't even think he realized what happened," I stammer. "Like how I…you know." My face burns and thank *god* she can't see me. Saying it out loud somehow makes the whole situation ten times more mortifying. "He didn't say anything."

"I find it *extremely* difficult to believe he made you orgasm not just once—but twice—and didn't notice." Monica says in her most disbelieving tone. "And now he's coming over? No way. He knows exactly what's going on. I think he likes you. All the evidence points to it." She says like she's giving a closing argument in court. I'm reminded this is why she's such a successful lawyer.

I giggle, then correct her. "I'm not sure. Maybe he likes…you know…doing things, but that doesn't mean he likes *me*."

"You said he's gorgeous, rich, and successful," she reminds me. "He could have any woman, right?"

I think back to his movie-star good looks and nod, which is silly. She can't see me over the phone. "Yeah. He's like god-level hot."

"But on this Friday night, a night he could spend with anyone, he's coming to see *you*," she argues, reminding me why she's my best friend.

I bounce happily on the couch, my grin so wide it hurts my cheeks. "That's true."

My phone chimes, vibrating in my hand. "Hang on, Monica, I'm getting a text."

"Is it him?!" Her voice pitches high with excitement.

"No, it's not. Calm down." I check the notification, expecting to see another message from Sarah, but this time it's from the principal at my school, Kent Wilson. I groan. This isn't exactly swoon-worthy content. "It's Wilson," I say, exasperated.

Wilson: I need you to cover crossing guard duty this week.
Jessica: I thought Hawkins was on this week. That's what the schedule says.
Wilson: Emily has to leave early to go to her second job.

"Who? Kent? The worst principal in the world? I can't believe you used to go to school with him." Monica's voice comes through my phone, faint and echoing. I switch her to speaker mode so I can text and talk at the same time.

"Just for one year. He's older than me, remember?"

"Proof older doesn't necessarily mean wiser. What does that weasel want?" Monica hates my boss, even though she's never met him.

"I have to cover crossing guard duty this week," I reply, already dreading it.

Monica makes an indignant squawking sound. "Why *you*? Didn't you freeze your ass off doing that last week?"

"Yes," I groan, remembering how the fall leaves had swirled, whipped up by biting winds off nearby Lake Michigan. My nose had run like a faucet that day, and by the end my feet had gone numb. "Emily can't do it. Something about her second job."

"Tell him to suck it."

From most people, this would be an empty threat, but not from Monica. She tells people to suck it all the time.

"I can't. Someone has to keep the kids from getting mowed down. You wouldn't believe how fast cars come around the corner."

"That's *his* problem. Let *him* stand out there in a reflective vest."

My phone buzzes with another text from Wilson.

Wilson: So you'll be there, right?

Jessica: Okay.

Wilson: Good. See you then.

I groan so loudly it echoes in my tiny apartment.

"Let me guess," Monica says dryly. "He's going to be there, too. Classic creep move."

I sigh, flopping onto my couch with its flat cushions and the broken spring that pokes my butt. "Yep."

"I *knew* it!" Monica exclaims. "That ass-wipe is trying to spend more time with you. He's probably sitting in his sad little office right now, planning which scarf he'll wear to impress you."

"Monica, stop." I can't help laughing.

"Don't pretend it's not true. He's the kind of guy who'd buy extra hand warmers just to be nice and then lingers awkwardly while handing them over like you're in a Hallmark movie."

I laugh so hard I can barely breathe. "Okay, that's way too accurate."

"I'm just saying," Monica adds, still smug. "Between Kent Wilson and Dr. Sexy, you're living a real *Choose Your Own Adventure* novel. And, girl, you *better* choose wisely."

I snort, relieved she's not giving me one of her trademark lectures about standing up for myself. Just when I think I've escaped, she mutters a huffy, "You're too nice. You know that, right?"

"I know," I admit, rubbing a hand over my face, then hastily redirect the conversation. "Anyway, about the hot doctor. What do you think?"

I expect her to crack another joke, but instead, her voice softens. "Okay, seriously." She hesitates, and there's a thread of something new in her tone...concern, maybe. "Are you actually okay with everything? Like, for real." A pause, as if she's choosing her next words carefully. "I could prosecute this doctor. He's crossed every line. I win malpractice cases like this all the time."

I bolt upright on the couch, gripping my phone so tight my fingers ache. "Monica! Don't you dare." Heat floods my chest. The urge to defend Dr. West, to somehow protect him, rises in me, so strong, so primal, it shocks me.

This is why I didn't tell her after the first exam. I was scared of the backlash. The judgment. I know most people wouldn't think this was normal, that they'd call it inappropriate. But the truth is, I don't care. Maybe I should but when I think about him—his eyes on me, his hands on my skin—I don't feel ashamed.

I feel *alive*. More than I have in years.

Monica lets out a slow breath, the sound crackling slightly through the phone. "Are you sure?" she asks, voice lower now. Measured. Like she's giving me one last out. "Because this could be...dangerous."

That should scare me, but it doesn't. It's true that my pulse spiked when Dr. West was near, but it wasn't out of fear. It was because I wanted more.

I square my shoulders and tell her a firm, no hesitation, "I'm sure. I want to see what happens with him. I—I need to know."

Monica's silent for a beat. Then, a knowing exhale. "Whoa." A short laugh. "You really *do* like this one, don't you?" There's a note of surprise in her voice, like she hadn't expected me to admit it.

"I mean," I pull at a loose thread on my couch, watching it unravel. "I barely know him, but there's something about him. Something...magnetic."

Monica is quiet again, but I hear the faint shuffle of fabric, like she's shifted in her seat. Finally, she sighs. "Alright. You're a grown woman. You make your own choices." Then, her voice turns sharp, protective. "But if he messes with you, if he hurts you, just know that I have a law degree and a deep well of rage at my disposal."

I bark out a laugh, tension easing from my shoulders. "You think he's trouble?"

"Absolutely. With a capital T," Monica deadpans. Then, her voice lifts again, playful, full of mischief. "But maybe he's the good kind of trouble—the kind you write about in your diary with little hearts in the margins."

I laugh at the thought of Dr. West and tiny hearts drawn around his name. "I don't even have a diary."

"Get one," Monica says. "This is diary-worthy. He's got 'sexy villain with a redemption arc' written all over him."

"Monica, this isn't a romance novel." I roll my eyes, but my lips betray me, twitching into a smile. "This is my actual life."

A life where Dr. West is coming here, to my apartment. The thought sends a shiver down my spine. What will happen, I wonder? Will we have sex? Can our relationship develop into something more? The anticipation, the not knowing where his head is at, is driving me insane.

"You know I'm loving how juicy this is, right?" Monica laughs again, then drops into a sing-song voice. "Jessica's hot for her doctor." She uses the same teasing tune she used when we were fourteen and she found out I had a crush on Tyler Dennis.

"Monica!" I laugh, kicking my feet against the couch cushion. "You're the worst."

We both know I mean she's the best. Because she really is. No one gets me the way she does.

"Oh!" She exclaims, "We should go shopping. You can't go on this date wearing your usual cotton panties and sports bra. That's not going to impress a guy like this doctor."

"Maybe that's his kink?" I suggest, giggling again. "Comfort-forward underwear."

Monica deepens her voice, imitating a man. "Why, Ms. Jones. How did you know granny panties turn me on?"

The thought of Dr. West saying that has me rolling with laughter. I pitch my voice high and breathless to play along. "Oh, Dr. West. Wait until you see my racerback sports bra. I've had it since college. It has sweat stains and gives me the best uni-boob."

Monica howls with laughter. "Oh, my god. Stop. That's too funny. If only men were so easily pleased. Like they'd be asking us *not* to shave our legs for once."

I snort. "Don't give me fantasies that can never be fulfilled."

We agree to meet the next day for lunch and lingerie shopping. I've been at a disadvantage so far when it comes to the good doctor. Every time he's seen me, I've already been naked. Not this time, though. This time, he's going to have to undress me if he wants to get me bare. Monica's right. I need to surprise him with pretty underwear…maybe the crotchless kind? My mind flashes forward to Friday night. His hands on me again. No paper gown this time. No rules. No excuses. Just me, him, and whatever the hell is happening between us.

Adam

I think about Jessica too much over the next week.

The anticipation builds, coiling inside me, growing sharper with every day that passes.

At work, I remain my usual self. Controlled. Professional. Unflappable. I've never blurred the lines before her—never even been tempted. Plenty of patients have made passes at me, some bolder than others. I've had patients proposition me indirectly, their intent written in the heat of their gazes, in the way they let their robes slip just a little too far and others outright ask me for sex.

I've always declined.

Until her.

Until Jessica was shivering and naked on my table, vulnerable in a way that set my blood on fire.

Something about her makes me break all my rules.

I almost hate her for it.

Sometimes, I feel resentment rise like bile in my throat—at this power she exerts over me without even trying. She invades my mind when she's not around, distracts me when I should focus. I want to punish her for that. Put her over my knee and spank that pert little ass until she learns her place.

Other times, the thought of her fills me with something... lighter. A feeling I don't recognize, definitely don't trust.

That's dangerous.

She's dangerous.

With one day left until I see her again, I act on a whim and place an order.

A gift.

I want to see her expression when she shows it to me.

To see if she understands what it means.

Jessica

Early Friday morning, before I leave for work, a knock on my front door makes me jump. Who could it be? For a brief moment my pulse leaps, hoping it's *him*, but quickly I crush that idea. Dr. West said 7:00 p.m., and he doesn't seem like the kind of man to change his mind.

My heart sinks. It's probably Brad, my annoying downstairs neighbor. We went on a date once. Just *one* time. He had too much to drink and groped my chest on the way home. I shoved him away—said I never wanted to see him again. That should have been the end of it, but it wasn't. Brad's been hounding me ever since. Phone calls, text messages, flowers left on my doorstep. I brace myself for another uncomfortable conversation and open my door.

It's not Brad though.

Instead, two burly men stand on my porch.

"Ma'am," the larger one greets me, tipping his head. "We've got your delivery."

My hand flutters to my chest. "Oh, there must be a mistake. I didn't order anything."

The smaller guy shoves a delivery notice in my face. I take it, wrinkling my nose at the dirty fingerprints smeared across the paper. Squinting, I read the tiny print. There it is, my name and address at the top and under it reads, "king bed." I'm about to open my mouth to protest that this is all a big mistake when I see that under purchaser it says one word. *West*. My jaw snaps shut, and my eyes widen.

While I stand reading the receipt, the delivery men barge into my apartment, carting large cardboard boxes in various sizes and shapes.

I point to the paper and ask the bigger man, "Who exactly bought this…bed?"

He peers at what I hold out and then shoots me a look like I must be stupid. "It says right there, lady." A stubby finger points. "Someone named West bought it."

I gape, shocked by this turn of events.

Dr. West is buying me gifts now? A *bed* of all things?

Annoyed by my speechlessness, the man asks in a gruff tone, "Where do you want it?"

I lead him to my small bedroom. A king-sized bed will take up almost all the space.

Not wanting to get in the way, I retreat to my tiny kitchen and let the men work. It doesn't take long before the bigger man, who must be the one in charge, brings me paperwork to sign. "We're all done." He glances at his watch like I've somehow put them behind schedule with my questions.

After they've left, I creep to my bedroom, almost scared to know what Dr. West has bought me. When I see it, tears prick the back of my eyes because it's *beautiful*.

When I was a child, I liked to think of myself as a princess. I would dream that I could ride a unicorn and that I had a gorgeous pink bedroom with a four-poster bed. In reality, my parents were poor teachers who could barely afford the small house I grew up in. They let me paint my room pink, but that was the closest my fantasies ever came to reality.

The bed before me is the bed from those little-girl dreams. It's white with twirling posts of wood at all four corners that rise almost as high as my ceiling. The posts are connected by pieces of wood that form a rectangular shape. There are even gauzy curtains hanging from the rails. They're on sliding hooks so you can pull the curtains and close off the entire bed, making it into a tiny room of its own.

I don't know what to make of it. This generous gift from this strange man. It's the last thing I expected.

On my walk to the bus stop, I make a hurried call to Monica to inform her of this new development.

"What do you think?" I ask her. "Why would he send me something like that?"

"It's obvious," she says. "You're going to get laid, and he wants it to be somewhere comfy. Not that crusty old mattress you usually sleep on."

"He doesn't even know what kind of bed I have."

I climb the steps of the city bus, tucking my phone between my shoulder and ear as I wave to the driver.

"Morning, Mikey."

His weathered face lights up, deep laugh lines crinkling around his eyes. He's been driving this route for as long as I've been taking it, five years now. Long enough for our daily greetings to feel like habit. For him to become a friend.

I slip a small paper bag into his hand as I pass.

"Sesame, extra cream cheese," I murmur. "Figured you might be hungry."

His grin widens. "You're an angel, Jess. You know that?"

I smile, covering the microphone on my phone, "Don't tell anyone. It'll ruin my reputation."

He chuckles, already unwrapping his bagel, and I make my way to my usual seat next to Julie, who also teaches at my school. We've arranged our schedules to ride together. It's more fun this way…and safer. Public transportation in this neighborhood is always a little dicey.

"Hey," I whisper to Julie. "Just give me a minute."

She nods, smiles.

Monica continues talking. "Who knows? Maybe he's been spying on you. Either way, I wouldn't complain. If a gorgeous doctor wanted to give me stuff, I'd take it happily."

"I *am* happy, just kind of confused."

"Well, you can ask him about it tonight." I hear the ding of an elevator through the phone. Monica's law firm is in a high-rise building downtown.

"I will." A thrill runs through me at her words, anticipation at the thought of seeing *him*. "Tonight."

Chapter Five

Adam

I shift nervously as I listen to the chime of Jessica's doorbell echo somewhere in her apartment. It's fall, the air crisp enough that I pull my jacket tight and shove my hands into my pockets. There's the sound of rushing footsteps and the rattle of chains as she unlocks her front door. I glance around one last time before she opens it, scowling. I don't like where she lives, not one bit. It's a run-down neighborhood. Not quite a slum, but the kind of place that will turn into one within the next decade. There's graffiti on the dumpster across the street, next to a neon-lit convenience store. The concrete steps that lead up to her place are chipped and stained.

It's all so disgustingly familiar. I used to live down the road in a shithole just like this one.

Bright light shines out when she swings the door open, making me squint. I blink against the glare and see her standing there, with the glow outlining her. It highlights her hair, lighting it up like a damn halo.

"Hi," she breathes out, smiling up at me.

Something pulls in my chest, sharp and fast. An answering grin lifts one corner of my mouth before I can stop it. I attempt to straighten my features. I've thought about it a lot and decided to keep my walls up this evening. She seems to enjoy the commanding doctor persona, and I like the distance that it places between us. The last thing I need is to fall for Jessica Jones.

Screw her, yes.

Love her, no.

My life is carefully organized. Everything in nice little compartments. I don't need her disrupting it more than she already has.

Without greeting her back, I push into the small living room of her apartment. My mood darkens even further when I see the threadbare carpet, worn couch, and tiny TV. Are those actual rabbit ears on her TV? Like the twin antennas that people used in the 1980s to get reception. Does she not even have cable, for god's sake?

I toss my brown leather satchel onto a chair near the door, followed by my jacket, then turn to her. I'm not sure what my expression reads, but it must be bad because Jessica takes a step back and raises her hands as if to ward me off.

"Are you okay?" she asks warily.

I take a slow, measured breath before answering. "Fine. And how are you this evening?"

She blinks, then brightens with a teasing smile. "So formal, Dr. West," she teases, batting her lashes. "I'm doing well. Extra good, actually, since I got a certain surprise gift from you today."

Some of the tension leaks from my shoulders. "Do you like it?" I ask, softer than I intend.

Her grin widens, easing a knot inside me I didn't know was there.

"I love it!" she exclaims, then grabs my hand and drags me after her, chattering excitedly. I snatch my satchel from the chair as we pass by.

"It's so pretty!" Jessica says. "Exactly what I would have picked out for myself."

She tugs me into her bedroom and waves to the large bed located in the center. "Look! Isn't it amazing?"

The bed looks good, but it takes up the entire room. That's how cramped her bedroom is. Irritation flashes through me that she lives like this. Jessica the prom queen deserves a real crown. A palace. Not this.

"What do you do for a living, exactly?" I demand, my tone harsh.

Again, she steps just out of my reach, until the backs of her legs are pressed against the mattress, and I instantly regret my words. I could have googled to find out more about her, but I deliberately hadn't. It's better not to know. I'm here for one thing only. To satisfy my desire and hers too. I'm not here to get to know her.

She lifts her chin, and even I can admire that spark of bravery in the face of an angry man.

"I'm a teacher. Just like my parents before me. High-school math."

My stomach clenches as a premonition occurs to me. "Which school?"

I know the answer before she says it. "Southfield High."

That place. The one I hate more than any other. That's where she goes every day. No doubt the boys there all ogle her when she's at the front of the classroom. They probably imagine her spread out on their desks. They probably masturbate to that thought.

Just like you do, says a little voice in the back of my mind. I tell it to shut the fuck up.

"My parents used to teach there," She continues, telling me information I already know. Her father, Mr. Jones, was my geometry teacher sophomore year. He was a nice man, even-tempered and patient.

"When I started teaching, the principal said it was full circle," She says with a note of pride. "That my parents worked at that school and now I do too."

More like circling the drain, I think. To be at a school like that.

"Isn't that place kind of rough?" I ask, remembering how the surrounding neighborhood was run-down when we went to school there.

"It is," she answers with a soft smile. "That's why I teach there. Those kids need someone who gives a damn. They need extra attention."

Great. She's a bleeding heart. One of those people who think they can make a "difference." Well, she'll learn soon enough that the world is fucked and all that matters is looking out for yourself.

Strangely irritated by the thought of her wasting her time on those delinquents, I tell her, "Get on the bed." I don't bother smiling.

Her face falls, just for a second, but I notice. "I thought you said this was a date."

"It is. A date where I fuck you." I gesture toward the king bed with my chin.

She glances back at the doorway that leads to her kitchen and living room. "But I made dinner."

For the first time, I notice the smell in the apartment. Something garlicky and aromatic. I quirk my head, confused.

"My grandma's spaghetti with garlic bread and spinach salad." Jessica winds her hands in front of her, probably nervous to see my reaction. "It's delicious," she adds, like she's trying to convince me.

I stand there, torn. On the one hand, I'm touched she made food for me. I can't remember the last time I had a home-cooked meal. On the other hand, when I said "date," I thought she would understand I meant sex.

Nothing more.

Dinner is definitely something more.

I take a step closer and then another until I'm towering over her, our chests almost touching. Her breathing hitches, then speeds up. I lower my lips to her ear and murmur, "There's only one thing I'm interested in tasting tonight, and it's not your grandmother's spaghetti."

I'm so close I hear when she takes a large swallow. "Are you sure? We could eat and then..." She trails off uncertainly.

"I'm sure." I shove her back, and her knees buckle. Jessica lands with a thump on the soft white duvet that covers her new bed.

I ordered that for her too.

Her breath catches, a small, delicate sound that tightens something deep in my stomach.

"I saw in the office how much you like it when I touch you."

Jessica blushes bright red, all the way to her hairline. Her fingers flex at her sides, her weight shifting. "I—I wasn't sure you noticed," she mumbles, staring at the floor.

I take a single finger and place it under her chin, tilting her face up to mine. "I did." I let the words settle between us. "I enjoyed it. I want you to lose control like that again."

Jessica's lips part slightly. A flicker of hesitation, and then—there it is—that moment of submission. The way her pulse jumps at her throat. The way her pupils widen, her body reacting before her mind can catch up.

I reach into the satchel and unzip it. Inside, several ropes lie neatly coiled. Jessica's eyes widen when I bring them out. "Made of hemp," I say, holding them up, "so they won't stretch when they're under tension."

"Umm," she stutters, eyeing the ropes like they're going to bite her. Her throat bobs in a swallow.

I remind myself to be patient. The women I usually screw are used to this. That's why I choose them and they choose me.

Jessica is different.

The thought that I can be the one to initiate her into this world makes my cock harden.

"You pick a safe word," I say gently, surprised I'm explaining all this. I had originally planned on coming over here and taking what I wanted, but I don't like the fear that ripples over her face. If we're going to do this, I want her to enjoy it as much as I do. That means I'll have to take my time. "If you say the safe word, we stop. No questions asked."

"Here." I hold out the rope. "Feel it. It's not too rough. It won't leave any marks."

Hesitantly, she takes it and unspools it slowly, running it through her hands. The moment her fingers skim the fibers, I see the shift. The curiosity in her eyes. The way she tests the texture against her palm. I want to tell her more, but I bite my tongue and give her the space to make her own decision.

She stays quiet, studying the rope. I can hear a clock clicking somewhere in the room. Probably the old-fashioned–looking one on her nightstand next to a pile of books. I examine them more closely and find they're all romance novels.

Figures.

She still hesitates, a war in her eyes, logic battling with raw, undeniable need. I soften. Just slightly. My fingers brush up her bare arm, barely a whisper of a touch. Goosebumps rise on her delicate skin.

Another minute of tense silence. Then, finally, she squares her shoulders. "What were you saying about a word?"

"A safe word. Pick the first one that pops into your mind."

"Cupcake," she blurts out immediately.

I laugh, a loud sound that bursts out of me, surprising us both. It's my first real laugh in—hell, I don't know how long.

Jessica grins at my reaction.

"Cupcake?" I wheeze, smiling. "You can't pick cupcake."

Her hands go to her hips and her lower lip juts out into a defiant pout, making me want to bite it. "Why not?"

"Well...because it's..." I flounder. "I mean, cupcake? Really?"

She crosses her arms over her chest and sends me a glare.

"I—oh, damnit." I take in her narrowed eyes and give in. "Fine, cupcake. That's the safe word."

"Good." Jessica swallows hard, but when she meets my gaze again, there's no fear. Only anticipation.

She hands back the rope, fingers brushing mine for the briefest moment.

I pause and stare down at the coil, feeling the weight in my hands. The weight of my choices.

Both equally heavy.

My thumb drags over the rope's fibers, rubbing them against my fingertips. My mind is already calculating where I'll tie each knot, where I'll wrap her wrists, how she'll look beneath me, stretched and bound. I push the thought away and inhale deeply, forcing my muscles to stay loose.

When I look back at her, the playfulness from before is gone. Jessica watches me carefully, breath slower now.

Something tightens in my chest. Maybe the last shred of my morality or maybe the ghost of a conscience I thought I buried long ago.

I step in and close the distance, then bend forward until my palms hit the mattress on each side of her hips. We're face to face now, closer than ever before. Her breath is a warm caress, ghosting across my cheek.

She stills. Green eyes wide, lips slightly parted.

"Tell me to stop." I say urgently, my voice low and husky. "Tell me no."

It's more of a plea than a command.

I know what comes next. She doesn't.

For a long moment, neither of us moves.

One second.

Two.

I wait for her to take the deal, reject me, but instead, resolve hardens behind those beautiful eyes. They blaze with a stubborn, reckless trust.

Like she's challenging *me*. Jessica deliberately lifts her wrists, pressing them together like an offering. A silent surrender.

That's when I know...I'm going to ruin her.

And even worse?

She wants it.

I exhale slowly, accepting her decision to move forward, a choice that suddenly feels inevitable. Like this was always where we would end up. Like we're race cars locked on a collision course, engines roaring, neither of us willing to hit the brakes, unable to stop the wreckage.

"Not like that." I gesture behind her. "I'm going to tie you to the bed."

Jessica whips her head around with her mouth hanging open. "The bed?" Her voice goes up an octave.

"Yes. The bed." Amusement stirs, brought on by her shocked expression. "Why do you think I got it?"

She looks at me, looks at the bed, then looks back at me again.

Her mouth opens and closes. On the third try she gets out, "You bought a bed…to tie me up in?"

It's not accusation.

It's wonder.

The air thickens between us. Jessica's pulse thrums at her throat, her breathing shallow. She wets her lips, her fingers twitching at her sides like she doesn't know what to do with them. A flush creeps across her collarbone, rising up her neck like she can already feel the ropes binding her.

That alone makes me chuckle. With a smirk, I slowly trail my fingers over her bare shoulder. I savor the softness of her skin, relish the way she trembles under my touch. I lift a brow. "Would you have preferred the floor?"

She exhales shakily, like she's trying to find the right words, but I already see the way her thighs press together. The way she bends toward me, just a little, her body betraying her thoughts. Whatever protest she might form has already slipped away.

Slowly, I lean closer. Her eyes dilate with what looks like a mixture of apprehension and desire. I let my lips hover next to her ear, my breath heating her already flushed skin and I hear the tiniest intake of breath.

She's waiting.

Wanting.

"Pretty girl," I say in my gentlest voice. "Move to the center of the bed so I can tie you up."

Jessica

My breathing picks up when he says that. It's not just the words, but how he says them, slow and seductive.

I do as he asks, scooting on my behind to where he wants me. The mattress gives slightly under me. It's perfect. Not too soft and not too hard. I lay on top of the comforter.

My heart stutters as Dr. West crawls in after me. He looks dangerous like this, on his hands and knees. The muscles of his forearms bunch and relax as he prowls closer.

Warm hands tug my shirt off over my head and release my bra. When he pulls down my pants and sees the lacy, black, crotchless underwear I picked out with Monica, he runs his hand over it with approval.

"This is nice." His fingers trace the swirling pattern of the fabric.

"I got it for you," I admit, my breathing already speeding up from his touch.

He rewards me with one of his closed-lip half-smiles. "Did you now?"

I nod vigorously.

A thrill runs through me when he says, "Then I think we should leave it on."

Once all my clothing, except for the panties, have been removed, he ties each wrist and ankle to a different post on the bed.

I can't move at all. My limbs are pulled taut, and my joints strain. It occurs to me that in this position Dr. West could hurt me if he wanted to. I'm helpless to stop him. I should be afraid right now—most people would be—but somehow, I'm not. Maybe because he's a doctor or maybe because he's never hurt me so far, I trust him to keep me safe.

Dr. West pulls the curtains closed all around us and sits back on his heels. He lets his eyes roam over my mostly naked body. "You're beautiful like this. Spread out. Ready to be used."

I shiver with anticipation, already aching for him.

With one hand he pulls off his shirt, revealing the most perfect torso and abs I've ever seen. Each muscle is sharply defined as if he were sculpted rather than born. He must spend a lot of time in the gym to look like that. Much to my disappointment, he doesn't take off his pants.

Instead, he positions himself down low on the bed, between my spread legs. "I've been wanting to taste you for a long, long time," he says, which is strange since I just met him, but I don't have long to ponder that mystery because his tongue is on me, a slow lick that makes my toes curl.

I moan when he suctions onto me. He draws my clit into his mouth, then releases it, then repeats the motion several more times. My chest heaves at the intensity of it. It's almost too much, but I can't pull away. Not tied up like I am. Dr. West pulls back and blows breath-warmed air over my pussy, making it clench. He nuzzles it almost tenderly and says, "You're delicious, Ms. Jones."

He sets to fucking me with his tongue, thrusting it into my entrance while his hand strokes my swollen clit. It's wet and warm and feels so good that within minutes my suspended legs tremble as an orgasm slowly builds in my center.

Just when I think I can't hold on any longer, he stops and sits up. He unzips his pants and pulls out his cock. I gasp at the sight of it, so big and rigid with serpentine veins that run its length. From his back pocket a condom appears. With practiced movements he rolls it on. I almost stop him, wishing I could feel him bare inside me, but don't.

The truth is that I don't know him, even though it feels like I do. Even though there's something familiar about him, almost comforting. No. It's better to use protection. Given how quickly he did the knots that bind me to the bed, I can safely assume I'm not the first woman he's done this with.

Once he's sheathed, his hand comes back to me, fingers slowly stroking. "Are you ready?"

I nod.

"What's the safe word?"

"Cupcake."

A hint of a smile, like he can't help himself.

I brace for him to penetrate me, but that's not what happens. He's left his bag on the end of the bed. I thought it was a mistake, that he'd forgotten it, but I was wrong. He put it there on purpose. He leans over my leg and fishes around in it for a minute. I gasp when I see what he's pulled out.

It's a speculum.

This one is made of clear plastic. Not cold metal like the one he used in the office. It's smaller, with a long slim design.

"I'm going to put this in your ass and then fuck you."

"Wh—what?" I struggle against my bound wrists, trying to sit up so I can see him better.

Dr. West isn't paying attention to me. He has a small bottle of lube that he's pulled out of his magic bag and is carefully coating the speculum.

"I'm not sure..." I trail off, alarmed by his plan.

Flat gray eyes meet mine. "It's like an anal plug. Have you ever used one of those?"

"No." Although I have heard of them.

He moves closer and separates my cheeks. His finger is still covered in lube, so it slides easily when he runs it along my behind. He localizes my rosebud and swirls his finger around it. "An anal plug goes here so you'll feel me even more when I'm in you. It presses everything together, so it's nice and tight. Which is good for you and good for me."

I never thought being touched back there would feel good, but what he's doing with his finger combines with the mental image his words paint, and my legs spread wider, giving him better access.

"Mmm," he hums. "That's it. That's my girl."

I whimper at the term of affection and at the possessive undertone in his voice.

My girl.

His.

He picks up the speculum. "Remember the safe word. You can say it anytime," he reminds me, using his free hand to hold me wide.

Slowly, he inches the speculum into my behind. I clench instinctively, then tell myself to relax. To breathe. Try something new. Surrender to this experience. I want him. Dr. West. I want to show him how far I can go.

He murmurs encouragingly as he advances the speculum, going deeper and deeper. He doesn't put it all the way in, just an inch or so, but it fills me up completely. I have to concentrate not to bear down and push it out. A few clicks and it widens until it stays in place without him holding it. He adjusts it some more, giving it one last click.

Once he's satisfied, he notches his dick at my entrance. He slips into me with agonizing slowness. His eyes never leave my face. His legs are spread wide as he kneels below me to accommodate the portion of the speculum that still sticks out. This wide-legged stance allows him to piston his hips back and forth with exaggerated movements as he begins to fuck me slowly. Each stroke of his cock combines with the fullness in my behind to create a warm, buzzing sensation over my entire pelvis. Everything down there feels alive, like it's tingling and tightening with pleasure.

He picks up the pace, watching me carefully. "Do you want to use the safe word?"

I shake my head no, all my concentration on the fire that's building in between my legs. I don't want him to stop. This feels too good, better than anything I've felt before.

He must have been waiting to see how I would respond because when I tell him no, he unleashes his own pleasure. He moves faster and faster, closing his eyes and tilting his head to the ceiling. A low, guttural groan leaves his throat, and it's the sexiest thing I've ever heard. "Fuck," he grits out. "You're so tight. It's incredible."

His hands land on my knees, which he pushes out, spreading me so wide that the rope bites into the tender flesh of my ankles. I barely notice the pain, though. I'm too busy focusing on the licks of heat from everywhere that our bodies connect. An orgasm winds tighter in my core with each touch, each thrust.

Another of those low groans from him. I slit my eyes open to see how his face is flushed and the muscles of his neck strain.

He's close and so am I.

He's pounding into me now as we get closer to release. My arms and legs stretch against my binding. I want to move my hips to his rhythm but can't. All I can do is lay there and react to the way his body teases mine. A pulsating sensation grows in me as I tense around him. Like my heartbeat has moved down into my core. With one last thrust, he buries himself in me and we cry out in unison, climaxing together.

Waves of pleasure wash over me, on and on as the orgasm undulates through my body.

"Fuck," he rasps out. "You feel so fucking good. I can feel you coming." He squeezes my knee and continues to move even as he softens. "Keep going," he encourages me. "Keep coming."

I do.

The orgasm stretches out longer than any I've had before. By the time it ends, I'm twitching and shivering like I touched a live wire. I barely notice when he pulls out and then removes the speculum.

Dr. West unties me. My legs and arms drop to the bed as if they weigh one hundred pounds. He draws back the blankets and tucks me under them, then lays down next to me. He's on his side facing me, with his head at the same level as mine. At this distance, I can see a thin rim of navy blue outlining the gray of his irises. His breath is warm as it mixes with mine. We stare at each other as our breathing slowly quiets.

"You did good," he whispers. Pride expands my chest.

Hesitantly, I stretch out my hand and brush it along his stubbled cheek. His eyes flutter shut, and he leans into my caress with a sigh.

In that moment, with the curtains pulled tight around the bed, it's like we're the only two people in the world. Like we're butterflies, trapped in a cocoon.

I lean forward and kiss him.

Want to *see* what just happened?

If your imagination is still spinning from that scene... you're not alone. I worked with an incredible artist to bring this moment to life with hand drawn *NSFW (Not Safe For Work) character art which I'm ONLY sharing with my newsletter subscribers.*

Want to see it? Join my newsletter, and I'll send the artwork straight to your inbox. It's intimate, steamy, and just for readers like you who want a little something *extra*. Click the link or scan the QR code below.

https://dashboard.mailerlite.com/forms/179195/149912545454458591/share

Come see what *Deeply Examined* really looks like.

Adam

Decades.

That's how long I've wanted her. Years of pent-up longing released in a single soul-shuddering orgasm. Muscles lose, every nerve satiated, I sink into the mattress, letting the rare sensation of contentment settle over me. A warm, unfamiliar weight.

After years of sex that blurred the lines of control and pleasure, I didn't think anything could truly surprise me anymore. But she has.

Jessica.

What we just did together exceeded my expectations. She fit like a glove, and when I was inside her the world for one fucking second made sense.

Usually after I have sex, I leave or my partner leaves. The women I fuck understand what this is—transactional, mutual gratification, nothing more. I make sure they're satisfied, and then we go our separate ways.

But this time, I don't go. I don't even reach for my clothes.

Instead, I climb into bed with Jessica and pull the blanket over both of us. It's not calculated. Definitely not part of my plan. It's just that I don't want this to end. I want to linger. To live with this sense of peace for a little while longer.

Peace that's shattered when she kisses me.

Soft lips touch mine, and my eyes fly open in shock. I rocket up in bed and scramble backward, my heart racing violently. My feet hit the floor.

She sits up too, her hand covering her gaping mouth. Stunned, wide-green eyes look at me. "I'm—I'm sorry. I didn't mean—"

"Why'd you do that?" I lash out, backing away from her. My voice is sharp, the bite of it only barely masking the raw edge of panic clawing up my throat.

Jessica clutches the blankets to her still-naked chest. "I'm sorry. I just—you were there and I—I wanted to kiss you."

"Well, don't. Don't do that. I don't kiss." I snatch my shirt from the floor and yank it over my head, then pull on my pants and grab my satchel. I'm moving on autopilot. My only thought is *get out, get out, get out.*

"What do you mean you don't kiss?" She blinks, trying to process, then shakes her head like she doesn't believe me. "Who are you? Julia Roberts from *Pretty Woman* or something? Everyone kisses."

"Not me," I spit out and spin around. Panic has hijacked my brain. I need to run, to escape.

"Wait!" she calls out as I dash down the narrow hallway. The tiny apartment closes in on me, claustrophobic.

I pause with my hand on the doorknob, momentarily distracted by the small table in the corner of the room. I hadn't noticed it when I walked in. It's set for two. Plates, silverware, cloth napkins folded neatly. Long tapered candles glow, flickering in the center next to a small vase of sunflowers. A single twinge of guilt before I jerk the door open and stumble out into the chilly night air, gulping it down.

I wipe the back of my hand across my lips, which burn from the phantom of Jessica's kiss.

No one's kissed me since my mother, and her kisses only came after the stinging slap of her hand.

"A kiss to make it feel better," she used to say.

That's when I learned that nothing ever made me feel better.

Chapter Six

J*essica*

Monica is fascinated when I tell her about the date.

"Wow," she says. "I can't believe he did all that. I bet he's into BDSM and all that kinky shit. Soon he'll be ordering you to crawl to him and call him Daddy."

I wrinkle my nose, not sure if I like the sound of that or not. "I think he's just bossy. Not a true dom," I say, proud I know that lingo. All those dark romance books I love to read have taught me a thing or two about that world. It sounds so thrilling and forbidden. So far my sex life has been pure vanilla, but late at night, after I've read about Mafia men, serial killers, and dirty-mouthed psychos, sometimes I've had to pleasure myself. To relieve the urges those books raise in me to do naughty, filthy things. Could I be that way in real life? Be that adventurous?

Probably not.

"Besides, he may never call again. Not with how fast he ran out." I sigh mournfully.

"He'll call. He'd be nuts not to. Look at you. You're pretty and kind and surprisingly okay with being tied to a bed. Oh! I was reading last night about this crazy thing. It's called urethral sounding." Monica's voice drops low, laced with the thrill of the taboo.

"Say what?" I ask, grateful to be distracted from my worries about Dr. West.

"Yeah. It's when you stick something up your partner's urethra. You know, where the pee comes out. They have special rods for it, or some people use household items."

I gape at the phone. "No way. You're making this up."

"I'm serious! Then you put the rod in your mouth and hum. In dudes it stimulates their prostate or some crap like that. They say it gives the most intense orgasm ever."

"You were reading about this why exactly?"

She laughs. Monica has always been more sexually free than me. She doesn't believe in the concept of a red flag. "One of my masked men was talking about it. You know, The Specter."

"Is that the guy you're obsessed with? The one that you're always forwarding to my Instagram?"

"That's him," she sighs wistfully. "He can sneak through my window any night. I'd let him stick anything into me, even into my pee hole."

I laugh at that. "Sometimes I worry about you."

"I know," she says cheerfully. "It's because you love me. Look, I get that you're upset with how the date ended, but trust me, that doctor will come around eventually."

"Maybe," I tell her, but the more I remember that look of abject horror on Dr. West's face when I kissed him, the more I'm sure she's wrong.

I blew it.

My one chance with sexy Dr. West and I had to go and get all sentimental and kiss him. *I'm such an idiot.*

* * *

He doesn't call me. I must be so stupid because I really believed Monica. I thought that in a day or two my phone would ring, and he'd apologize or at least say he wanted to see me again. Surely, he recognized how mind-blowing that sex was? Wouldn't he want to do it again?

I have long conversations with myself about how this is for the best. After all, I don't want just a fuck buddy, no matter how good they are in bed. I don't want a man who can never kiss me back. Dr. West obviously has issues if he likes to go around tying women up but not kissing them. That's not exactly well-adjusted adult behavior.

Forget him, I tell myself. *That relationship, or situationship, or whatever was never going anywhere.*

I've almost got myself convinced by the end of the second week after he bolted out of my place. Almost have accepted that he's irreversibly damaged, incapable of normal human affection. But every night, right before I fall asleep, a single memory flickers behind my closed eyelids. It was when I put my hand to his cheek, and he leaned into that touch. How he melted into my palm. I felt it, when all the tension left his body and that ever-present furrow in his brow smoothed out. It was so fleeting, but I know that for a split second I held his beating heart.

One question remains.

Was it the heart of a man or of a monster?

Chapter Seven

Jessica

The pounding on my front door blends into the pounding of my feet on pavement in my dream. Dream me is running, chasing something or someone. I can't make out what lies before me, but I stretch my hand toward it as I race forward.

"Jessica!" slurs a voice loudly, followed by knocking.

I lift my head and blink the bleariness out of my vision. "Wh—what?" My bedside clock says it's only 10:00 p.m. I must have dozed off while reading my romance book.

"Let me in!" The double chain locks I have installed on my front door clink together.

I recognize the voice now.

It's Brad.

Drunk and angry from the sound of it.

"Please, I just want to talk to you," he cajoles.

I throw off my blankets with an annoyed sigh and pad toward the front door. I've reached the living room when something slams into the door, making it rattle.

"Let me in, you bitch!"

I freeze at the hatred in those words.

Behind me, back in the bedroom, my phone rings.

Shit!

I rush back to silence it, but it's too late.

"I know you're in there, you whore! I hear your phone." The pounding on my door intensifies like he's kicking it.

My heart hammers nervously in my chest. Alarm bells chime in my mind.

I can't let him in. If I do, something terrible is going to happen. I just know it.

In my haste, I barely notice that I've picked up my phone and answered it.

"Hello?" A deep voice faintly emanates from the speaker. "Jessica?"

The screen reads Dr. West.

Double shit!

Of course, he would call me now of all times.

I hurry into the bathroom and shut the door, but it's no use. I can still hear the commotion Brad is making. At this rate, I'll have to call the police. What a mess that'll be.

Flashing lights. Filing reports. All the neighbors gossiping behind my back.

"Hello? Are you there?" says my phone.

I put it to my ear and whisper, "Hey, I can't talk right now."

Before I hang up, Dr. West interjects, "Listen, if this is about last time, I can explain."

"No, no. It's not that," I whisper, ignoring the creak of wood from my living room. If I don't hurry, Brad's going to break down the door.

"What then? Why are you whispering?" he demands. I don't have to see his face to know he's scowling.

"Jessica!" Brad bellows so loudly I hear it through the bathroom door.

"What's that racket?" asks Dr. West. "What's going on?"

"It's my neighbor, Brad," I admit as I peek around the door frame and peer down the hallway. "He's drunk and trying to get into my place."

"What!?" Dr. West exclaims.

"I think I need to call the police, but I don't really want to," I babble. "What if it causes a big scene, and the school finds out? If they think I'm involved in something unsavory, they might fire me." Saying it out loud pierces through the denial that was keeping me calm. I'm in trouble, and the reality of it brings a choked sob up my throat. Tears prick the corners of my eyes.

"I'm going to kill you, you stuck-up bitch!" screams Brad, so loudly that even Dr. West must hear it.

In an eerily calm voice, Dr. West says, "Jessica, I want you to go into your bathroom and lock the door. Stay in there, no matter what you hear, until I call you." There's rustling sounds, and I can tell he's on the move. "What apartment does Brad live in? What number?"

"A13. It's downstairs," I reply, sniffling. Tears leak from my eyes and race down my cheeks. "I'm scared."

"I know you are, but don't worry. I'm on my way. Everything's going to be just fine."

I heave a shuddering sob. "Hurry, please."

"I will. Be my brave girl now and lock the door. Okay?"

I do as he asks and shut myself in the bathroom. After I hang up, I crawl into the cold porcelain bathtub and pull the shower curtain closed. The flimsy fabric wouldn't stop Brad for a second, but it hides me, gives me a false sense of security.

Brad continues to rant and rave outside. He sounds unhinged, like he's lost his mind.

Terror claws the pit of my stomach. My imagination supplies every horrific scenario that might happen if Brad reaches me. Throat tight, I bury my face in my crossed arms and cry.

Adam

I floor the gas, the needle climbing past one hundred, but I barely notice. Jessica's whispered, terror-stricken voice plays on a loop in my mind, each word slicing through me like a blade. Fifteen minutes. That's all that separates her apartment from my condo, but it feels like an eternity—a torturous stretch of time where anything could happen to her.

A dark, all-consuming need grips me to protect her, shield her, and destroy anyone who dares to harm her. No one will touch her. Not while I'm breathing.

God knows, I've been there—cornered, broken, betrayed. I know the hollow ache of fear, the scars it leaves. I'll do whatever it takes to make sure she never feels that pain.

Knuckles white, I clench the steering wheel and fly through the last red light, narrowly avoiding a honking truck. My wheels squeal on the pavement as I slide into a parking space in Jessica's lot.

Brad's hollering penetrates my car before I even have a chance to step out of it. Rage colors my vision red when I see him angrily hammering on her door with both fists. I check for security cameras as I walk up. Of course, there aren't any. In my neighborhood, if something like this happened, the perpetrator would be filmed from five different angles and the police would arrive within minutes.

Not here, though. This asshole has been making a ruckus for over twenty minutes and not a single person has stuck their head out to see what's going on. No one's offered to help. There's fear here. People cowering behind closed doors, just glad it's not happening to them.

I hate it.

Hate that this is where she lives.

The lack of cameras is in my favor now. No one to watch how I'm going to deal with this guy.

A grim smile touches my lips.

Brad's so focused on reaching Jessica that he doesn't hear me come up behind him. I grab him by the back of his collar and haul him away, like an errant schoolboy about to be taken to the principal's office. He sputters, swiping behind him with ineffectual punches that I dodge easily.

I drag him down the stairs, not caring when he trips over his own feet and falls on the last two steps, scraping his knees. His door is easy to find. A13. It stands wide open like he was in such a rush that he forgot to close it. My nose wrinkles when I enter his living room and slam the door closed behind us. The source of the rotten smell is obvious. There are old half-eaten take-out containers and empty vodka bottles everywhere.

Looks like Brad went on quite the bender.

I toss him onto his couch, where he slumps to the side and stares at me with red-rimmed eyes. Bending, I crouch in front of him. I keep my hands loose and balanced on my knees, ready to grab if he makes a run for it. He's got frat-boy good looks, but the kind that're fading. Hair going thin at his temples. Stomach bulging from one too many keggers.

This close I notice his dilated pupils and the erratic way he breathes. I frown, leaning forward for a better look, but the signs are unmistakable. This man isn't just drunk. He's high and not from weed. He's hopped up, cocaine or methamphetamine or maybe both.

Jesus.

He's even more dangerous than I thought. The idea that this lunatic might have broken into Jessica's apartment makes me furious. I have no illusions about what he would have done to her.

"Who're you?" he slurs, eyes shifting from side to side like he can't focus on one thing at a time. "Do ya know Jessica? That whore. Thinks she's so great. Are you fucking that slut? She—"

Whatever he was about to say is lost to the crunch of his nose as I break it. My fist slams into his face quicker than a lightning strike. Blood gushes down his chin, staining his shirt and the dirty couch cushions.

I grin wickedly at the gruesome sight. I used to get into fights all the time, back when I was a kid and a teenager. I miss it sometimes.

The copper smell of blood. The grunts of pain. The tears.

"Gah!" he exclaims and raises his hands to ward me off, but there's no stopping me now.

I punch him again, holding nothing back. "Do you like it?" I rain blows down on his upper body, thrilling with each thud and gasp. "Hurting women?" Another crack. This time a rib buckles under my fist. "Does it make you feel like more of a man? Messing with people smaller than you? Weaker?" His head rockets to the left when I hit him in the temple. I follow up with a punch from the right.

In a distant part of my memory, there's the echo of mocking laughter. The flush of the toilet. Water flooding into my lungs. I'm dying. Drowning. Fury grips me. My vision tunnels down to the sight of my hands hitting his bloodied and battered face. Over and over. Another bone breaks, and it feels so fucking good. Like salvation. Vindication.

This goes on for so long that Brad passes out. I get a glass of cold water from the kitchen and pour it over him. He wakes up and gapes at me, blinking stupidly.

"Oh no," I tell him with a grin. "I'm not done with you." His head lolls forward. I grab him by the hair and hold him up so I can stare into his rolling eyes.

"I bring life into this world every day, and I can take it out just as easily." I give his head a shake. "What do you know about potassium, Brad?"

"Huh?" he mumbles, incoherent.

"Potassium," I repeat pleasantly. I'm calming down now. A plan is forming, rearranging its pieces as I think through each step. "It's a very important nutrient," I inform him, nodding wisely. "The heart in particular needs potassium to function properly. Too much or too little and it stops beating."

"Glurb," he mumbles.

I might have broken his jaw.

"*I* have access to potassium." I jerk his head back, making his teeth rattle. "Someday I'll inject you with a small dose. It won't take much to kill you." I sing out the last part, cheery at the thought of ending his miserable life. "I'd do it now, but the police would blame Jessica. Everyone heard you out there."

I rub my chin, musing if there's any way I can kill him now. I've never murdered anyone before, but I'm not opposed to it. Not when it comes to this piece of shit. Finally, I drop my hand with a sigh and tell him, "It's okay, though. I'm a patient man. I'll wait until you least expect it."

Getting beaten has sobered him. Brad's eyes go wide with understanding.

I lean closer and wince at his putrid breath.

Deadly serious, I say, "You'll never see me coming."

Jessica

I'm not sure how long I sit in the cold, hard bathtub and bawl, but I've just stopped crying when my phone rings next to me. I've put it down, and it stutters across the porcelain as it vibrates, chiming loudly.

"Let me in," Dr. West says when I pick up.

Silence outside. I open the front door a crack and peek out. He stands on my doorstep with his hands in his pockets, like it's a normal night and he's here to pick me up for a date.

Except he's not normal...and he doesn't date.

He gives me a reassuring smile. "It's okay. Brad's gone."

I let Dr. West into my apartment. The room is dark. It's midnight now. With a click, I turn on the small lamp on my end table. It lights with a soft, golden glow. Cautious, my nerves still jangling, I return to him.

"What happened?"

Dr. West doesn't answer. He pushes past me and heads to my bedroom. Once there, he opens the top drawer in my dresser and pulls out stacks of my underwear, bras, and socks, flinging them onto the bed.

"Get your suitcase," he tells me. "Pack as much as you can."

"Wh—what?"

"Start packing. Bring what we can carry. I'll send for the rest later."

I stare, mortified at my lingerie in his hands. He's looking at me with impatience, waiting for me to follow his instructions.

"What are you talking about?" I sputter. "What happened?" I hurry after him. Taking my panties from him, I shove them back into the drawer.

Immediately, he gets them out again and adds them to the growing pile on the bed. "You're leaving this hellhole."

"I can't leave. I don't have anywhere to go. My parents are gone, my family's too far away, and my friends—" My voice breaks. "They have their own lives." I snatch the underwear from the bed. My movements frantic, I cram it into the drawer, not caring that it's a wrinkled jumble now.

I'm frightened, angry, and overwhelmed. It crashes into me like a tidal wave, how close I came to disaster with Brad. My shoulders hitch with a sob. Embarrassed, I bury my face in my hands to hide my tears. Strong hands grip my arms and pull me forward until I stumble into Dr. West's arms. He cushions my head on his chest and rocks slightly, making soothing noises as I cry big, shuddering sobs.

"You can't stay here." His breath is warm against my hair. "There's nothing stopping Brad from coming back tomorrow or the day after that. You're not safe."

"I don't have anywhere to go," I repeat in a whisper, my voice breaking.

"Yes, you do," he says, his voice firm. "With me."

I stiffen, pulling back just enough to look up at him. "I can't," I say, shaking my head. "I barely know you."

"You know me better than you think," he counters. His gaze is steady, unwavering. "At least come for one night—or two. Just until we figure something else out. I won't let anything happen to you. You'll be safe with me. I promise."

I search his face for any sign of hesitation, any hint that this is a mistake, but all I see is certainty.

And yet, I pause. "I don't know..."

"It's late," he says gently but firmly. "You're exhausted, and you've been through hell. Let me take care of you, just for now."

I exhale shakily, the weight of his words sinking in. He's right. I can't stay here. Not after what happened. But going with him feels terrifying in a completely different way.

"Okay," I murmur, the word barely audible.

"Good," he says, stepping back. He resumes his methodical packing.

My shoulders slump in defeat. I fetch my dusty suitcase from under the bed. It belonged to my parents. They loved to travel, mostly road trips around the United States since we didn't have a lot of money. We'd pack up the car and go, sometimes without a clear destination. Just roamed around, wherever the wind took us.

We had a tradition of getting a sticker from every place we visited. At the end of the trip, we'd slap the stickers onto the suitcase until its sides were covered in them. I run my finger over an image of a colorful beach, the sun setting into the ocean like a flame about to be extinguished. I haven't gone anywhere since they died. Too busy and too poor. It's ironic that this is the first time I've left home in years. Not to travel the world but to run away. To escape.

We work together in silence. Dr. West hands me items, which I neatly fold and pack. Soon, the suitcase and another bag bulge with my things. He takes one in each hand and asks, "Are you ready?"

No, I think. *I'm not.*

I swallow hard, forcing air into my lungs and reach for a strength I'm not sure I have. "Yes," I whisper at last, my voice steadier than I feel.

And with that, I follow him out the door.

Chapter Eight

Jessica

Dr. West leads me to his sports car, which is sleek and black, so shiny it reflects the full moon high above us. His head swivels side to side. "Where's your car? You can follow me. I have an extra parking spot you can use."

"Don't have one. I had to sell mine years ago to cover my parents' medical expenses. They died within the same year, so it was a lot all at once."

Dr. West's head snaps up. His eyes widen with shock. "They're *dead*? Both of them?" He seems truly shaken, which is sweet considering he didn't even know them.

"I told you earlier they were gone." I shift my purse higher on my shoulder, unable to believe how this night has turned out.

"I thought you meant on vacation. I didn't think you meant they were *gone*."

"Well, they are." My shoulders sink as the memory of those dark days takes over. "My mom had breast cancer, and shortly after she passed my dad had a massive stroke. He never woke up from it. Eventually, I had to stop life support."

"That's terrible." Dr. West halts by the front of his car, his brows pinch together. "I had no idea."

I quirk my head, confused by his reaction. "How would you?"

He sticks his hands in his pockets and rocks on the heels of his feet. "Oh…er…Were you close?"

I let out a sad sigh. "Very. I'm an only child, an oops baby. My parents were in their late forties when they had me. They'd been told they could never have children. To say they spoiled me, doted on me, is an understatement. I was their entire world, and they were mine."

His voice is low when he says, "It sounds like you had a good childhood."

"We didn't have much, but we had each other and that was enough."

The air is heavy with sadness. My tears were used up by Brad—otherwise, I'd probably be crying again. I miss my parents *so* much. Miss being part of a family.

Before grief can overwhelm me, I return to the topic that started this conversation. "That's why I use the bus. The reason why I picked this apartment." I wave back toward the concrete three-story building. "It's on the direct line to school."

My answer makes him frown, deepening the well-worn grooves in the middle of his forehead.

"Oh!" I clamp my hand over my mouth. "How will I get to work if I'm with you? Is there a bus stop near you?"

The frown turns into a glower. "You're not taking a fucking bus. I'll drive you or get you an Uber." He opens my car door so hard it bounces back and he has to shove it open a second time. Then he stalks over to his side and does the same thing with his door.

I raise my eyebrows, wondering what I did to piss him off.

It's quiet in the car as we wind through the streets, which are nearly deserted this late at night. As traumatized as I am by everything that's happened, I'd be lying if I didn't admit I was also a little bit excited to be going home with Dr. West. What will his place be like? Fancy? Or mundane? Does he live in a mansion? Or a bat cave?

By the time we pull off the street, I'm dying of curiosity. So much that I press my face to the cold glass window of the car and stare out, not wanting to miss anything.

He guides the car onto a ramp that leads to the underground parking for a tall condo building downtown. The building has to be at least thirty stories high, with dark tinted windows and thick external steel beams that make a repeating X pattern across the sides.

From the garage, we take an elevator to the top floor. The penthouse. The elevator doors slide open and Dr. West murmurs, "After you." Carrying my bags, he ushers me down a short hallway to a door. A silver plaque next to it reads "3512-P."

He doesn't use a key to get access but rather his thumbprint pressed to a small black pad located under the plaque.

My mouth drops open. "Wow. That's high-tech. I didn't know they had fingerprint door locks."

"It's a prototype. I invested in the company a couple of years ago. They should go public soon," he responds absently. He's got his cell phone out and is punching something into it.

"Put your thumb on it now."

"Me? Why?" I do as he says, pressing my thumb on the cool glass surface.

"I'm programming you into the system. Now you can use it too."

I'm oddly flattered to have such intimate access to his home. "Thanks. That's so kind of you."

"It's fine. I'll erase you from the server once you're gone. It only takes one step on the app."

And now I'm not so flattered. "Thanks," I repeat again, this time with much less enthusiasm.

Oblivious, he reaches past me to push open the door.

I gasp when we enter the room. It's two stories tall, a great room with a living room and kitchen open to each other. The kitchen is super-modern, with shiny white cabinets without handles. *How does he open them?* Double stainless-steel refrigerator and freezer. *Does he cook?* The kind of oven that has red knobs on it. *I can make cookies!*

The elegant living room is dominated by a large sectional in a U-shape. It faces tall windows that show off a nighttime view of the city. Twinkling lights from distant buildings look like a fairy village from up this high. The long stretch of the Navy Pier is visible, its large Ferris wheel flashes with a multitude of colors.

Of all the things that impress me in this space, there's one that stands out more than any of the others.

Books.

The back wall of the room has rows and rows of bookshelves. They reach up two stories tall. A ladder on wheels can access the top shelves.

Without thinking, I reach out and clutch Dr. West's sleeve. "Oh. My. God! You have your very own library."

He follows my gaze and shrugs. "Yeah. I like to read."

I give his arm a small shake and say in an awed whisper, "You even have a ladder!" The last word comes out as an excited squeak.

"It's no big deal," he says.

"Shh." I hold up my hand, almost wanting to cry over all the beautiful books. "Don't ruin this. I'm having a *Beauty and the Beast* moment. I mean, you have a *ladder*!"

"I assume I'm the Beast in this scenario?" he asks dryly.

"Well, *duh*." I release his arm and turn to him, grinning. "Of course."

"Don't get too excited. Unlike the Beast, I'm not giving you my library."

"Aha!" I point at him, bringing my finger so close to his face that he flinches backward. "So you admit that you *have* seen the movie!"

He shoves my hand away with an irritated scowl. "Everyone's seen that movie."

"No," I say, shaking my head. "Lots of people, especially guys, haven't seen it. Only secret romantics have watched it closely enough to remember a small detail like that. Men who go around saving damsels in distress, for example." I send him a pointed look.

He fixes me with a stare. "Trust me. I don't have a romantic bone in my body."

I wag my finger at him, teasing. "I'm not buying it. As matter of fact," I say as I lean forward and pretend to sniff his shirt, "I think I smell marshmallow because deep in your soul you have a secret soft side."

He rolls his eyes. "If my soul had a smell, it would be decay from all the grudges I've buried down there."

I give him a knowing look. "If you say so."

He heaves an exasperated sigh. "You're loopy from all the adrenaline. Let me give you a quick tour and then you can go to bed."

Quickly, he shows me the downstairs. Besides the kitchen and living room there's a hallway bathroom, office, and professional-looking gym. Each room is illuminated by a night light in the corner, small but surprisingly bright.

"This place is gorgeous," I say as we continue down the hall. "Good to know what doctor money can buy."

He laughs, the sound gravelly and delightful since it's so rare. "Oh, no. Doctor money didn't buy this. Doctors make a lot less than people think."

I quirk my head. "If not doctor money, then what? Trust fund money?"

He scoffs. "Hardly. I used to get bullied for wearing the same dirty pair of jeans to school every day." His expression contorts into something bitter, but when I put a soothing hand on his arm it quickly morphs into irritation.

He jerks away from my touch with a scowl. With short, clipped words, he says, "This is stock market money."

"Stock market?" I come to a standstill and tilt my head, looking up at him. It's late now and my eyes feel gritty, but he looks as fresh as ever, although annoyed with his mouth turned down at the corners.

He lets out a deep breath and shakes his shoulders slightly, like he's forcing himself to relax. Calm again, Dr. West glances around, then turns those shiny gray eyes back to me. "I've always been good at math, and I like analyzing things, so I've been day trading since I was a teenager. I used to take everything I made and invest it. Even if it was just $5 from some busboy job. Eventually I made enough to put myself through school and then I bought this condo."

"That's quite an accomplishment," I say, impressed.

He ducks his head and rubs the back of his neck with one hand. "I guess so." Then he straightens and gestures to the end of the hallway. "Anyway, down there is my bedroom."

I look to where he points but only get a glimpse through the partially open door. Enough to see a *very* familiar-looking bed. His is made of a dark brown wood, but it's the same curtained four-poster bed that he bought me.

My breath catches at the sight and all the memories it invokes. There's a tingling between my thighs. I open my mouth to say something witty about it but stop when another door catches my eye. "What's that? The door next to your bedroom?"

"Oh...that holds all my electronics. You know, the stuff that controls my audiovisual equipment. Nothing interesting."

"Cool. This is a real smart home, isn't it?"

"Yep. Full of the latest technology. You must be tired by now." He takes hold of my elbow. "I'll show you to your room."

"My room?" I ask, confused. "I'm not sleeping with you?" I don't know why, but given all the—*ahem*—intimate moments we've shared I assumed he would put me in his bedroom.

"I don't sleep with anyone."

"That's just not true," I counter, for a second wondering if I imagined all those orgasms.

Again with the eye roll—he's really good at those. Must have had a lot of practice. "You know what I mean. I sleep with women, but I don't *sleep* with them."

"Still not understanding."

"I like to sleep *alone*. In my bed. Without anyone else."

"Oh." That stops my upbeat mood immediately. "Gotcha."

He tugs me to a wrought iron spiral staircase in a corner of the room that I had somehow missed. "You're up here."

We wind up the stairs, with him in the lead. Our footsteps clang like Sunday morning church bells on each metal rung, the sound reverberating in my ears.

Feeling awkward about the bedroom conversation, I try to distract him with chatter. "These stairs are steep. Have you ever fallen down them after one too many glasses of wine?"

He looks back over his shoulder. "I don't drink often, only when I'm out."

"You don't?" I ask, surprised. "Why not?"

"I like to be in control."

A flashback to how he tied me up. How he bossed me around.

Spread your legs.

"That does seem like you," I agree, which earns me a quizzical glance.

We reach the bedroom at the top. It's beautiful, with pristine white walls and a tufted bedspread. Pedestal nightstands painted dove gray flank the bed. A wingback armchair sits in the corner next to a small table and a floor lamp with a cream-colored shade.

There must be something wrong with me, because my first thought upon seeing the white iron frame headboard is to wonder if he can tie me to it.

Stop, I chide myself. *You're roommates now. Maybe he won't want to do those things with you anymore.*

To my surprise, I find this thought even more depressing than the realization that I'll never be safe in my old apartment again.

Since the staircase is narrow, it takes two trips for Dr. West to bring up my suitcase and bag. He sets them on the floor.

He shoves his hands into his pockets. Looking everywhere but at me, he says, "Hope you get a good night's sleep."

"Thanks," I say, trying to ignore the hollow feeling of longing I get when I look at him. I wish so badly that he would touch me, but he doesn't. As he turns to go, I call out, "Good night, Adam."

Immediately, his back stiffens. Slowly, he faces me. In a quiet voice that hides deeper emotions, he says, "Don't call me that."

I take a step back, stricken by the dark, shuttered expression that's taken over his face. "I'm sorry. I thought that was your name? It's written on the door to your office. Adam West, M.D."

"It's my name, but I don't use it. Don't like to hear it."

"What should I call you?" I let out a single, high-pitched, nervous laugh. "I can't be here and call you Dr. West. That would be weird."

A pause, then he says, "You can call me West. That's what most people do."

I nod with understanding. "West. Got it. Good night."

A solemn "good night" from him. Then he leaves, the metal spiral staircase creaking as he descends.

Once he's gone, it's eerily quiet. Not a sound in the whole place. I put on my pajamas but don't wash my face. I'm too tired to navigate those stairs again. Instead, I slip under the covers and try unsuccessfully to sleep. I'm not dreaming, but my mind is haunted.

Not by Brad, like I expected, but by *him*...West.

Adam

The next morning, Jessica slowly comes down the stairs with one hand on the railing. She's lovely, with her feet bare and her hair loose around her shoulders. Back in high school, I used to be obsessed with her hair. I'd wait every day, wondering how she was going to wear it. Up or down. One ponytail or two. Now, the morning sun slants through the window and illuminates her from behind, lighting her up like she's an angel.

I sit at the wide, marble-topped kitchen island, perched on a bar stool and sipping coffee while I read the newspaper. I watch, waiting to see how she'll react when she sees the neatly stacked boxes by my feet. They're labeled "J's kitchen," "J's bathroom," and "J's bedroom."

As I predicted, she halts and stares at them, her eyes running over the words. "Wh—what is this?"

"I got the rest of your stuff last night. It's all here, except for your furniture, which is in storage."

She gapes, like she can't believe what she's hearing. "Why?! I'm only staying a night or two. That's what you said."

I blow on the surface of my coffee, making it ripple. The steam twists and curls under my breath, then breaks apart to float away. "Stay as long as you want. This way you never have to go back to that place."

Her gaze bounces between me and her belongings. "*How*? How did you get into my apartment?"

"You must've been distracted. You left the front door unlocked when we closed it last night."

Her mouth twists. "I'm usually good at remembering that. I never forget."

I give her a pleasant smile. "You were upset. It was a stressful evening."

A suspicious glare from her, mouth downturned and flattened. "I could've sworn—"

"Don't worry. It could've happened to anyone."

There's a bite of guilt when I see doubt creep into her expression, but I can't tell the truth. She would freak if she knew about the locksmith and movers that met me at 4:00 a.m. Better not tell her about that part.

Jessica's still trying to figure out the logistics of it. I can tell from the furrow in her brow. She glances down at her wristwatch. "We didn't even go to bed until 1:00 a.m."

"I don't need much sleep." I take a drink and scald my tongue, the one I'd like to put between her legs.

Not yet. Give her time to adjust.

I push aside my desire for her. Ignoring it for now.

She's still not convinced, and I'm a terrible man because I'll do anything to keep her safe—even lie to her.

"Brad was hanging around the stairs, looking up at your door."

I checked. Brad's in the hospital, regrettably very much alive, though in critical condition. Turns out, he's a trust fund baby. Never worked a day in his life, just burns through his inheritance, snorting half of it and spending the rest on women, each bad decision landing him in an even worse apartment. That's how he wound up in Jessica's building, one eviction away from rock bottom. What a waste. Now I wish I'd hit him harder.

"I guess my conversation with him wasn't enough to make him stay away."

Jessica's face falls. I've got her now.

"I don't know what his problem is." Her lower lip sticks out, and her eyes swim with unshed tears. "We went on one date. *One!*"

I shake my head like I'm commiserating. "Some guys are crazy. I'm sorry you can't go back there. You understand why, don't you?"

She sniffles and says, "You're right. It's not safe there for me anymore. It was nice of you to get my stuff."

Tension eases in my chest, making it easier to breathe. She's not going back to that apartment, I'm sure of it.

Using my chin, I gesture to the boxes. "Make sure nothing got missed."

She kneels before the first box, her face dangerously close to my dick, which perks up at her nearness.

Crap. Don't want her to see that.

To distract myself, I think about all the times I got beaten up in high school, like the time my worst bully, Kent, gave me a busted nose in the parking lot. It works, and the erection quickly fades.

Jessica sorts through the boxes, moving clothes and trinkets aside before repacking each item neatly. When her hands pull out an old cheerleader's uniform, my composure shatters and my dick forgets all about my attempts to calm it. Like Pavlov's dog, it's been trained to respond to that ruffled red skirt. It quickly rises, so hard it's painful. I subtly shift, trying to hide it.

God. I'd love to fuck her in that outfit.

This thought doesn't help my hard-on. It strains against my scrub pants. I can only hope she doesn't notice because there's no way to tame it now. Not without my hand or, better yet, her warm, wet mouth.

"Were you a cheerleader?" I ask, aiming for casual curiosity. Inside, I'm holding my breath, as I wait for her answer.

Her fingers trace the thick sweater that matches the skirt, *Jessica* embroidered across the chest in bold red letters. "Yeah," she murmurs, her voice soft. "All four years."

There's no pride in her tone. Instead, there's a wistfulness, a shadowed kind of sadness that catches me off guard.

"Isn't that a good thing?" I press, brow furrowing.

She shrugs, exhaling a resigned sigh. "I guess. Everyone else sure thought it was great."

Not the answer I thought I'd get. Again, I probe. "They thought it was great, but *you* didn't? What didn't you like about it? All the practicing?"

She lets out a humorless laugh. "I actually liked practice. No. It wasn't that. It was so much more than just practices or games. It was the pressure—always having to look perfect, to smile no matter what. Worrying about disappointing my parents, my team, my entire school. And the friendships…" She pauses, her expression tightening. "Never being able to trust my so-called friends. Guys wanting to date me not for me, but just so they could say they were with a cheerleader."

Ouch. That last one hurt. Didn't I used to daydream about that? About how I'd brag to everyone if she were mine. Was I no better than the kids who used her as a rung in the ladder of popularity?

She keeps going, her voice quieter now, tinged with a raw vulnerability. "Most mornings, I'd stand in front of the mirror before school and practice smiling—praying no one would see how fake it was. How fake *I* was."

Fuck.

The idealized image of her I'd held onto for years—the girl with the perfect life, the loving parents, the endless friends—disintegrates in an instant. She wasn't untouchable or flawless. She was tired, lonely, and trying to survive in her own way.

And now, the real Jessica sits before me, bowing her head over that uniform, the weight of her past written in her posture. She's bruised, imperfect, and heartbreakingly human, and, somehow, I like her even more for it.

They say trauma recognizes trauma, and though I'm still sure my childhood was *way* worse, something in her quiet pain calls to me. My hands itch to reach for her, to pull her into my arms and kiss away her sadness.

What the fuck!

What's wrong with me?

I raise a shaky hand to my forehead and rub it. I'd brought her here without thinking it through. There'd been nothing but a need to save her last night, to get her out of danger as fast as I could. Now my breath catches as the realization crashes into me. This is more than lust. More than a desire to protect. It's something deeper, more dangerous. *Forbidden.* Something I can't afford to feel.

She's fucking with my head. Her beauty, her vulnerability…it's unraveling me.

I shoot to my feet so fast my coffee sloshes over the countertop. I don't bother wiping it up. "I've got surgery all morning and clinic after that. I won't be home until late," I say, my voice clipped. "Make yourself comfortable. Help yourself to whatever's in the fridge."

Jessica blinks, startled by my abruptness. "Oh. Okay." She looks up at me, her golden lashes catch the light and reflect it back. "I…um…have a nice day?"

"You too."

I don't dare meet her eyes as I grab my jacket and stride to the door. Once outside, I pause in the hallway, leaning against the wall as I drag in an unsteady breath.

Years ago, one of my many therapists told me I have a problem identifying my emotions. I've worked on it since, but, still, I probably have the emotional maturity of a toddler.

I close my eyes and force myself to follow the steps the therapist taught me. Breathe. Name the emotion.

What am I feeling?

The answer is stark and simple.

I'm scared.

Chapter Nine

A^dam

For weeks I avoid her, leaving early in the morning for work and staying extra hours at the gym in the evening. I'm already lean, but with this workout schedule I'm burning so many calories I might just disappear. When I come home at night, Jessica's door is closed and her lights are off. She's probably dreaming about the time she was crowned prom queen. How she smiled and waved. I watched it from the crowd, a random face she doesn't remember.

My dreams are all nightmares, which is why instead of sleeping I prowl around my condo like a detective trying to solve a case. There's evidence of Jessica everywhere. It's not that she's messy. She does her dishes and puts away her trash. It's more like she's distracted and leaves a trail of items behind her.

I find lipstick on the kitchen counter, pink like cotton candy.

Why was she putting on make-up? To impress some guy?

An aluminum tin of spicy-smelling mints on the end table. I sniff them, then sneeze so hard my eyes water.

Why does she care about her breath? Is she kissing someone?

Butterfly earrings in the bathroom, with a matching necklace. I hold them up to the light and inspect them, observing how the tiny rhinestones glimmer.

Are they special to her? A gift from a boyfriend, perhaps?

These questions drive me crazy, so much that I turn to the security cameras that cover every inch of the condo. They're discrete, hidden in bookshelves or high in the corners of the room.

Jessica doesn't know about them.

She also doesn't know what's in the locked room next to my bedroom. I told her it was my audiovisual equipment, but that was a lie. The room contains a row of TV monitors to observe all those security cameras. It also has some other...pieces of equipment in it. Things I doubt Jessica is ready to experience.

Late at night I go into that room and lock the door behind me. Like a peeping Tom, I review footage from her day. I expect she'll be gone most of the time, probably out on dates with men I'd like to throttle. It turns out that she's a bit of a homebody. She goes to work in the morning and is home by 4:30 p.m. every day. Then she spends her time grading papers, reading books from my library, or texting on her phone while sipping a single glass of white wine.

Whoever she's messaging must be hilarious because one time Jessica giggled so hard that she spilled her wine on the couch cushions. She immediately jumped up, cursing, and, after a furtive look around the empty condo, wiped the droplets off with the hem of her shirt, revealing the smooth curve of her waist. I'd replayed that tape several times, mesmerized by that strip of bare skin.

Eventually, I can't take it anymore. I have to know who is on the other end of that phone, so I wait until 4:00 a.m. and creep into her bedroom. She's asleep, her lips pursed and hair tangled. One arm hangs off the side of the bed, her wrist bent at an awkward angle.

Her phone is on the nightstand, plugged in and charging. It emits a faint ding when I disconnect it. I freeze, my heartbeat loud in my ears, and watch to see if the noise will wake her. She doesn't stir. I slink to the top of the spiral stairs and shut her door enough to block the light from the phone as I fire it up. I've zoomed the security footage in close enough that I know her security code. I've watched her punch it in countless times.

131313.

I gasped in disbelief when I saw that. It was the easiest code to crack in the world. Who lives like that? So trusting and vulnerable? If it wouldn't reveal my invasion of her privacy, I'd have a serious discussion about cybersecurity with her.

I tap the passcode into her phone, shaking my head with disapproval, and scroll to her text messages. Based on the timestamp, the ones that made her laugh are to someone she's labeled as M.

Who the fuck is M?

Michael?

Matthew?

Miguel?

Jesus, can't she spell the entire name out?

I run an aggravated hand through my hair, then look over the rest of her call log. More time talking to this mysterious M. The night before Brad tried to beat down her door, Jessica spent two hours chatting with this person.

Another name catches my attention. A missed call from a Stewart Stralla, who lives in Las Vegas. I drag a hand over my face. *Crap.* Who is he? A sigh of relief when I see in the notes section under his contact information it reads, "Cousin Stewart. Son of Aunt Marie (deceased) and Uncle Johnny (deceased)."

Thank God.

Just a cousin.

Besides that, Jessica occasionally talks to some other women. Another cousin named Sarah. A Meredith, Samatha, and someone who's labeled as "Julie from work."

No one that interests me, besides this M.

I scroll through her texts, my teeth grinding as I see the string of messages to M. They're hidden under her phone's private settings. Why? What are they talking about? The thought of her keeping secrets from me, of her laughing with someone else, twists my insides.

Frustrated that her phone hasn't satisfied my curiosity, I return it to her bedside. I'm about to go down the staircase when I pause with one foot lifted. Two steps and I'm back inside, staring at Jessica like a stalker. She's beautiful, there's no doubt about it. Lightly flushed cheeks and rose petal lips. Tangled hair that begs to be wrapped around my fist. Asleep, she looks younger, more like the girl I used to furtively watch from across the school yard.

I liked her back then because she was pretty, but even more because she seemed kind. She floated around, talking to everyone, jocks and geeks alike. I daydreamed she would cast those green eyes on me. That she would laugh at my jokes, maybe touch my arm in that unselfconscious way she had. Whenever she came near, reality would hit. I'd duck and hide, like the coward I was. I couldn't stand the thought of her laughing at me the way everyone else did.

For a fleeting moment, I imagine climbing into bed, letting her wake up with me already buried inside her. She'd be startled but helpless beneath me—*no*—I can't do it. She looks too sweetly peaceful, so I discard that plan. Instead, I gently lift her arm, then tuck it in next to her side. Moving slowly and quietly, I pull the covers higher until they cover her chest, which rises and falls with shallow breaths.

For longer than I'd like to admit, I watch her sleep, marveling at her delicate beauty, unable to believe she's here in my home. Like a fantasy brought to life. She's grown even more gorgeous with age. I can't be the only one who's noticed. Imagining those lips touching another man, like this M guy, makes my fists curl by my sides.

Part of me wants to possess her in the most brutal way.

The other part wants to protect her, even from myself.

I wonder which will win?

Jessica

He's avoiding me. It's been weeks, and I've barely seen him. This morning, I deliberately set my alarm for earlier than usual, hoping to catch West before he leaves for work. I make it to the top of my stairs just in time to see the front door drift shut. I run after him, out the door and into the hallway, wearing only my short nightgown, but it's too late. The elevator shows the numbers going down, level 12, 11, 10, until it reaches G2, the underground garage where he parks. I return to the empty condo with a disappointed sigh.

My phone chimes with an incoming text message.

Sarah: Any news?
Jessica: No, which is bad. If I got the job, they would've responded by now.
Sarah: I'm so sad. You'll apply for a different position, right?
Jessica: Of course. I'll keep you posted.
Sarah: Okay. Don't worry. We'll find something for you here.

Jessica: We totally will. I need to get to NYC.

Sarah: I know. Love you.

Jessica: Love you back.

I sigh and set the phone aside. I should be devastated that I haven't heard back from the school I applied to in New York, but honestly, with all the Brad drama and moving in with West, I'd almost forgotten about it. I've been so distracted looking for a new place to live here in Chicago that I've let my job hunting in New York slip.

No more, I tell myself. *You can't live like a queen here forever. Soon, West will get tired of you cramping his style. He'll want to bring other women here. He'll ask you to leave.*

My vision blurs as I contemplate that moment, when West says he doesn't want me here anymore. That he doesn't want *me*. Maybe it's already happening. Maybe that's why he's never home.

Confront him. That's what I need to do. Living here and not seeing him is driving me crazy. *I'll talk to him tonight,* I decide over my morning coffee.

He can't hide forever.

Adam

It's 3:00 a.m. I'm in my study, researching a new cryptocurrency I'd like to buy, when she walks in.

Jessica.

Dressed only in a short white nightgown, so translucent I can see the outline of her legs, illuminated by the tall floor lamp by the door. I like it bright, even though by this time of night my eyes are dry and the contacts I wear all day burn. I blink, watching as she crosses the room, headed straight to me.

"Aha!" she cries out, waving her finger in the air. "Gotcha!"

She sways unsteadily, and I suppress my smirk. I already reviewed the security footage from the evening. She drank *three* glasses of wine tonight, and, judging by the glassiness in her eyes, this lightweight is tipsy.

I put down my pen and lean back in my chair, letting it tilt. "It's late. What're you doing up?"

An exaggerated pout from her plump lips. "Can't sleep. My mind keeps worrying about everything."

I cross my arms over my chest. "Like what?"

There are two large leather chairs in front of my desk. She flops into one dramatically and slings a leg over the armrest, followed by her other leg, until she half reclines, lying sideways. I try to ignore the flash of pink panties I got during that movement. My dick definitely noticed, though. It twitches and stiffens.

"I need a place to live. I can't mooch off you forever. But there's nothing I can afford. The neighborhood by the school is awful, and anything beyond that is too expensive. It's all renovated brownstones and modern apartments. I don't want to commute two hours every day, but that's what I might have to do." She sighs mournfully.

"You're fine here," I counter, alarmed by the idea of her moving into that derelict neighborhood or so far that she has to spend hours on the bus. "I've arranged for that car service to take you to school and back. Isn't that working out?"

"It is, but I can't accept your handouts forever." She slumps further in the chair, her chin falling to her chest. "Besides, *you* don't want me here. You've been dodging me." An accusatory pointing finger jabs my way. "Don't try to deny it, mister. I've barely seen you." One leg slips off the chair and again I get that tantalizing flash of underwear. A thong from the looks of it.

"You're right." I rip my eyes from the sight. "I've been staying away on purpose."

She stares down at her toes and asks in a small, sad voice, "Why? Do you not like me?"

"Come here." I hold out my hand and beckon.

Jessica rises and comes over to where I sit. I grab her by the wrist and pull her into my lap so suddenly that she lets out a startled yelp.

Raising my hips, I press my erection into her rounded backside. I lower my mouth to her ear and whisper, "Does it feel like I don't like you?"

She shivers deliciously in response.

"Just because that one part of you likes me," she says, pushing her butt down on my hard-on as I groan at the sensation, "doesn't mean the rest of you does."

She grinds against me, and it releases something primal in me, making my heart rate spike. For the past few weeks, I've been holding back. I've suppressed my desire for her, worried about getting too close, but now with her in my arms all that lust roars to life.

I stroke my hand from her cheek, down her neck, and finally to her breast, which I cup. Her eyelids flutter shut, and her breathing picks up at my touch. It's a powerful thing, to affect her like that.

"All of me likes you, Jessica," I breathe into her ear as she swivels her hips, digging into me harder. "I'm just not used to sharing my space. I haven't lived with anyone since I was fifteen."

That makes her eyes pop open. "Fifteen! Why so young?"

Crap. I don't want to explain about my mom and my shitty teenage years. Not to her. I shift my hand and slide it beneath the thin strap of her gown. Her skin is warm and soft. Her heartbeat thrums against my palm. Moving slowly, so she feels every caress, I stroke the tender skin along the underside of her breast, then shift higher, moving closer and closer to her nipple. When I finally reach it, she arches and moans, letting her head fall back on my shoulder.

I'm tuned into her response. Every shift of her hips, every little whimper that falls from her lips, make me harden even more until it's too much. My restraint shatters. I stand, pulling her along with me, then shuffle us to my desk. Firm pressure applied to the back of her neck bends her forward over the desk's surface. She throws her hands out, palms flat and fingers spread to stabilize herself. The hemline of her nightgown rises, showing the half-moons of her ass. I was right. It is a thong. I run my index finger along its embroidered edge, then hook it and pull it to the side so I have access to her core, which is already slick with arousal.

I rub my hand into that wetness, let it coat my fingers so I can tease her clit with no resistance. My fingers catch on that sensitive bundle of nerves and circle it slowly. Then, using two fingers, I penetrate her and pump in and out. Trembling, she moans and bucks against my hand, riding it. I adjust the pace to synchronize with the rolling of her hips, letting her guide how hard and fast she wants it. With one hand on her back and the other fingering her, I have her completely at my mercy. Once she's so close to orgasm that her walls flutter around me, I pull away.

She makes a disgruntled sound in the back of her throat and breathes out a pleading, "West."

I chuckle, delighted at the sight of her bowed over my desk with her hem shoved up to her waist, her ass on full display. I give it a light smack with the flat of my hand, enjoying the sting.

"Ow." Jessica looks over her shoulder with a frown, uncertain why I did that. I can't explain to her my frustration over the past few weeks. The torture of having her so close and not knowing every thought in her pretty head. I have questions, and I know exactly how to get the answers I want.

The desk drawer next to me slides out easily. I fetch a condom from it and quickly fit it over my swollen dick. I'm throbbing for her, my tip leaking with pre-cum. It would be so easy to satisfy us both with a couple of quick thrusts, but I'm good at denying my pleasure. I wait and bide my time.

Two tugs and her panties slide down her legs. I lean over to help her step out of them, bringing my face to the globe of her ass. I gave it a quick nip, which makes Jessica jump in surprise and half-rise to look at me. My hand on her lower back, I inch her back down until her cheek presses to the hard wood of the desk.

With my foot, I widen her legs so there's plenty of room for me to step between them. My cock presses into her center with little resistance. I enter her, and she moans loudly. I pull out slowly and then slam into her as far as I can go. She cries out, and it's the sweetest music I've ever heard. With a brutal pace, I take her from behind, seesawing my dick in and out of her wet pussy. She feels fucking amazing, tight and hot. She's vocal, which I love, crying out as I move within her. My dick is so hard it feels like the skin might split. I push her harder against the table, lifting her slightly. At this angle, the table edge should be brushing against her clit with each thrust. It doesn't take long for her to tighten around me.

That's when I stop. Our combined harsh panting fills the air. Leaning forward, I wind my hand into her long hair and give it a light tug, asking, "Who's M?"

"Wh—what?" Lust-dazed, she's slow to understand.

"On your phone. Who's M?" I repeat, anger and frustration buzzing under my skin. The thought of someone else touching her like this makes me want to set the world on fire. I'd rather burn it all down than share her. Deliberately, I loosen my grip on her hair and slow my breathing.

"What? How?" she mumbles, then catches her breath as I move in and out of her in tiny centimeter-long motions, just enough to remind her I'm there. To motivate her.

"M," I prompt, with my mouth close to her ear, slowing down the pumping of my hips.

She groans, frustrated that she's so close. A huff from her with a furrow in her brow as she thinks.

"Jessica..." I don't hide the threat in my voice.

"Oh! Monica. My best friend. I didn't remember her name the first time we met, just that it started with the letter M."

Her best friend...or is she lying?

Without warning, I give her ass a hard spank. A surprised squeak flies out of her lips.

"Why is M set to private?"

Another smack, this time softer. Already guilt churns in my stomach. I like spanking women, but only when it's consensual and out of passion not anger.

Get your shit together.

In my own pathetic way, I made amends by stroking her wet pussy until she's moaning again, her fingers scrabbling against the desk.

More gently I repeat, "Why would your text messages to M be hidden, if it's just your friend?"

Another thrust and Jessica gasps out, "She sends me thirst trap videos of masked men all the time. I don't want the kids at school to accidentally see them."

A wave of relief pours over me, shocking me with its intensity.

That actually makes sense.

Thank God.

I place my forehead on her back and rest for exactly ten seconds, counting in my head.

1, 2, 3, 4...

Then my hands move to her hips, one on each side, and I give her a sharp thrust angled upward so I can go as deep into her as possible. She groans, throwing her head back. "Yes. Oh my God. That feels *so* good," the words drag out. I continue to fuck her, experimenting with speed and pressure. I'm learning there's a spot that makes her gasp aloud every time I hit it. I aim for that location, making sure to drag my tip along it. Within minutes, she's screaming my name into the wooden surface as her walls clench and pulsate around me. I had planned on making her come again, but the sensation takes me over the edge right along with her. I empty into the condom so hard I have to grab onto the sides of the desk so I don't lose my balance and fall over.

Chest heaving, I pull out and stand with a twinge in my back from being bent over for so long. Jessica's hair is tangled and sweaty at the base of her neck, I brush it aside and help her stand, straightening her nightgown. Then, I fall back onto my office chair, dragging her back onto my lap.

Jessica snuggles against my chest, tucking her head under my chin. She gives a contented sigh, which makes me smile. We sit in silence for a few minutes, as our breathing slowly returns to normal.

She breaks the quiet with the question I was waiting for. "How did you know about my phone? About Monica?"

I'd practiced my answer in my head several times earlier this evening, preparing for this exact moment. Jesssica is a smart woman. I knew she wouldn't let it go.

I lie. "I heard a buzzing from your room one morning. I came up to check it out, and it was your phone. You were sleeping with it going off right next to your head." I chuckle lightly as if this is just a silly anecdote I'm sharing with her. "I shut it off so it wouldn't wake you. The message was from M, so I wondered who that was, calling at such an early hour. I tried to read the text to make sure it wasn't an emergency, but it was set to private."

She shifts, sitting up to look at me with the corners of her mouth turned down. "I don't remember that."

I brush a lock of hair back. "Of course not. You slept right through it."

Jessica looks like she wants to argue, but before she can begin a huge yawn splits her face. Her hand rises to hide it. "Sorry," she mumbles once it's passed. Her head drifts back down to settle against my chest, and I breathe a sigh of relief that she's letting the topic drop, at least for now.

"I can hear your heart," she tells me, pressing closer.

"What's it saying?"

"That you're going to start coming home."

I laugh at that but don't make any promises. The reality is that I can't decide which is worse—ignoring her or being obsessed with her.

Another yawn. This one smothered against my shirt.

"I think it's time for bed." I scoop her up in my arms and stand.

"I can walk," she protests, squirming to get down.

I grip her tighter. "You're drunk on wine and orgasms. I'll carry you."

That makes her giggle, the sound light and happy.

"Besides," I continue, "you're the one who once pointed out that the staircase is dangerous if you're under the influence."

That settles her down. Jessica wraps her arms tighter around my neck. I take her up to her room, winding around the stairs carefully so I don't trip. By the time I get her to her bed, she's almost asleep, her eyes drifting shut with long, slow blinks. I tuck the covers up to her chin. I've just turned away when she says one word that makes me freeze.

"Stay."

I turn back to her. "You know I can't."

"Not can't. Won't," she argues, words trailing off at the end as she fights against her drowsiness.

I sigh. "It's just not something I do."

"No exceptions?" she asks plaintively.

"*None.*"

As I leave her room, closing the door behind me, her words echo in my mind. She's right.

It's not that I can't stay.

It's that I'm afraid of what will happen if I do.

Chapter Ten

Adam

It's 6:00 p.m. when I arrive home the next night. I push open my front door and am greeted by the sight of Jessica's ass as she bends over to look in the oven. It's an exquisite sight. My condo smells like brown sugar and butter just had sex, which makes sense when I see the rack of chocolate chip cookies cooling next to the sink.

"You're here!" she cries out warmly once she stands and sees me. A wide smile spreads over her face.

I freeze like a gazelle that's been spotted by a lion. My heart thuds painfully, and a claustrophobic panic swirls in my gut.

This is too much. Too domestic. Too happy. Too goddamn *nice*.

"I'm going to go change," I mumble and turn on my heel, fleeing down the hall to my bedroom. I move fast but not before I see the disappointment on Jessica's face. The way her shoulders slump.

Fuck.

I made her feel bad, which makes me feel bad. This is the problem. I'm not cut out for this. I'm not designed to make people happy. I don't know how to act normal. I never saw what that looked like growing up.

In my bathroom, I peel off my scrubs and throw them in the hamper. Standing only in my boxer briefs, I place my hands on the edge of the sink and let my head drop forward. Closing my eyes, I count to twenty-two and give myself a pep talk.

You can do this. Just go out there and talk to her. Eat her food and wash the dishes and say thank you. You've watched enough sitcoms to figure this out, you moron.

Even my internal dialogue thinks I'm an idiot.

I straighten, square my shoulders, let out a deep breath, and get dressed in gray sweatpants and a black T-shirt.

She's at the table when I come back out, the food in front of her so fresh it's still steaming. A matching plate sits at the place setting across from her. I take the seat there and admire the Pasta Carbonara she's made along with a leafy green salad and crusty garlic bread.

Jessica sips her wine and eyes me silently as I serve myself. Her gaze is sharp, which makes me want to hide but also warms me. I want to bask in her attention.

"What was that?" she asks.

I pretend not to understand. "What?"

"You running away just now. You looked like you thought I was going to attack you with a knife and serve you up for dinner."

I laugh, the sound artificial even to my ears. "I had to change out of my scrubs. That's all." I set my jaw and give her my frosty stare, the one that sends the nurses scrambling back at the hospital.

It doesn't work.

Jessica isn't scared of me, although she should be.

"I don't think so." She focuses on me, laser sharp, and I resist the urge to shrink into myself. "I think you got spooked. I think you're wishing you were on your own right now. That you could do whatever you do when I'm not here. Like walk around naked or masturbate while looking out your window at the city below."

"Jessica!" I say, slightly scandalized, which I know is hypocritical given what's in the locked room.

She's on a roll now. My protesting doesn't even slow her down.

"I've snooped all over this condo," she admits with her chin resting in her hand. Her food sits before her, uneaten. "Know what I found?"

Alarmed, I ask, "What?"

"Nothing. Big fat nothing." Those green eyes never leave my face. "Being here is like living with a ghost. There's nothing personal. No photos or scrapbooks or even documents, beyond your medical license and that kind of stuff." She looks over at my bookshelves. "You have a ton of books, every genre imaginable, which is a perfect example of what I'm talking about."

"How so?" I ask. There's a part of me that wants to know more. To see how she views me.

"Usually, you can tell a lot about someone based on the books they read. Sci-fi, they like politics and have a good imagination. Historical fiction, they like war and figuring out how events in the past affect us today. Romance readers are hopeful—they think everyone can be redeemed. But *you*," accusation mixes with her words, "*you* read it all. As a result, when I look at your bookshelves I'm left knowing you no better than I did two months ago when I first walked into your office."

No idea what to say to that. I've lived my life trying very hard *not* to be known, and, according to Jessica, I've done a damn good job of it.

I should feel proud of myself...but I don't.

"Do you need to know me?" I ask, not sure what answer I want to hear.

"Yes," she says simply. "I would like that."

I swallow, look away. "I have a past I'm not proud of, so I'd rather not talk about it."

A long silence as she considers this. "Fine. Then don't. Talk about the present. Tell me about your day, about your favorite food so I can cook it for you. Teach me about the stock market, about medicine. If you don't want to look backward, we can look forward."

Some of the tension drains out of my body at that. I was worried she'd pry. Dig up all the bones in my graveyard and, worst of all, find out who I *really* am. How can I explain it now? That I knew her back in high school. The time for that conversation was months ago.

"I think I can do that. At least I'll try," I promise. I raise my wine glass to her. "To the future."

She clinks her glass against mine. "The future," she echoes, her voice soft but weighted. She takes a sip of her wine, her eyes lingering on mine, searching for truths I'm not ready to reveal. If she knew everything, she wouldn't be sitting here. She wouldn't be smiling at me, cooking me dinner, or hoping for a future.

She'd be running.

Jessica

Things shift after that first dinner together.

Not like a landslide. West doesn't just open up and start telling me all his secrets.

No. He lets me in like a leaking faucet, in dribbles and drabbles. Some nights when he gets home, he's tired or extra wary of me. Those times I get one-word answers and an excuse about needing to go to bed early. Other nights he's more energized. Those are my favorite times, when he speaks long paragraphs about an interesting patient he had that day or about how he wants to invest in a new company that uses external brain wave stimulation to control epilepsy. In those rare shining moments, he loses his brooding man vibes and gains a boyish quality, open and unguarded.

In return, I tell him about my day—about my students. Milo, who aces every test but never turns in his homework because he works two jobs after school to help support his family. Kieke, whose family has moved three times in the past five months, bouncing between couches and unable to find stability. I slip granola bars into her backpack when she's not looking, and, though we never talk about it, she always leaves her bag unzipped.

Not all my stories are heavy, though. There's Beck, who just won the local science fair, and Ari—quiet, withdrawn Ari—who, with a little nudge from me, went from never speaking in class to starting his own e-sports club. Now he's leading it with the kind of confidence I always knew was there.

At first, I'm hesitant to tell West everything. Sometimes, the things I share make him frown, a flicker of judgment in the downturn of his mouth. I hold back, editing out certain details, afraid he'll say I'm too invested. Over time, something shifts. He starts to show interest in these students he's never met, asking about them over dinner. How did Sam do on his test? Is Cheri still dating Nick? Slowly, the judgment fades, replaced by a curiosity that makes me feel a little less alone in carrying the weight of their stories.

Before I know it, a month has passed, and this condo, which once felt overwhelmingly opulent, now feels like home. I shouldn't get too comfortable, though. This is only temporary. Every day I still search for Chicago apartments and New York jobs online. Eventually I'll find a new home here or a new job in New York and then I'll have to leave.

The thought fills me with sadness. I wouldn't have called myself lonely before. I had friends and went on dates, but now that I've lived with West, I see that I *was* lonely. Going out with friends and dates all ended by 11:00 p.m., and the empty hours that followed were hollow. I used to putter around my apartment until 2:00 a.m., vacuuming my already clean floor and overwatering my houseplants until they all died in an effort to keep myself busy. I don't do those things anymore. Now I stay up with West, talking or reading next to him until my eyelids droop and I yawn. Then I climb up the spiral stairs to my room and fall asleep with the echo of his voice and the flash of his mirror eyes in my mind.

West would never admit it, but the contented sigh he lets out as he sits beside me on the couch, paired with the subtle glances he keeps sneaking my way, tells me he was lonely before too.

As comfortable as everything is, two mysteries nag at me. One, why aren't we having sex, and two, what's in that locked room downstairs?

To answer number one, I run through the possibilities. Maybe he doesn't find me attractive anymore? To test this theory, I wear my shortest skirt, the one that shows my butt when I bend over. It's black and pleated, almost like my old cheerleading skirt. I pair it with a tight white crop top and my favorite beaten-up Vans.

That day West comes home and skids to a stop in the doorway. He stares at me with wide, gray eyes, which he then tilts to the ceiling and squeezes shut. Hand rubbing his temple, he stays there muttering to himself. I hear the whisper of his voice, counting 1, 2, 3, 4... The rest of the night he barely looks at me. The one time I put my hand on his shoulder when I walk by, he jumps like he was bitten by a rattlesnake.

By the end of the evening, I'm convinced he doesn't like me that way anymore. Most likely, I've been friend-zoned. A common occurrence for me since I'm so "nice."

Ugh.

No woman wants the hottest man she ever saw to just think of her as "nice."

I give up on the idea of being more than friends with West and focus instead on the locked door. When I pass the room, I hear a low whirring sound, like the noise a computer makes when its fan turns on. Even more strange is that when it's dark a flickering white light shines out from under the door. It strobes flashes of white, gray, and black across the hallway floor.

Intrigued, I search for the locked room's key in every drawer and cupboard but find nothing. West either carries it with him or keeps it at his office. I try to pick the lock with an old bobby pin. In the movies that always works, but in real life half of the bobby pin breaks off and gets stuck in the lock mechanism. I spend a sweat-filled thirty minutes using every tool—kitchen knife, toothpick, another bobby pin—to get it free. I'm already rehearsing what excuse I'll give West for ruining his lock when I finally get the piece out using my favorite eyebrow tweezers.

Thank God!

At that moment, the front door opens, and West strides in. I hide the tweezers behind my back, which is ridiculous because there's nothing inherently suspicious about them. The weird thing is that West is also hiding something behind *his* back, except his is harder to hide because it's a huge white box tied with a shiny red bow.

Is that for me?

It can't be, right?

If it's not for me, that means it's for another woman, which makes me want to melt into a puddle of tears and then throw these extremely pointy tweezers at his head. Seeing what these things do to my eyebrows, I could do some serious damage with them. I grasp the tweezers more tightly in my hand and ask, "What'cha got there, West?"

The guilty flush that climbs his cheeks has me gritting my teeth. I'm about to play dartboard with his face when he clears his throat and says, "I need to talk to you."

Oh God, here we go. This is when he tells me to move out so his seven-foot-tall supermodel girlfriend can move in. I bet he won't make her *live up the spiral staircase tower like Rapunzel.*

I send him a glare that makes him flinch backward, a puzzled frown pulling at his mouth. "Are you okay?" he asks me.

"Fine." I put the tweezers in my pocket and slouch into the living room, where I fling myself on the couch, already planning my next steps.

Monica will let me sleep on her couch if I ask.

West sits next to me. He carefully places the box between us, handling it like it's a stick of dynamite that'll explode if he moves too fast.

I eye the package, resisting the urge to childishly knock it onto the floor and stomp on it.

"Well?" I prompt.

"You're coming with me to the charity gala on Friday," he says, his lips pursed and jaw set. He stares at the carpet like he's inviting it rather than me.

"What?!" My brows hit my hairline. That definitely wasn't what I was expecting. A pleasant warmth runs through me. He's not kicking me out. He's *taking* me out. My happy feeling is quickly replaced by annoyance once I fully process the arrogant way he just said it.

"Are you ordering me or asking me?"

Gray eyes drift to mine and then bounce away. "Um, asking, of course. Didn't I ask?"

"No. You didn't," I answer, my tone flat.

He clasps his hands in his lap and manages to look contrite. "Sorry. I'm a little nervous."

At that admission, my hard feelings melt away like a snow cone on a summer day. "Where's this gala? What's it about?"

"It's at the Art Institute of Chicago downtown," he explains. "It's in their conservatory. They have it every year. There's an auction to raise money, and they always ask me to donate a prize. I usually say no, but this year they're fundraising for a charity that supports homeless children and teenagers."

"You want to help out?" I scoot closer, loving this generous and bashful version of West. I've never seen him like this, but I guess he's never had to ask me for anything before. I've always been the one begging for favors.

He nods, staring at his hands. "I always want to help kids. When I started medical school, I thought I'd be a pediatrician."

"What made you change your mind and go into obstetrics/gynecology instead?" I've wondered about his choice of specialty before. It's not common to see men in that profession.

"I realized that by the time you see a kid with something wrong, it's already too late. I figured the most important person in a child's life is their mother. Give a kid a healthy mom, in both mind and body, and the kid has the best chance for success."

My heart warms, thinking about how selfless he is. To make his career choice based on the needs of others.

"I guess we have that in common," I tell him, lightly bumping my arm against his. "We both want to help kids."

A small smile from him. "I guess so."

"You want me to go to this gala?" I ask, refocusing on his earlier question.

"I need you to help me with the prize."

"The one they're auctioning off? What is it?"

"Me." He lifts his head. "They're auctioning off me."

"Come again?"

"It's a date with me. That's the grand prize. I think it's stupid, but one of my partners' wives is organizing the whole thing. She gave me this big speech about how I'd be doing it for a good cause and everything. Next thing I knew, I'd agreed to it." He leans close to me and, in a scratchy whisper, says, "She's like a wizard. You listen to her talk in circles long enough, and you'll agree to anything she says. Wait until you meet her, and you'll see what I mean."

I blink, trying to wrap my head around this plan. "If you'll end up with a date from this thing, why do you need me?"

"Because I don't want to date any of the women who will be at the gala. There's several who've already said they're going to bid on me, including a top hospital administrator who I detest." He leans back against the couch, scrubs his hand across his face, and groans.

"I can't get you out of it if you already said you'd do it." My rule-following instincts rebel at the very idea. I was always the kid who ended up as the only guest at the unpopular kids' birthday parties because I'd agreed the moment they gave me the invitation. Even if a better party came up at the same time, I'd stick with whoever I said yes to first.

"I'm not asking you to get me out of it. I need you to bid for me. You have to win the date, so the other women don't get it. You can use my money. Spend as much as it takes. Sky's the limit."

"You want *me* to spend *your* money to win *you*?" I clarify.

"Exactly." He nods, a hopeful expression lighting his face. "Plus, you'll get a good dinner and free booze. They have an open bar."

I hold up my hand. "Wait. You're telling me I get free food *and* alcohol *and* I get to spend your money?"

His lips twitch with a smile.

With a grin, I throw up my hands and say, "I'm in! I mean, how could this get any better?"

"Well..." He nudges the box my way. "This might make it a little better."

I gather the package into my lap. "You got this for me?"

West ducks his head. "I was worried you'd take a lot of convincing, so I wanted to sweeten the pot."

I laugh, the sound lifting into the air. "You underestimate how easy I am." West gives me one of his famous eye rolls, and I chuckle. A few tugs on the end of the bow unties it. The silky ribbon slips to the floor by my feet.

West bends down to fetch it, his face at the level of my knee. He pauses there, then tentatively reaches out. I'm wearing shorts so I feel every cell in my body rejoice when his warm hand wraps around my ankle and slides with agonizing slowness up the front of my leg to my knee. He stares at his hand on my leg, his eyes unfocused like he's mesmerized.

It's the first time he's voluntarily touched me in forever, and just that slight contact has my heart racing. His gaze flicks up to mine, and the spell breaks. West snatches his hand away like I'm on fire and he doesn't want to get burned.

"Open the gift," he says, suddenly brusque. He crosses his arms over his chest.

I try not to take offense. I'm getting used to it now, this push and pull. He's like the ocean—advancing to high tide and then retreating, leaving broken seashells in his wake. I focus on the box, letting the childish excitement of opening a gift displace any awkwardness between us. When I lift the lid and brush aside the gauzy pink tissue paper, I gasp out loud.

"West!" I cry out as I pull the dress from the box. It unfolds in my hands, yards of scarlet silk and tulle cascade to the floor. "It's gorgeous!" Standing, I hold it up to myself and give a little twirl.

The dress has thin spaghetti straps, the bodice shaped like a corset with a wide ribbon that ties up the back in a crisscross pattern. The skirt is full but not too wide, with an overlay of tulle studded with tiny crystals and rhinestones. It shimmers and glitters as I sway.

West watches me, a small smile playing on his lips. "Do you like it?"

"Like it?!" I exclaim. "I love it!"

"Why don't you go try it on? Make sure we don't need to call in a tailor before Friday."

"Good idea," I agree, turning to go to the bathroom, but then I stop. That lingering touch on my leg has given me hope. Maybe romance between us isn't a total lost cause. I turn back to him and gather up my courage. Right there, in the living room, I strip off my shirt and shorts so that all I am wearing is my bra and matching lavender panties. West stares at me without blinking, his chest rising and falling rapidly. Just when I'm about to claim victory, his expression hardens and he glares up at me.

"Try it on," he says through gritted teeth.

"Okay. Jeez." I widen my eyes. So much for attempting to seduce him. I was hoping that seeing me half-naked would end up with us doing it on the living room floor, but no such luck. Quickly, I pull the gown over my head. Of course, it gets stuck halfway so my arms are poking from the top but I can't get them out far enough to push the dress all the way down.

"A little help here," I say, my voice muffled from the layers of fabric that cover my face.

Even through the dress I can hear his impatient sigh. It takes both of us working together to yank the dress down and straighten it out.

Once that's done, I present my back to him. "Tie me up?"

I can't see his face, but I hear the strangled noise that rises from the back of his throat. *Oops. Didn't mean it like that.*

I have a Scarlett O'Hara moment as he takes the ribbon and pulls it tight, cinching the top of the dress close to my body. It forces my breasts upward, so they look fuller than usual.

With one last tug on the laces, he says, "All done."

I spin to face him, arms outstretched, grinning because even without a mirror, I know I look incredible. The dress molds to my body like a second skin, the silky fabric whispering over every curve. I hadn't noticed before, but now that I'm wearing it, I feel the way the plunging neckline frames my cleavage, how the fitted bodice accentuates my waist before flaring into a skirt that flows like water when I move.

Then, there's the slit.

High—dangerously high—running up my thigh to reveal flashes of bare skin with every step, every shift of my hips.

West's gaze travels down, slow and deliberate, lingering first at my exposed neckline before dipping lower, tracing the curve of my leg where the dress parts. His eyes darken slightly, his jaw tightening. For a long second, he doesn't speak.

Finally, his eyes return to mine. I almost pass out from joy when he says a simple, "Beautiful."

I want to ask if *I'm* beautiful or if the dress is, but I'm too scared of the answer so I just beam at him and say, "I love it. Thank you."

That makes him smile, the full relaxed grin that extends all the way to his eyes. I can count on one hand how many times I've seen that expression on his handsome face.

"I bought shoes to match," he tells me. "The same color. Hopefully they'll fit. I looked at the heels in your closet the other day when you weren't back yet so I could figure out the right size."

My hand goes to my chest. "That was so thoughtful of you."

I get another of those special smiles. We lock gazes, and there's a frozen second where I feel it—a connection zinging between us. Intense and intimate. I lean toward West, and he bends to me. I zero in on his lips, the need to kiss him so strong that I'm already imagining what he tastes like. We get inches apart when the hazy expression on his face suddenly clears. He rears back and jerks his head to the side, narrowly missing my mouth.

Shit.

I lost him again.

His expression shutters, and there's a purposeful harshness when he says, "Yeah, everyone's going to be looking to see who's bidding on me, so I need you to look the part."

I deflate. My arms drop to my sides. I sigh, reminding myself not to take it too personally. I know this is a defense mechanism of his, but still...he's lucky I'm not holding my tweezers.

Chapter Eleven

J essica

Work is busy over the next few days, with my students taking a series of state-mandated, standardized tests. I always hate this time. The kids are stressed and irritable, which means they act out and get into more trouble than usual. Twice on Thursday I have to send a student to the principal's office, one for threatening me and another for cheating. Normally, I pride myself on being an ally for them, an advocate, but sometimes they push me over the edge. Boundaries have to be in place so they don't walk all over me. It breaks my heart, but I've learned the hard way that it's best for me and for them.

I'm rushing to get ready on Friday night. My hair is still warm from the curling iron as I slip on the high heels West got to match my dress. They're taller than I usually wear, at least five inches, but fit well enough that they're comfortable.

Carefully, so I don't fall, I gather up the skirt of my dress and make my way down what I've come to think of as *my* stairs.

West waits for me in the kitchen, leaning against the counter and scrolling through his phone with one ankle crossed over the other. He looks up when he hears the tap of my shoes on the marble floor. Once he sees me, the hand that holds his phone drops to his side, forgotten. His eyes widen, and for a minute he seems at a loss for words.

I feel the same way. He got dressed at the gym after he worked out, so this is the first time I've seen him in his black tuxedo with its clean white shirt and red tie. His hair is carefully styled, gelled back from his face so his strong jaw is emphasized. Black dress shoes and silver cufflinks finish his outfit.

"Nice tux," I tell him, noting how his broad shoulders fill it out.

"Nice dress," he responds, his voice lower than usual.

"It should be." I unleash my grin and send him a wink. "You bought it for me."

He chuckles at that, bowing his head to hide his smile. He holds out his hand. "Come on, funny lady."

I take his offered hand and hold it, letting him pull me toward the front door. We stop to put on our jackets since it's winter now. Cold air off Lake Michigan blows snow so hard it flies horizontally to strike the penthouse windows, creating a tap-tap-tapping sound. West has been lighting the fireplace in the corner of the room every night. I've enjoyed its crackling heat as I've snuggled under a fuzzy blanket, reading on the couch next to him. Now the fireplace is unlit. I spare it a glance before he closes the door behind us. Hopefully we'll be back in time to sit beside it later this evening.

The drive to the Art Institute is quiet. West is nervous. I can tell from the way he grips the steering wheel tightly and how his shoulders hunch up close to his ears. Most people wouldn't notice details like that, but when you live with someone who doesn't like to communicate with words you learn to interpret their body language. To watch for the small signals that indicate their mood. I've done that with him. Studied him, searching for the key to unlock all the mysteries in that dark head of his.

Do you need to know me?

Yes. I'd like that.

We park and walk to the front entrance with me tottering slightly in my high heels. Right before we enter, West reaches out and clutches my hand. If I mentioned it, he would say it was just for appearances, but I know the truth. I work with kids every day. I can sense when they need the comfort of touch. When they crave a hug or a squeeze on the shoulder.

He may be a grown man, but I'm realizing more and more that there's the hint of a child in him, underdeveloped and potentially neglected. Why else would he have been on his own by fifteen?

Tall signs labeled "special event" point the way to the conservatory. I come to a standstill when we walk into the room. It's huge, with soaring ceilings made of repeating triangular panels of glass that come together to form a dome over our heads, the center of which is a large piece of stained glass, ruby red and faceted like a jewel.

It's a true conservatory, filled along the perimeter with plants, including tall palm trees—a complete juxtaposition to the blowing snowstorm that we drove through to get here. Along with the palm trees, there are spiky ferns and tropical flowers, including hibiscus and bird of paradise. The air has a faintly humid feeling to it, like they pump moisture into the room to keep the plants healthy. I reach up to confirm it's making the curls at the base of my neck spring up into even tighter spirals.

Round tables with red tablecloths and gold chairs are placed around the space, all oriented toward a large, raised stage with a microphone on a stand.

Using our joined hands, I point to it. "That's where they're going to sell you off like cattle, huh?"

West doesn't laugh at that. He just looks grim and with a resigned sigh says, "Yeah. That's it. They'll do it during dinner. When everyone is sitting down to eat. That way the audience gets food, and I guess I'm their entertainment."

Hoping to lighten him up a bit, I suggest we get a drink. We move through the growing crowd to the bar, where, as promised, there's free alcohol. I choose a glass of red wine and West gets a gin and tonic. He's just stuffed a couple of bills into the tip jar when the big-chested nurse from his office breezes up to us.

"Why, hello," she purrs, her eyes bright and locked on me. "I know you from the clinic. What's the name again? Jennifer? Jasmine?"

I open my mouth to answer, but West beats me to it.

"Jessica," he tells her. "Jessica Jones." His hand once again finds mine, maybe more for my sake this time. The woman reminds me of a shark, calculating and predatory. She stares with fascination at our intertwined fingers.

Gesturing to the woman, West tells me, "This is Tracy Jensen, one of our nurses and the wife of my partner, Jeremy."

Wife! I don't have to worry about her after all.

"Ah! Yes, Jessica. So nice to see you again." Without hiding it, she looks me up and down. "What a pretty dress and your shoes go with it so well."

"Thank you," I tell her, tracking her hand, which has landed on West's arm.

She squeezes it and tells him, "Jeremy wants to speak with you. Something about the Surgery Center merger."

West frowns. Dismissively, he says, "I'll talk to him about it later."

"He said for you to come now. Dr. Barnet is speaking with him about it, and you know how hard it is to pin that guy down." She squeezes harder.

West shakes her off with an irritated scowl. "Fine."

"You can leave your pretty new friend with me," she says to him. "I'll take care of her until you get back."

He opens his mouth to protest, but Tracy cuts him off.

"It'll be fine. I promise not to bite her. Now hurry before Barnet takes off." She makes a shooing gesture with her hands.

There's indecision in his face as he glances from her to me and back again.

It's petty, but I can't stop myself from touching his arm—just to prove that I can. "It's okay. You go. I'll be fine," I reassure him.

"Are you sure?" He's frowning again, his brow so low it shades his eyes.

"Of course." I give him a small shove away. "I can handle it."

Right before he leaves, West leans forward and whispers, "She's the wizard."

His lips brush the shell of my ear when he says that, and I shiver, a tremor that rolls though my entire body. Tracy observes the interaction closely.

It's impossible to miss how the crowd parts as West walks away. How the women, and even a lot of the men, stare at him admiringly. I stare too, until I can't see him anymore. There's a small ache in my chest with his absence.

"Almost two decades I've known West." Tracy shakes her head, again looking me over. "Never seen him with anyone. No friends. No dates."

"Really?" I ask her, curious to hear more. "That long?"

She swirls red wine in her glass. "My husband, Jeremy, went to medical school with him and then they did their residency together. Now they're in the same practice. All those years, he's only come out alone."

I flush, feeling special that he chose *me*, then remind myself that this evening is for West's benefit.

Not mine.

This isn't even a *real* date.

"I was starting to think he was asexual, which would be such a waste of that gorgeous body, when he finally told me he likes a *certain* kind of woman." She eyes me shrewdly, waiting for my reaction.

"What kind of woman?" I ask, wondering what that could mean.

A dominant? A submissive? Young or old?

The possibilities are endless.

A shrug of her slim shoulders, "He wouldn't say. I'm surprised I got that much out of him. You know how he is."

I sigh and nod because I *do* know.

She takes a sip of wine and stares at me over the rim of the glass. "He is incredible at his job, though. So smart and good in the OR. Do you know what he's known for in the office? What he does best?"

I shake my head no and lean closer, curious to learn more about my sexy housemate.

"Mental health," she says. "That man has a sixth sense for when one of our patients is struggling. He can spot postpartum depression a mile away. Makes three times more referrals to therapists and counselors than the rest of our physicians."

"That's amazing," I say, remembering how West told me his theory about how helping moms is the best way to help kids.

"Is he good in bed?" she asks, giving me whiplash with her sudden change of topic. "Please tell me he is. *All* the ladies in the office have a bet that he's fantastic."

My shoulders stiffen. "I don't think that's any of your—"

She continues on as if she can't hear me. "I mean, I love Jeremy, but he has a tiny dick."

It's a good thing my dress is red, so it hides the drops of wine that I spit out. "Ex—excuse me?"

Tracy explains patiently, "It's like one of those little sausages in a can. What're they called?"

"Vienna sausage?" I venture cautiously. *Surely she's not comparing her husband's penis to a piece of lunch meat!*

"Yes!" Tracy places her wine glass on a nearby table. "That's it. How short are those?"

"Umm." I hold up my hand and make a pinching motion with my fingers. "This small."

She shakes her head sadly. "He tries, poor man, but there's only so much you can do with a Vienna cock. How's West? Hung like a horse?"

I have a sudden vivid recollection of West taking me from behind in his office. How the wood of his desk rubbed my cheek raw as he thrust into me. My face burns with the memory.

Tracy notices right away. "Aha!" she crows. "Knew it. Are you in health care too?"

"I'm a teacher. High-school math. I'm out at Southfield High."

"Isn't that in South Side? Like the bad part?"

I nod. "Yeah. It's a Title One school, meaning most of the students are well below the poverty line."

"Yikes. That sounds rough."

"It can be, but I love the kids. They have so much potential. They just need help seeing it."

Some of the sharpness leaves her features, making her appear softer, younger. "*Shit.* You seem like a nice person, Jessica." She turns to gaze at the space where West was a few minutes earlier. "I know it's none of my business, but be careful. There's something off about West. He's always so fucking controlled. All these years and he's never been upset, angry, or excited. Never lost his cool, and there's something eerie about that." Her expression is somber when she turns back to me. "It's not normal. I think—"

"What do you think?" West interrupts, reappearing like he's psychic and knew we were talking about him.

A twinge of surprise mixed with fear causes Tracy to startle. "Jesus! You scared me," she cries out with her hand hovering over her chest.

West gives her a slit-eyed glare. "What were you saying?"

"Nothing! I—" Tracy's next words are lost in the hiss of a microphone.

Together, we turn to the source of the sound. A white-haired man stands onstage. "Ladies and gentlemen," he announces. "Please take your seats. We're about to begin the dinner and auction portion of the evening."

There's a shuffling sound as everyone gathers their cocktail glasses and goes to sit down. Right before we leave the bar area, Tracy's eyes flick to West, who stands close to my shoulder. "See you at work on Monday, West." She holds out her hand to me. "It was nice to meet you, Jessica."

"You, too." I shake her hand, which is cool and dry. My mind is still buzzing from our conversation.

Certain women.

Be careful.

Not normal.

What does it all mean?

West takes me by the elbow and guides me to our seat at a table close to the stage. He quickly introduces me to the other guests who sit there, a couple of pathologists with their wives and a radiologist with her husband. Their names and titles all merge together.

A stunningly handsome man saunters up. He comes to stand next to West. The contrast between them is so stark that it's startling. West is all brooding darkness, but this new guy—he's pure sunshine. Bright blond hair and big blue eyes. A wide grin on his face.

"Hey there," he booms, shooting his hand out toward me. "I'm Parker. You must be Jessica. West told me all about you."

I'm pretty sure my mouth drops open in shock as he shakes my hand, pumping it enthusiastically.

West has been talking about me?

Parker gracefully ignores my sudden inability to speak. "I'll be sitting with you while West is up on stage. I've been given strict instructions not to touch you."

"Don't fucking touch her," West growls quietly so that only Parker and I hear.

My eyes snap to Parker, expecting him to be angry or fearful, but Parker just laughs and socks West playfully in the shoulder. "Down, boy," he teases West cheerfully. "Don't worry. Your date is safe with me."

I watch to see how West will react to me being called his date, but there's no flicker of emotion in his frosty gray eyes.

Still grinning, Parker shakes his head at West. "Can't believe Tracy finally talked you into this."

West shoves his hands into his pockets. "Yeah, well, I can barely believe it myself."

Parker laughs again, loud and unrestrained. "It's your funeral, buddy. Just glad it's not me up there." He gives West a friendly smack on the back, the kind that athletes give each other after a particularly good play. I stare, fascinated by this display of intimacy between them. Tracy just told me West has no friends, but given the warm way Parker looks at him I think she might be wrong.

Not sure the feeling is mutual, though. West rolls his eyes at Parker, more annoyed than entertained.

We chat for a few more minutes, long enough for me to learn that Parker is a surgeon who works in the same hospital as West.

"Did you two meet there?" I ask, curious to know more. "In the hospital?"

"I'd just started working here," Parker tells me. "Had no idea how to get around. The OR was paging me saying they've got a patient on the table. I'm rushing around, trying to find the elevator, when I run into this guy." He hooks his thumb toward West.

West takes over, glowering from the memory. "*Literally* ran into me. This asshole comes flying around the corner and knocks into me so hard we both fall down."

"It was so funny," says Parker.

"It was a mess," interjects West. "I was carrying a bunch of old reports to medical records, and they scattered all over the place."

"I helped you pick them up," Parker reminds him.

Charmed by the story, I clasp my hands to my chest and gush, "Aww! It was a meet cute! You guys had an actual meet cute!"

Parker wrinkles his brow and asks, "What's a meet cute?"

West answers, "It's when the characters in a romance novel first meet in a cute way."

"How the fuck do you know that?" Parker lifts his brows at West, incredulous.

"Never mind," mumbles West. I swear he's blushing. Quickly, he changes the topic. "I've got to get going." West warns Parker, "Remember what I said. I don't want to unmask all your secrets." He lowers his eyebrows threateningly, and something unspoken passes between them.

Now it's Parker rolling his eyes. "As if. Just go already. I told you, Jessica's my bestie. She's like a little sister to me." He sidles closer and throws an arm around my shoulder.

West's eyes narrow dangerously, but he doesn't say anything. He just turns to me and sends me a questioning look. It's an unspoken, *Are you going to be okay?*

I smile up at him. "Go raise some money for a good cause."

Once West is gone, Parker proves that he takes his role as my caretaker seriously. He chats to me and carefully includes me in every conversation. I'm grateful for his attentiveness. I might be intimidated in this grand room surrounded by people I don't know, but Parker is easy to talk to. Soon he's got me cracking up with his silly jokes and sarcastic comments.

In the background the auction begins, with the white-haired man from earlier calling out the bidding. I can't tell if he's a real auctioneer or one of the physicians who's been trained for the role. Most of the early bidding is on smaller things, such as gift certificates to a local restaurant, golf lessons, or a day at the spa.

We're finished with dinner and working on dessert by the time that West takes the stage. He swaggers up there, looking cool and confident. If he really wanted to sell himself, he'd smile, but he doesn't, just looks out over the crowd almost as if he's bored. When his eyes meet mine, they hold for a second before moving on.

"Who wants a dinner date with this handsome man, Dr. Adam West? Shall we start the bidding at $1,000?" the auctioneer asks.

Immediately, a black-haired woman two tables over raises her hand. I lean around Parker to check out my competition. The woman must love the color purple because her pantsuit is made out of a purplish fabric. Her shoes and nails are the same color. "$3,000," she bids.

Other hands are raised in rapid succession, all by other women in the crowd. Soon it's at $10,000 for a dinner date with West. As the price goes higher, more and more people drop out from the bidding.

It's down to the purple-loving lady and a younger blonde woman who sits over by the bathrooms.

"$10,000," the auctioneer repeats for a second time.

"$15,000," says the purple lady, her attention fixed on West with something like hunger.

"That's Marsha Stussman," Parker tells me in a whisper. "The hospital CEO."

Oh, so that's the administrator West was worried about. I'm so busy looking her over that I almost miss the auctioneer as he repeats, "$15,000. Going once. Going twice..."

West clears his throat loudly, and my head snaps his way. He's pointedly staring at me with lifted eyebrows.

Shit!

I raise my hand like one of my students when they have to use the restroom. "Wait! I'll pay 20. $20,000."

The room hushes, and everyone looks my way. Maybe I should have offered $16,000 before jumping to $20,000, but heck, I haven't done this before. I have no idea what I'm doing.

Even the auctioneer is befuddled. He takes his glasses off and wipes them before replacing them and peering at me. "$20,000?"

I nod yes, holding my head high. Let everyone be surprised. The truth is, I think West is worth the money. Plus, it's not coming out of my pocket. Didn't West say to spend as much as I need?

"$20,000," I confirm, swallowing hard.

The crowd gasps when Mrs. Stussman follows up by bidding $23,000. She stares at me when she says it, smiling gleefully.

That grin dries up when I counter with $30,000. I wipe my sweaty palms on the linen napkin in my lap.

The room is quiet, tension thick in the air, as the auctioneer counts down. "$30,000. Going once. Going twice." He bangs his gavel on the metal stand that holds his papers, emitting a ringing sound. "Sold to the young lady for $30,000, a new record for this event."

Everyone claps, they break into cheers and excited chatter. Around the table the doctors shake my hand and smile.

Parker congratulates me. "You did it!" he exclaims, but he's distracted, with his attention held by something over my shoulder. I turn to follow his gaze and find that he's looking at a statuesque brunette in a tight-fitting green dress.

"Do you know her?" I ask.

He straightens his tie, oozing confidence. "Not yet, but I will in a few minutes. Are you okay if I leave before West gets back or do you need me to stay?"

"I'm fine. Go get your prize, Tiger," I say, laughing at the eager puppy-dog expression on his face as he bounds off in pursuit of the woman.

"It was nice meeting you, Jessica," Parker calls over his shoulder.

"You too," I yell back, really meaning it. I laugh at the saucy wink Parker shoots me just before he taps the lady on her shoulder.

Jessica

"I guess you own me now," says a deep voice in my ear. The tiny hairs along the back of my neck raise at the sound. I don't know how he always sneaks up on me like that.

"Did I do okay?" I turn and ask West. "Was it too much money?" I shrink back, nervous about his reaction.

He sits in the chair next to me, where I've kept a plate of food waiting for him with a napkin over it. "It's fine. I would've donated that amount anyway."

My breath whooshes out in relief. "It's wonderful that you want to help kids at risk like that."

Something flits across his face, gone before I can identify it. "Yeah. I suppose."

I sniff dramatically, lifting my nose into the air. "Do you smell that?"

Confused, West glances around. "No. What is it? Food? Perfume?"

I send him a triumphant grin and declare, "Marshmallow. That's what I'm smelling and it's coming from you, Mister Softie."

He pretends to be disgruntled, but I see how his lips twitch. "Hardy-har-har. You and Parker should go to Netflix, do a duo stand-up comedy routine."

The thought of that makes me giggle. "You know, Parker really likes you. I can tell."

West leans closer like he's sharing a secret. "Don't *ever* repeat this to that insufferable knucklehead, but I kind of like him too. The days when he's in the OR are way more fun."

I gasp, widening my eyes. "Why, Dr. West," I tease. "Did you just admit that you can have fun?"

I expect him to laugh with me, but instead his expression heats. His eyes drop to my lips, and an electric tension grows between us. I scour my mind, wondering what I did to make him look at me like this.

Was it when I called him doctor?

A single finger unfurls and reaches out to trace my lower lip. My mouth parts automatically, and he slips in a little deeper. Right there in the crowded room, he drags my lip down with agonizing slowness. I resist the urge to take that single digit fully into my mouth, to suck on it like it's his dick.

What would he taste like?

His eyes darken like he can read every dirty thought in my mind. He lowers his voice until it's a sexy rasp. "Oh, I know how to have fun," he whispers so low that I lean closer to hear. "It's just that my idea of fun and yours might be radically different." There's a hint of warning in how he says it that should scare me off but instead has me clenching my thighs together beneath the table. This is a conversation I want to explore further, but not here. Not with all these people around.

I clear my throat, the sound loud. "Eat your dinner," I say, slightly breathless. With a quick wave of my hand, I gesture to his plate, "before it gets cold."

He picks up the napkin and sets it aside, then cuts into his steak with surgical precision.

Now that dinner and the auction are over, guests get up and wander, networking with each other. I look around for our waiter, but he's nowhere to be found.

"Do you want a drink?" I ask West. "I can get you another gin and tonic."

"That would be great, and a glass of water, too. Thanks." He chews his food with his head down, one arm curled protectively around the plate.

Tracy waves at me from across the room as I walk over to the bar. She's talking to a short man, and I can't help but wonder if it's her small-dick husband. Vienna sausage. I'm not getting that image out of my mind for a *long* time.

Everyone waited until after dinner to refill their drinks, so there's a line. I take my place at the end, behind a tall man about my age. He's good-looking with brown hair cut short and a well-fitted tux. He glances back at me, and we exchange the pleasant half-smiles of strangers. I figure that will be the end of it, but he does a double take and turns to me with a soft, "Good evening."

"Hello," I answer back, my attention drifting past him to count the number of people ahead of us. *Six*. I tap my foot, impatient to go back to West.

The stranger notices. "Are you in a hurry?" he asks. "You can cut in front of me if you need to."

I force myself to still. West will be fine waiting, I remind myself. He won't lose it without me. Heck, he might not even notice I'm missing. "No. That's kind of you to offer," I tell the man. "It's not necessary, though. I can wait."

We move forward a couple of steps. I expect him to turn around and ignore me, but he doesn't.

"Do you work at the hospital?"

"No. I'm a teacher."

He quirks his head, wrinkling his brow, until I explain, "My friend works here. He asked me to come with him."

"Ah, well that was nice of you." He smiles warmly. "A teacher. What an important profession. I wish it were paid that way."

"You and me both." I give him a rueful smile, remembering my old apartment with Brad screaming at the door. Maybe if I had lived somewhere nicer—safer—that wouldn't have happened.

"How about you?" I ask, attempting to hold up my side of the conversation. "Do you work in the hospital?"

He holds up both hands like I'm about to rob him and grins. "Guilty as charged. I'm an interventional cardiologist." He sticks out his hand and says, "Dylan. Nice to meet you."

The line inches forward as I introduce myself.

"Have you been here before?" Dylan asks, indicating the conservatory with a wave of his hand.

"A couple of times," I answer. "Once I brought a group of kids from the Student Council on a field trip. I had them bring paper and colored pencils. They sketched a copy of their favorite piece of art. They liked it and spent over an hour working on their drawings, which was longer than I had expected."

"Sounds like a wonderful activity thought up by a wonderful teacher." Another smile from him. His cologne is nice, woodsy with a hint of spice.

We move up in line, with him walking backward, while we talk about how great the gala is, how the weather had been so cold, and how he prefers beer, but I like wine. I don't miss the appreciative glances he sends over my body and how every time we go forward he steps a bit closer. Normally, I'd be flattered, maybe even interested, but right now all I am is annoyed.

The bartender talks to each person in front of us, flirting with the women. I want to scream at him to hurry up. West is waiting, and I have so many things to say to him. I want to tell him how proud I am that he's donating all that money. I want to ask about those other women bidding on him. I want to know why we never have sex.

When we finally get to the front of the line, Dylan orders his beer and then turns to me. "I'd offer to buy you a drink, but since it's an open bar that kind of defeats the purpose."

I laugh politely. "That's okay. I can get it on my own."

He moves aside and waits while I order my drink and West's. I shuffle to the side while the bartender makes the gin and tonic.

Dylan's eyes drop to my lips and then to my bare shoulder and finally to my chest. We're crowded together, hemmed in by the wall on one side and the line of people at the bar on the other. It's claustrophobic, the press of strangers and Dylan, whose elbow rests against mine.

"Jessica." He reaches an arm around me and pulls me close, bending his mouth to my ear like he needs to be in this position for me to hear what he's saying, but that's bullshit. I could hear him just fine before he touched me. I stiffen at the contact, my stomach turning over uneasily.

"I'd love to take you out sometime. Is there any way I can get your number?"

"Thanks for the offer, but no." I pause and then say, "I'm kinda seeing someone right now."

Dylan's wide smile dims. "That's a shame. What can I do to convince you?" His thumb caresses the bare skin of my shoulder. I shudder at the sensation, a quiver that he mistakes for desire.

"See?" he says, drawing me closer so that our hips touch. "We have instant chemistry. I knew it the first time I saw you."

I flashback to West walking into that exam room months ago, the zing that went through my body at the sight of his gorgeous profile.

That was chemistry.

This is not.

"I'm sorry, but I'm really not interested." My drinks are waiting for me at the end of the bar. I twist in Dylan's arms and reach for them, but he holds onto me, his grip tight. I'm just about to tell him to let go when a deep voice has me wheeling back around.

"Get your filthy hands off my date."

West stands there, his expression pinched with anger. If he were a cartoon character, steam would be coming out of his ears.

Dylan doesn't budge. He just glares back. "Fuck off, West. I'm talking to the lady."

"You're about to be talking to my fists." West balls his hands by his sides and takes a menacing step forward. "I said, *Leave. Her. Alone.*"

"Why?" Dylan asks. The congenial man from a few minutes before is gone. Instead, he morphs into someone who oozes bitterness. He raises his voice until it's loud and mocking. "What are you going to do, West? Count?"

West's face darkens even further with that, but he doesn't back down.

Dylan continues, "We've all heard you do it. 1, 2, 3. You fucking psycho." He speaks even louder, catching the eyes of the people in line to make sure they're listening to this exchange, which they are. More and more heads turn our way.

"Everyone talks about how insane you are behind your back," Dylan sneers, so focused on West that he doesn't notice me ducking under his arm to escape. "You think just because you're good-looking and did well at school you can get away with murder, but that's not the case."

West steps closer and quietly hisses, "You're jealous of the grant money I got from the University of Illinois. Don't try to pretend this is about me when, really, it's about you."

A whining tone comes into Dylan's voice. "That was *my* money, and you know it. I had the better proposal." Just as I squirm free from his arm, Dylan grabs my wrist and drags me back. "You take something from me, and in return I'll take something from you."

If I weren't so busy trying to get away, I'd smack myself on the forehead for not seeing it sooner. Dylan's flirting with me was a set up. He knew who I was all along. Probably noticed me bidding during the auction and thought I'd be the perfect weapon for revenge.

The realization infuriates me. I yank my arm out of Dylan's grasp just as West winds up his fist to punch him in the face. Before West can make contact, I grab his arm and pull it down. His strike misses Dylan by inches. The crowd gasps, people gathering around now to see what the fuss is all about.

"West," I say, willing his eyes to meet mine. "West, stop. He's not worth it."

West doesn't hear me. His venom-laced stare is directed at Dylan. He brushes me off and brings back his fist. I throw both my hands over his forearm and yell, "I said, knock it off!"

West tries to shake me loose for a second time, but I hold on and hiss, "Are you really going to give up medicine for this loser? Because that's what'll happen if you hit him. Then how can you help those women in your clinic? The depressed ones? The ones who need you?"

That gets his attention. He lets out a frustrated growl, but he drops his hand and allows me to drag him away. I lead him past the whispering crowd and out of the room, into the long hallway that goes to the lobby. A set of bathrooms is off to the side, hidden behind a large potted bush with glossy green leaves and white flowers so large they droop under their own weight.

I head for the plant, intending on tucking us behind it until West cools off, but that's not what happens. As soon as we reach the restrooms, he takes over, grabbing me by the wrist so hard that I wince. With one foot he kicks the door to the women's restroom open. He barges in, lugging me behind him. Two women dressed in fancy ball gowns are inside washing their hands at the double sink.

"Get out," West barks at them with so much authority that they don't even question him. The ladies gather their beaded handbags and scurry out of the room. West lets me go with a small shove forward. I stand and rub my aching wrist as I take in the elegant bathroom with its dimly lit wall sconces, rubbed bronze fixtures and paneled walls. A vase of fresh flowers sits next to the sink. Without a word, West turns his back to me and flips the deadbolt on the door, locking us in together. Keeping his back to me, I hear him whisper, 1, 2, 3, 4. He gets to twenty and then takes in a deep breath.

When he turns to face me, his expression is so dark and murderous that I move backward, away from him. I continue back, each step matched by one of his own as he comes closer. The wall behind me stops my back-pedaling.

"Why are you mad at me?" I squeak, alarmed by the rage I see blazing in his eyes.

"I fucking hate it so much. What just happened." His palms land on each side of my head. He cages me in with his body, so close I can feel the heat of his skin burning against mine.

"I'm sure they'll forget those things Dylan said," I rush to reassure him, to smother his anger.

"I don't give a fuck what that dickhead said. Don't care what anyone thinks about me." His face is inches from mine. His chest presses against me, flattening me against the wall.

"Then why are you so upset?" I cry out, baffled by the intensity of his reaction.

His lips move to my ear, his stubble chafing my cheek. "I hate that he touched you. If you hadn't stopped me, I would have killed that bastard."

I search his face, sure he must be bluffing, but find only fury, which is terrifying. My mouth gapes open, and my mind empties until some primitive part of my brain takes over. It tells me to run.

Be careful.

Tracy was right. This man is dangerous. I prepare to flee.

West presses closer, trapping me. His gaze pierces mine, unrelenting, as if he's not just looking at me but through me—stripping away all my layers.

I tremble under those intense gray eyes, my breathing erratic and my heart speeding up.

That's when he says two simple words.

"Fuck it."

He kisses me.

His lips descend on mine, brutal and demanding. His tongue plunges into my mouth, seeking, touching, exploring like he's the conqueror and I'm the territory he's invading. It's the best kiss I've ever had, completely overwhelming. Endorphins flood my brain. Arousal explodes through my body, making me instantly want him. I whimper against his mouth, my hands fisting his shirt so I don't slide to the floor from the dizzying rush of it all.

When he finally breaks away, I'm a panting mess of need. I gaze up at him through half-lidded eyes. "What was that?" My words come out slow, my brain dazed.

"A kiss." His lips are already on the move to suck and lick along my jawline. I tilt my head to the side, exposing the vulnerable soft skin of my neck to him. He could bite me there, lacerate my carotid artery and let me bleed out on the bathroom floor, but he doesn't.

"You don't kiss," I say, my voice a breathy whisper so soft I'm not sure how he hears me.

"I don't date either, yet here we are." His hands are as busy as his mouth, sliding along my sides to my hips. West gathers bunches of fabric from my skirt, drawing the gown up until he reaches the hem. Then he slips his fingers under the yards of tulle. He grasps my bare hips with both hands and pulls my pelvis forward. His hardness presses against me, so big that I gasp from the feeling of it. He takes advantage, returning his mouth to mine. Soon, I'm giddy from it. From the way he kisses me like there's no other place he'd rather be. Like the only thing he cares about in the entire world is *me*.

West has reached my panties now. With a quick tug he rips them off. They shred into pieces and a rush of cold air hits my exposed core.

My eyes snap open to watch as he casually tosses them into the trash can by the sink.

"West!" I exclaim, distressed since that was my nicest pair of underwear.

"I'll buy you new ones. Fly you to Paris to pick them out," he says against my collarbone. His hands dig into my ass as he pulls me against his length. His upper body leans into me, holding me still.

There's a questioning knock from the bathroom door. I jerk my head up at the sound, my heart rate spiking even higher.

Oh no! We can't be discovered!

"West! We have to stop. This is a women's bathroom," I hiss, embarrassment warring with lust as he teases my earlobe with his tongue.

"So what?" he murmurs as his fingers slip into my folds, parting them.

"You're not supposed to be in here!" I protest.

He snorts. "I already told you. I don't give a fuck what people think, and you shouldn't either." Without slowing the prowling of his mouth or hands, he sends a firm, "Go away," toward the door.

I can hear a woman's incredulous voice outside ask, "Was that a man?" The words grow fainter as the speaker retreats, moving back to the conservatory.

His lips are on mine again, erasing my embarrassment, eradicating the thought of anyone besides the two of us. All my life, I've followed the rules, but when he touches me like this, I want to break every one of them. It only takes a minute to make my decision.

I want this.

I want him.

Here and now.

Don't give a fuck. That might be my new motto.

He swallows my moans when he takes both hands to the place where I need him most. His fingers brush, rub, and circle my clit. A heady rush of pleasure radiates out from my core, warming me. I cry out when two fingers enter me, filling me as they move deeper.

"Such a needy cunt, isn't it?" he asks, the filthy term turning me on even more.

"Yes. Yes," I babble mindlessly. "Need it—you." My hips thrust against his hand.

"Whose pussy is this?" He adds another finger and moves it in and out.

"Yours," I pant, my legs trembling as pleasure sends electric waves dancing up my spine.

He kisses me, hot and hard, his lips bruising. "Whose mouth is this, Jess?" He's stroking me from the inside now, quick thrusts of his fingers that drag along the tender skin in my core.

"Yours. Yours." An orgasm is building in me, tension tightening each muscle. Pleasure spreads until it's a warm blanket over my entire pelvis.

"Whose body to be used as I see fit?" He increases the speed of his hand, winding me up like a spinning top. It's overwhelming, the pleasure he sparks in me. The urge to come is so strong.

"Yours! I swear it." I scream as he flicks his thumb over my clit, releasing my orgasm with that simple movement. My entire body clenches hard and then releases. I shake like I'm in the middle of a world-ending earthquake, like my bones are going to rattle apart. West keeps me steady, his hold firm until the worst of it subsides. Dampness streaks my cheeks, tears or sweat, I can't tell. My head lolls against his shoulder, heavy and spent. My eyes close, dragged shut from the weight of my eyelids. I'm drowsy now, my body wrung out.

There's a zipping sound and the rip of a condom. I feel the press of his sheathed cock against my entrance. He nudges me gently. I widen my legs and hitch one knee over his hip to give him better access. He grunts when he pushes inside, then goes deeper until he's fully seated. The sensation of him inside me wakes me up. My heart thumps so hard I'm sure West can feel it. Our harsh panting fills the room with sound. It echoes off the walls and marble floor, making it seem like there are a hundred of us having sex in here.

I open my eyes to find West staring down at me with such a mix of emotions that I can hardly separate them. There's the residue of his anger from earlier, a hint of wonder, a bit of tenderness, and of course desire. He looks at me like I'm the only woman on the planet, in a way that makes me feel truly *seen* for the first time since my parents died.

"I missed this," I tell him, dragging my fingernails down his back. I cup his bare ass and yank him closer, burying his cock in me as far as it'll go. We both moan. "I thought you didn't want me," I say, confessing my worst fear. "Earlier, when you were mad. I thought maybe you hated me."

He leans his forehead down to touch mine. "I hate that I don't hate you." He pulls out of me with agonizing slowness and pushes back in the same way. He kisses me, open-mouthed, full-lipped kisses, his tongue tangling with mine. The air between us heats, warmed by the mingling of our breaths.

"Let me in," I tell him, my breath sputtering with each deliberate stroke of his body into mine. "Show me who you are."

"You're not ready," he counters, just as breathless as I am.

"Try me," I challenge and lift my lips to his. I kiss him with every ounce of confidence I possess.

West returns the kiss. His teeth graze my lower lip, then gently bite down. Soon he's thrusting harder and faster. My back slides higher against the wall with each movement. My orgasm grows more gradually this time, enough that I maintain my senses. I watch West's face as he gets closer, entranced by how he licks his lips and his eyes squeeze shut.

"Mine. Mine. Mine," he chants each time our bodies slam together. "Only me, Jess."

"Yes." The rolling of West's hips gets me closer and closer to my climax. I press my lips to his ear and in a clear voice say, "Only you."

We come together in a chorus of moans and cries. West kisses me again. I gasp into his mouth, my body humming from the orgasm.

Later, when my breathing has returned to normal and my dress once again falls to the floor, I tease him. "Do you always walk around with condoms in your pocket?" I don't know why, but that little detail seems hysterical to me.

He finishes zipping his pants and smirks. "I do with you around. Wouldn't want to miss the opportunity to fuck you."

I lift my chin and send him a mock glare. "I feel like I should be offended by that."

He grins back at me, a completely different man than the one who entered this bathroom. "Don't be. You're very fuckable. Especially in that dress." His grin widens as his eyes travel over my body, head to toe. Ever-changing, his mood shifts again and settles into something more serious.

"You want to know me better? *All* of me?"

I match his tone, to let him know I'm sincere. "I do."

West holds out his hand to me. "Then let's go home. I need to show you something."

I take his warm palm and nestle it against mine, lacing our fingers together.

We exit the gala. Bypassing the conservatory, we head straight for the lobby and then out to the car. We're mostly silent on the drive back, each of us lost to our own thoughts. I don't know what's on his mind, but in mine there's a single word that repeats over and over.

Home.

Chapter Twelve

Adam

Jessica's eyes bulge when I take the key off my keyring. It's nothing special, a standard silver key. The kind you can have made at any hardware store. But in this moment, it holds all the weight of Pandora's box. She knows what it is immediately. Her gaze flies up to mine, her breath catching, when I hand it over to her.

"To the room?" She glances back at me, her green eyes shining with nerves and defiance. Neither of us need to clarify which room. I've reviewed the security footage. I know all the times she's pressed her ear to the door. Even the one time she got on her hands and knees to try to peer through the crack under it. I'd chuckled when I'd watched that, knowing there was nothing she could see from that angle. She clutches the key tight in her hand, and I can see it in her eyes...she wants this, even if she's afraid of it.

I follow her down the hall to the door leading to what I jokingly like to think of as my "lair." It's the place where I hide my darkest desires. As she fits the key into the lock, I lean against the wall and observe her.

Jessica is stunning in the red dress I picked out for her. It clings to every luscious curve of her body, lines and swells I itch to trace with my tongue. Her hair is messy from our tryst in the bathroom, with tangled curls that tumble down the nape of her neck. There's a love mark, a hickey, right beneath her left ear. It's so small that it would be easy to miss, but I smile when I see it. I like her this way, mussed with evidence of me all over her. Physical proof she's mine.

Mine.

I'd been so furious when I saw Dylan's arm around her. My brain had red-lined the way it had with Brad at her apartment. If she hadn't stopped me, I would've fought Dylan, right there in front of my colleagues. All the rage I push down every day would've bubbled up to the surface. A volcano of anger that I wanted so badly to pour out on him.

That hadn't happened, because of her. Jessica's voice had penetrated through the fog of my anger. It had calmed me, stopped me from making a mistake I would have regretted for years to come. I'm used to protecting her, but in that moment, *she* protected *me*. It blew me away. I can't remember any other time that someone had bothered to stop me from self-destruction.

New feelings rise in me, ones I'm not familiar with.

Gratitude.

Trust.

It makes me want to do something for Jessica. Something special to repay her. So I give her the thing I know she wants.

The room.

I just hope she understands one simple fact.

Be careful what you wish for.

Jessica

The key turns smoothly in the lock. My heart thumps with a combination of nervous anticipation and excitement. I've waited months to see what's in here.

The door swings wide to reveal a large windowless room with stark white walls. I step through the threshold and enter. The air inside this room feels colder, sharper. Directly across from me is a bank of TV screens. Black and white images, slightly grainy, flicker across their surfaces. I step closer to observe them. Each one shows a different room, all of which I recognize.

There's the kitchen, the living room, the office…my bedroom.

I suck in a breath and spin to West.

"You've been watching me!"

He doesn't even blink. "Every day."

"What?!" I think back to all the times I dressed in that room and, even worse, when I masturbated under the covers thinking about him. Did I say his name as I came?

How humiliating.

I look over the monitors again. "Do you have cameras in the toilet too? Do you watch people there?"

"No. Those are the only unmonitored rooms."

I cast my voice high and sarcastic. "*Gee.* How nice of you."

He doesn't flinch. He just stands there, still as a statue. I drag in a shuddering breath and try to control my outrage.

"Why would you need this?" I flap my hand at the security monitors. "Before I arrived, you lived here alone, right? And you already had these?"

He nods confirmation.

I turn to the screens, where nothing stirs. "What are you watching?" I ask, baffled. "This building is secure. You have a doorman downstairs, for fuck's sake."

My hand rises to my chest as a new idea occurs to me. "Oh, my gosh! Are you in the Mafia or something? Does someone have a hit out on you?"

West heaves an exasperated sigh, raising his eyes to the ceiling like he's praying for patience. "No, that's not it."

My hands go to my hips. "So?" I challenge. "Why the cameras and the secret spying?"

"I hear noises sometimes." A muscle ticks in his jaw as his eyes dart away from mine. "I used to search this entire place to make sure everything was okay. With this installed, I can see everything at once. It makes me feel…" He hesitates so long I start to wonder if he's ever going to complete the sentence. Then he finishes with a simple, "better."

I have no idea how to respond to that. *Is he saying he's scared? That he comes here in the middle of the night to check for bogeymen?*

Before I can question further, West's voice cuts through my thoughts. "You're missing the bigger picture. What this room is really about." He looks over my shoulder, and I follow his gaze.

A curtain hangs from the ceiling in a corner of the room. It sways slightly, teasing me with whatever lies behind it. It's the kind you would find separating the patient rooms in an Emergency Room or in post-op where the patient waits after surgery.

Like Alice going down the rabbit hole, I wander toward it, wondering what could be behind that pale green fabric.

West doesn't stop me. He just eyes me carefully with his chest still, as if he's holding his breath.

Determined to know the truth, I pull the curtain aside with one swift yank. It slides easily, revealing a scene so odd my brain can't comprehend it.

I stare, unblinking, for a very long time.

West whispers behind me, counting 1, 2, 3, 4. Then he's talking, his voice distant, like I've fallen down a well and he's yelling at me from above. "Jessica, we can leave now. Forget about this and go back to how things were—"

"West?"

"Yes?"

"Why do you have an exam room in your home?"

That's what is in front of me. A medical exam room, eerily similar to the one where I first met him. There's the table with its stirrups tucked away. There are the shelves full of medical equipment. There's a handwashing station against the wall. A rolling stool and a silver tray covered with a dark blue towel.

"Do you see patients here?" I ask.

"Not exactly."

"Who comes here?" There's something dreamlike about this moment. It's so unexpected that it feels like I've been kicked out of my own body. Like I'm watching this from afar, totally uninvolved.

There's a heavy pause, but I don't look over. I'm too transfixed by the glass jars of cotton balls and tongue depressors on the counter. By the blood-pressure cuff on the wall.

Finally, he answers in a low voice, "Women. The ones who like this kind of thing."

"Thing?" I echo, not comprehending. Of all the possibilities I thought I'd find in this room, this wasn't it.

"It—it's called medical play." He takes a single step closer, and I flinch. He halts. "It's my kink. One of the ways I like to have sex." His explanation speeds up. "Listen, I know it's unusual, but this has *nothing* to do with my real job as a doctor. I would never take advantage of a patient. *Ever*. I can separate what happens in this room from what happens in the hospital or the clinic. I don't mess around with real patients, don't even want to do that."

"What about me?" My voice is a faint echo, so soft. "You messed around with me."

"That's different."

I finally look at him, taking in his drawn brow and how his jaw works, clenching and unclenching.

"How?" I can't help but ask, so confused.

"It was *you*, Jess. *You* sitting in my clinic. *You* waiting for me to come in. You change everything. Make me break all my rules."

His answer has a familiar ring to it. Didn't I think the same thing earlier this evening? When he fucked me in the bathroom with a hundred people outside. Jessica from months ago would never have let that happen. I would have been too embarrassed. Too worried about what other people thought of me. Always trying to be the good girl, the nice one.

Break all the rules.

Was that what he did to me? Yes. *Is it really so crazy to think I do the same thing to him?*

"Okay. I believe you when you say this kind of behavior stays at home, in this room, but who are these women? The ones who come here and do these things with you." I try to keep my voice steady, to be reasonable, but jealousy licks its fiery way through my body, the burn scorching. It's hard not to look at that exam table and imagine West naked, screwing another woman on it. The thought makes me want to vomit.

West answers slowly, concern etched on his face. "There are places, chat rooms and such, where people who like this connect and agree to meet up." He takes a small step closer and, when I don't protest, another one. He keeps advancing until he's by my side, close enough that I can feel the wisp of his breath against my cheek when he talks. "Those women, they were only here for this, Jess. They never sat on my couch or cooked in my kitchen. No one has been up the spiral stairs besides you. *No one.*"

I must have started crying at some point because West catches a tear with his fingertip. He holds it up to the light so I can see how it sparkles. He puts that finger in his mouth and sucks on it.

"Are you drinking my sadness?" I ask.

"You want to know me—well, guess what? I want to know you too. Inside and out. I want to know what makes you cry, what makes you laugh, what keeps you up at night. I want to know how best to hold you, kiss you, make you come so hard you lose consciousness."

He brushes another tear from my cheek, his fingers dancing along my skin. He offers the tear to me, holds it up to my mouth, and whispers, "I want *you* to know *yourself* better than ever before. To know how to demand what you want, what your boundaries are, how much pain and pleasure you can withstand."

"It's just," I say as my chest hitches on a suppressed sob. My dreams are changing, rearranging themselves into something new. "It's a lot to take in."

"I know."

He doesn't say a word after that. Doesn't push or pull at me. This will be my decision and mine alone.

I stare at his offering, the physical embodiment of my sorrow held on the tip of his finger. What should I do? Pack my bags and leave? Forget all about him and the things he's made me feel. Or accept him, *all* of him. His kinks and idiosyncrasies too.

This strange man.

The man I'm falling in love with.

It's almost scary how quickly I make up my mind. It makes me wonder exactly what I'll do for him. How far will I go?

I open my mouth and let him press the tear to my tongue until I taste the saltiness of it. It reminds me of the ocean, that timeless mixture of brine and minerals. I close my lips around his finger and suck it into my mouth, swirling the tip with my tongue.

"Fuck," West groans, hemming me in until I'm caught between him and the exam table. My hip bumps up against the upholstered surface, and I cast a glance back, my heart hammering with fear and lust.

West notices. He backs away with his hands up, muttering, "We don't have to do this. I can get you a cab and pay for a nice hotel for you to stay in until you find an apartment. You don't owe me anything."

I consider his offer. He's sincere. I know it. He'd let me go if that's what I wanted.

But is it?

What I want?

The thought of walking out of here and never seeing him again is pure torture. Things are finally getting good between us. He's letting down his walls, brick by precious brick. If I go now, I'll never learn his story. Never figure out why he counts and what made him hate the sound of his own name.

He's a puzzle I want to solve.

A code I need to crack.

I can't leave.

I'm too addicted to his presence. Obsessed with those gray eyes and the weight of his body on mine.

I place my hand on his chest, over his heart. West freezes, watching me with wide, cautious eyes as I reach behind my back and pull the laces that secure my dress. Once they're loosened, the gown falls to the floor, puddling at our feet. Goosebumps rise on my bare skin like flowers blooming.

West's breath stutters, then speeds up. He says a soft, "Jessica..."

I stare up at his beautiful face and in a loud, clear voice say, "I'm here for my appointment, Dr. West."

Adam

And just like that, I know—this woman isn't afraid of the darkness.

She's drawn to it.

And God help us both if she ever finds out just how deep mine runs.

With the kiss in the bathroom and now with her in my secret room, I've broken all my rules. Just like I'd break myself for her. Just like I'd fight for her, kill for her.

I'm not a good man. I know that. All the dark desires that swim in my heart. I view the world with a mixture of distrust and hatred. But I tried to be a better man for her sake. I offered her a way out of this.

Like a gentleman, I let her choose.

Now she stands before me nearly naked and trembling. A sacrifice on the altar of our mutual lust. I grin, knowing she doesn't fully understand how there's a part of me I keep caged at all times, a wild feral beast that claws at my insides. No, she doesn't understand what she's just unleashed.

Not yet.

But she will.

"You've wanted this for so long," I murmur, my voice low and dangerous. "Do you like what you see?"

She hesitates, then nods, but her throat bobs as she swallows hard. Her nerves betray her.

I step closer, brushing my fingers lightly over her bare shoulder. "Good. Because now that you're here, you should understand something."

She turns to face me, her eyes wide, searching mine.

"This room," I say, letting my words hang in the charged air, "isn't just about desire. It's about trust. Surrender. And once you step into my world, there's no stepping out."

Her lips part, a mix of fear and exhilaration crossing her face.

I glance around at the shelves lined with carefully arranged instruments and to the sleek leather-topped examination table that I had custom made so it's wider and longer than usual. Big enough for two people to lie on it. My gaze moves to the polished mirror above the sink that gleams in the bright light. My reflection stares back, my eyes alight with dark anticipation.

This is my world, laid bare before her.

Can she handle it?

Chapter Thirteen

Jessica

West goes to the wall of cupboards and drawers. He gets out a cloth gown, the kind that you get in the clinic with ties in the back. I'm only wearing a bra since he ripped off my underwear back at the gala. Just like in a real doctor's office, this room is cold, so I'm grateful for the small amount of warmth the gown provides when he wraps it around my shoulders.

"Why don't you look around?" West's voice is a soft, sexy purr.

Hesitantly I follow him, eyeing the medical equipment with trepidation.

"It's okay," he encourages. "You can explore."

I open the drawer closest to me, the one on the end. It glides out silently. My sharp inhalation is loud in the room, where the only other sound is the hum of the security monitors. Inside the drawer are neatly arranged dildos that go from small to large. West's eyes are on me, likely trying to gauge my reaction, but I don't look his way. I'm too focused on the contents of the drawers and cupboards that I open one after another. There are sex toys: vibrators, handcuffs, ropes, and other items that I don't recognize, next to rows of medical instruments. West says the names as I run my fingers over their smooth surfaces. "Forceps, retractors, hemostats, EKG leads…scalpels."

I hold up something that looks like a tiny version of the jumper cables you use to start a car when the battery dies. "What're these?"

"Nipple clamps."

"Oh." My cheeks heat at that, and a forbidden sort of arousal swirls low in my belly. Another drawer has whips and what looks like a riding crop.

I jump when West speaks directly into my ear. He's snuck up on me yet again.

"I don't get those out much. If I'm going to spank you, I'd rather use my hand."

"Oh," I say, which apparently is the only response my short-circuiting brain is able to form at this moment.

His hand slips through the open back of my gown. Gliding along my skin to wind around my waist, he reels me in gently until my back is pressed to his hard chest. Butterflies explode to life as he whispers in my ear.

"I can fulfill all your fantasies in this room, Jessica. Even the ones you're too scared to imagine, too timid to admit to yourself. You can be your true self here. There's no judgment. Only pleasure. Only *you* and *me*."

The images his words paint send shockwaves through my body, lighting it up like a thousand suns, warming all the places where I'm the most sensitive. His lips find the tender spot behind my ear. He kisses me there, sucking and licking. I moan, arching into him like a cat in heat.

"I'm going to make you feel *so* good, Jess. I promise," he murmurs into my skin like it's an oath.

"Pick something out," he rasps softly. "One thing you want to try."

Fuck.

I've lost my mind.

A day ago, I was a normal schoolteacher living with a slightly eccentric and incredibly irresistible man. Now I'm in his sex den picking out which toy to use.

Who am I?

Is this a false version of me, or the most real I've ever been?

With shaking hands, I select the nipple clamps and hand them over, unable to look West in the eyes as my cheeks burn with shame.

"Hey." He turns me so our chests are pressed together, so my heart slams against his. His finger is under my chin, forcing it up until my gaze collides with his. His hand raises to brush my cheek and then tangle in my hair. I draw in a ragged breath. A million emotions battle in my chest. Fear, humiliation, excitement, desire. My chin quivers.

"It's okay," he says gently. "You're going to be okay."

"I'm not sure what to do," I confess, as he helps me up on the exam table.

"Play along," he whispers back. "Remember the safe word."

Cupcake.

"Trust me," he says, and I must believe him. That's the only explanation for why I follow his instructions, for why my core aches for him, even in this strange room.

I watch, captivated, as he lifts a long lab coat from the counter where it lies neatly folded. In hospitals and clinics, lab coats are always white—a symbol of purity, of trust. But not this one. This coat is black, so dark it devours the surrounding light. The choice feels deliberate, symbolic. A silent declaration that this version of West is different. Darker. Dangerous.

Gray eyes study me, and a slow, playful smile curls his lips. "Shall we get started?"

Quickly, he strips the gown off me, followed by my bra.

I'm naked now. Exposed.

I lie on the table with my knees bent. In this position, my pussy is bared to West. His gaze flicks down, and his expression heats. When he gets out the stirrups, he doesn't have to instruct me. I know exactly what to do. I put a foot in each one and spread for him, as wide as I can go.

"How have you been feeling?" he asks in his professional voice as he washes his hands.

"Bad," I say, which isn't true. Since I moved in with him, I've been content, happy even, but this is role playing. I understand that. I'm not sure if I'm doing it right, but I want to try.

For him.

For us.

Drying his hands with paper towels, he turns to me with a furrowed brow. "Tell me your symptoms."

I think quickly, trying to come up with something good. "I can't sleep. Can't eat. I'm agitated, anxious."

His gaze warms with sympathy and understanding. "It's just as I thought. You *are* sick."

"Yes," I tell him. This, at least, is partly true. I'm nauseous from all his revelations. "I feel awful."

He shakes his head mournfully. "Poor Ms. Jones." He pulls two yellow rubber tubes from a drawer and holds them up. "Do you know what these are?"

I squint at them. "Are those the things they use to squeeze your arm when you get your blood drawn?"

He nods with approval. "They're tourniquets. I'm going to need you to be still for this next procedure. I can cure you, but I need you to submit fully. These will help. Do you understand?"

A flashback to when he tied me to the bed.

You're beautiful like this. Spread out.

"I understand," I tell him, proud there's no waver in my voice.

"Put your arms above your head." West demonstrates, raising his arms up to the ceiling.

I do as he asks, stretching my arms out long.

He comes up to the head of the table. There are tall silver poles, the kind you would use to hang an IV, on each side of me. Quickly, he ties a tourniquet to each side. He grabs my wrist and tugs it up until it's at the level of the pole. He wraps the loose end of the rubber tube around the pole and my wrist twice and ties it into a knot. He repeats the process on the other side. By the end, I'm bound to the IV poles with my arms taut above my head.

An experimental tug proves that I have a very limited range of motion. I panic a little. My heart thunders in my chest, nervous and excited all at once.

West steps back and strokes his chin thoughtfully. "Yes," he says, his voice raspier than usual. He examines me like I'm his favorite science experiment. With a hint of satisfaction, he says, "That'll work."

I'm at his mercy in this position. He can do whatever he wants. With effort, I relax into that knowledge. Letting my inhibitions go, I embrace the loss of control. In my regular life, I have to plan and work and strive. Now I don't have to do anything. I *can't* do anything except take whatever he decides to give me.

I stare at him, taking in the curve of his bicep, the width of his thighs, the sharp angle of his jaw, now shadowed with stubble since it's late.

Fuck. He's sexy.

What's he going to do?

Anticipation quickens my breath and pulls my muscles taut.

"You're a beautiful woman, Ms. Jones." My heart leaps at his words, then stops when he lays the back of his hand on my cheek. He runs his hand down to my jaw, then pinches my chin lightly, tilting it up toward him. "Gorgeous face." His hand moves to the sensitive skin of my throat, where my pulse flutters wildly. He wraps his hand around my neck. I hold my breath when he squeezes lightly.

He trails his hand down to my right breast, where he rubs his thumb over my erect nipple, making it peak even more. "Perfect tits." His fingers warm with friction as he trails them down my side and around to my butt, which he palms. "Sweet ass." His hand slides around my hip and reaches between my legs, hitting the spot I've been waiting for. "And such a pretty little pussy." With that, his fingers toy with my clit, flicking it rapidly.

I moan loudly. I can't help myself. His touch sends waves of desire roaring through my body.

"Why, Ms. Jones." His eyes widen with mock surprise. "You're drenched. Is this all for me?"

Embarrassed, I turn my head to the side and avert my gaze.

"Eyes on me," he commands in a no-nonsense tone.

My eyes whip up to meet his frosty expression.

"Don't look away," he warns.

Our gazes locked, he continues to stroke into my wetness until I'm panting, trembling. It feels so good, but I want more. I need to be filled, to ease the pulsing hollowness between my legs.

He doesn't give me that.

Not yet.

Instead, he gets out the nipple clamps and holds them up so I can inspect them. A delicate silver chain connects the metal clips. They're tipped with black plastic or rubber over the part where they'll attach to my nipples.

I'm scared. I almost ask him to stop, but he's already opening the first clamp. He brings it to my nipple, and I wince against its coldness. Slowly he releases it, letting it pinch my tender flesh. I suck in a breath because it hurts, an exquisite kind of pain, the sensation sharp and burning. He places the other clamp more quickly, hurrying now. I bite my lip to stop from complaining as my vision swims with unshed tears.

Pain overwhelms my arousal, but then he's back, stroking between my legs. West pushes two fingers into me, followed by three. He pumps them slowly, his eyes glued to my face. There's a war in my body. Pain and pleasure fight each other. Each demands my attention until they all blur into one. Slowly, I relax and let the sensations overwhelm me. The bite on my nipples, the friction between my legs where he rubs faster now. I moan loudly, dropping my legs farther to the sides and arching my back.

West reaches up and gives a gentle tug on the chain connected to the nipple clamps. It stretches out my nipples, making them sing with an erotic buzzing intensity. I feel it then, the heightened desire. How everything sharpens until all the world is forgotten. I'm not me anymore. I'm a wave, a vibration, a shuddering pulse of tension that begs to be released.

"See? It's good, isn't it?" West murmurs. The quickened pace of his breathing matches mine.

I glance down and notice a sizable bulge in his pants, between his legs. He sees where I'm looking. I whimper when his hands leave my body. He steps back and slowly, with no change in his expression, unbuttons and unzips his pants. Once they're undone, West pushes his pants and underwear down his thighs to reveal his thick, erect cock. He wraps his hand around the base and strokes up to the tip where a tiny drop of fluid beads.

"Is this what you've been wanting? Will this make you feel better?"

All of my longing for him over the past weeks comes crashing back. I want him, any part I can get. I nod silently.

"Louder," he demands, his steely gaze flat and his mouth in a straight line.

"Ye—yes, please," I stutter, intimidated by him. "That—you—that's what I need."

"I like it when you tell me what you want." He rewards me with a rare smile, and my insides melt.

He looks me over, naked and restrained before him. An appreciative lingering gaze that feels like he's touching me, even though he's not. He steps closer, kicking off his clothing as he goes. He stops between my legs, which are still up in the stirrups.

A lazy smile this time. "Someday, I'm going to fill up all your holes. You'll be dripping with my cum by the time I'm done with you."

My nipples pinch, from the clamps, but even more from his words.

His hands land on my thighs as he continues. "Today we'll start slow," he says in a tone like he's talking about the weather. "Today, I'm going to fuck you until you scream so loud you can't talk tomorrow."

Warm hands caress my inner legs as they slide higher until they reach the apex. A thumb brushes over my aching clit. I moan and widen my legs, inviting him in. The tourniquets bite into my wrists as I strain toward him.

"Please," I plead. "I want you inside of me."

He circles my clit harder now and whispers huskily, "I like it when you beg. Tell me more." A condom appears in his hand like he's a magician and has pulled it out of thin air. He puts it on quickly, then returns to stimulating me.

"Yes, doctor. Please give it to me." I rock my hips against his hand, needing more.

"Since you asked so nicely." West keeps rubbing my clit while he uses his free hand to position himself at my entrance. He takes his tip and runs it up and down my center. Up and down. Up and down.

I'm panting now, awash with need. "Please."

"Such a good girl, begging to be filled up." He pushes his tip into me, and I come off the table, arching my back.

"Yes," I pant. "More."

He pulls out, and I whimper.

"Remember, Ms. Jones, this is my exam room. I'm the one in charge here," West scolds. He slams into me with a single forceful movement.

I cry out with pleasure. He pushes all the way in, which is easy since I'm so wet. He places his hands on my hips and pushes me back before pulling me toward him with a quick thrust. My back scrapes against the exam table. My wrists are suspended taut above my head. I want to reach out and touch him, but I can't in this position. He picks up the pace, hands on my hips as he drives into my body over and over again. His eyes glaze, and his breathing increases, short bursts of air. He's enjoying this.

"Such a dirty girl. You like getting fucked. Don't you?"

I gasp, breathing erratically. "Oh yes. Please do it to me."

Without stopping the movement of his hips, Dr. West leans forward and pulls on the nipple clamp chain. Not gently this time. It's a sharp prolonged tug, but it doesn't hurt now, just feels good, like he's electrocuting me there, firing up every nerve. That sensation combines with the feeling of his cock moving inside me. It's overwhelming, having him stimulate my breasts and my pussy all at once.

My orgasm grows, building from deep in my core and slowly bubbling up to the surface with each of his controlled strokes. When he pulls on my nipples even harder and pushes in as far as he can go, I climax, screaming for him as I come. The sound bounces off the ceiling and echoes around the room.

I open my eyes to see his neck muscles strain. West throws his head back and closes his eyes as he lets go. As soon as his shuddering stops, he pulls out, leaving behind a void.

I get a view of his sculpted ass when he walks over to the sink, where he wets a pile of paper towels. He uses them to wash himself off and then tugs his pants back on. Once that's done, he comes to me. The towels are warm as he gently wipes the sticky residue of my arousal from between my legs. I'm still twitching from the aftershocks of my orgasm. He releases my wrists and rubs them gently. They hurt with pins and needles as the blood flow returns. When he takes the clamps off my nipples, I cry out in pain. The rush of the cold air over my abused flesh cuts like a knife.

West dims the lights slightly, until the room is bathed in a soft glow, then climbs onto the table beside me. The upholstered top dips under his weight, and I tense, my body screaming with exhaustion and tenderness. He slides his arm around my shoulder, pulling me into him. We fumble awkwardly for a minute, readjusting ourselves, until my head finds its place against his chest. The steady rhythm of his heartbeat soothes the raw edges of my nerves.

I bite back a whimper, my skin aching, my body bruised, my emotions a tangled mess.

"Shh, shh," he murmurs, his voice a low hum against my ear. His fingers stroke along my arm, slow and grounding. "You did so well, Jess. So, so good."

His words seep into me, easing the ache. Pride flickers faintly in my chest, a fragile warmth that spreads with every word of praise he whispers. I draw in a trembling breath and nuzzle closer, seeking his heat, his reassurance. His scent wraps around me—clean and warm with a hint of something darker, uniquely West.

As I'm pressed against him, his voice becomes my anchor. He speaks softly, a mantra of devotion and awe. He calls me beautiful, brave, remarkable. His words are unrelenting, sinking deep, filling every empty, aching space inside me. Each one chips away at the lingering doubt, replacing it with something new, something I don't have the strength to name yet.

My eyelids grow heavier with each gentle stroke of his hand, each murmured endearment. The world fades, the edges of reality blurring, until all that remains is his warmth and his voice.

What we just did—what he guided me through—was foreign, unsettling in its intensity, yet strangely liberating. Now, here in the stillness, close to him, I feel a comfort I haven't felt in years. It's as if he's rewriting my definition of safety, reshaping my concept of home.

Adam

The alley where I wait is tucked around a corner, hidden from anyone passing by on the sidewalk. My hands are covered in thick gloves, the leather insulating them against the chill. I flex my fingers, the material stretching taut over my knuckles with a faint creak. In a couple of hours dawn will break, but I'll be long gone by then. Back home to where Jessica sleeps, exhausted by her time in my special exam room, my lair. She'd barely stirred when I'd carried her up the winding stairs and tucked her into bed.

The door next to me squeaks on its hinges as it swings open. It's the back exit of a strip club in the seedier part of downtown. A blare of music cuts off abruptly when the door closes. A man steps out, a cigarette glowing red between his fingers. He tosses it carelessly on the ground, not bothering to crush it under his heel.

I grab him by the arm and jerk him into the shadows. "Don't you know littering is a crime?" I hiss into his ear.

Dylan snaps his bloodshot gaze to mine. His jaw hangs wide open with shock. "West? What the hell? What're you doing here?"

I shove him against the graffiti-sprayed brick wall and pin him there with my elbow. "I think a better question is, what are *you* doing here, Dylan?"

"Uh." His eyes roll as he searches for a plausible lie.

With my free hand, I tap my chin and look up with my head tilted like I'm thinking. "It's strange because your wife thinks you're on call tonight. That you're staying late at the hospital admitting patients, but I checked the schedule and you're definitely not on. *Hmm.* How do you explain that?"

"Uh, I—um—I thought I was on call, so I came down here to—uh, check in on some former patients and—"

Sick of his blathering, I interrupt. "Oh, really? Scarlet is one of your patients? Or maybe we shouldn't use her stage name. How about her real name, Marcia Crosby. I don't remember you treating any seventeen-year-olds recently."

Dylan blanches when I say the name of his mistress. He's quick to correct me, "She's eighteen. Not seventeen."

I laugh, throwing my head back like that's the funniest thing I've ever heard. "Oh, Dylan. Dylan. You poor stupid sucker. Is that what she told you?" I laugh some more, raising my voice to be heard over the scream of a siren as a police car rushes past us. Dylan watches it with hungry eyes, like he thinks the cops can save him.

Idiot.

No one can save him from me.

I stop laughing as quickly as I started, the silence resoundingly loud after my outburst. More serious now, I tell him, "You got played, you moron. That girl is seventeen, which means sleeping with her is statutory rape." I lean against him and whisper in his ear, "How do you feel about jail time?"

He trembles, his eyes dilated with fear. "No. No, that's not true. I—she—"

"She lied. Just like you lied to your wife about where you are right now. Just like you lied to Jessica when you were hitting on her to get back at me."

I can't get out of my head the sight of Dylan's hand on Jessica's arm as she twisted against it, trying to get away from him. How, once she broke free, I could still see the angry red imprint of his fingers on her soft, ivory skin. The memory of it ignites something primal inside me, dark and uncontrollable.

Dylan quickly recovers from my truth bomb about his girlfriend. He's always been like this. Shifty. Selfish. A real asshole.

"I can't be checking on some whore's age," he whines. "Why the fuck do you care about it, anyway? It's not your problem."

"*You* became my problem when you touched what's mine," I seethe through gritted teeth while rage roars in my ears, drowning out what little morality remains in me. "You put your hands on *my* woman. You threatened *my* career. You think I'll let that go? That I'll turn the other cheek?" I gather the fabric of his shirt in one hand and shake it. Dylan's head whips back and forth so hard his neck pops audibly.

"Do you know what happens to people who touch what's mine?" I lift him by his shirt so that his feet scramble, trying to find purchase, but I've got him so high that he gives up and lets his legs dangle uselessly. I bring his face to mine, so close that our noses graze. "Do you?!"

Dylan flops like a fish out of water. "No! No, I don't know, you fucking maniac. Get your hands off me."

I grin in his face, secretly glad he's resisting because it gives me the perfect excuse to punch him. "People, like you, who touch what's mine get destroyed. It's as simple as that."

With my free hand, I make a fist and slam it into his cheek. His skin splits under the impact, and blood runs in a red rivulet down his face. The rage-filled beast inside me roars in approval, happy to be released from his cage. I continue to beat Dylan, aiming my blows mostly on his soft belly and flanks. Don't want to leave too many marks. A lacerated cheek he can explain away, which will be good for what I have in mind. Even as I'm lost in the mist of my fury, there's a part of my brain that remains calm, calculating, scheming. I have to be more careful with this one. I can't totally let go like I did with Brad.

In the beginning, Dylan tries to fight back, but he quickly realizes the futility of it. Soon, he reveals the coward I always knew he was. Cursing, he begs and pleads for me to stop. When my arm tires, I drop him to the ground. He tries to make a run for it, but I catch him easily and shove him against the wall. My forearm goes to his throat, pushing hard enough that his words come out choked.

"You fucking asshole," Dylan swears at me, squirming. He stops to spit out blood. It stains his lips red, a macabre kind of lipstick. "I'm going to ruin you for this," he hisses. "Your medical license is as good as mine. Wait until the police and the medical board hear about how you assaulted me."

"*Tsk, tsk,* Dylan." I shake my head like he's disappointed me. "You won't be doing that. Not unless you want everyone, including your wife, to learn about your teenage girlfriend. You fucking pedophile."

"I don't care about my wife. Fuck that bitch. I'm going to leave her anyway." Dylan sends me a triumphant glare, thinking he's outsmarted me. Without warning, he kicks out, trying to trip me, but I sidestep and he ends up kicking air.

"Aww," I croon with a sarcastic lift of my brows. "That's so sweet. Are you planning on making your stripper the new Mrs. Dickhead? Make sure you send me an invitation to the wedding."

"You'll get an invitation to your own funeral. That's what you'll get."

"I don't think so." I cock my head and give him my sweetest smile. "Remember back at the gala? When you were saying such nice things about me?" I pretend like I'm lost in the memory. "You said I was good-looking and did well in school. Remember that?"

Dylan twists under my grasp, desperate to break free, but it's no use. I lift weights every day, and I doubt this wimp has seen the gym in months.

Finally, he gives up his wild thrashing. With pure unadulterated hate in his eyes, he grits out, "Get fucked."

I continue as if I didn't hear him. "You left out the other thing I'm good at. I mean, sure, it's not as sexy as those other qualities, but it's just as useful. Do you know what it is?"

He rolls his eyes, knowing this is a hypothetical question.

"Math. I'm good at math or, more specifically, financial statistics." I reach into my coat pocket and pull out a thick sheath of papers, which I wave in front of his face. "That's how I know for a fact that you've been embezzling from your physician group. Millions of dollars, from what I've uncovered."

The blood drains from Dylan's face, a beautiful sight, but I don't need to see his reaction to know I'm right. People, I've learned, cannot be trusted, but the numbers never lie. I shove the papers in his face, unable to hold back my grin. "I have bank statements, wire transfers, and stock trade records that document in lurid detail exactly how naughty a boy you've been, Dylan. If I were you, I'd be much more worried about *your* medical license than about mine."

If I weren't holding him up, I'm sure he would slide to the ground. That's how boneless he's become.

"Wh—what are you going to do with that?" His gaze bounces between the papers and my face.

"Good boy." I give him a hard pat on the top of his head, which makes him wince. "I'm glad you're not wasting my time trying to deny it. That's the first smart decision you've made."

Now that I've got his full attention, I ease back enough that his feet land on the ground. He rubs his throat, glaring at me like he'd kill me if he could.

I'm not offended. If our roles were reversed, I'd feel the same.

"You want to know what I'm going to do?"

He nods, his cheeks an angry red.

"Nothing," I say simply. "I won't do anything, as long as you leave this city, actually this state. Get out of Illinois. Take your wife or your mistress or both. I don't care as long as you leave. Get a new job at a different hospital. You can carry on with your idiocy if you like, as long as it's far away from here."

Quick as a flash of lightning, my hand shoots out to grasp his throat. Slowly, I squeeze. "If I ever see your face again, or if you so much as think about coming near Jessica, I'll make sure you lose everything. Your career, your freedom, your life."

When I let go, Dylan crumples against the wall, coughing. I wait patiently until he recovers. A couple of ragged breaths later, he blinks at me owlishly. "Really?"

"Really." I rock back on my heels, grinning. "I don't give a fuck. Just go."

His posture slumps with relief. He scrubs his hand over his face with a quiet, "Thank god."

"You should be thanking *me*. You waste of space." I kick, landing my foot on his shin.

Dylan yelps, then hops comically on his good leg, holding the injured one in his hand. Again with the baleful glare directed at me. Just when I think he'll admit defeat, a cunning gleam sparks in his eyes.

He's so predictable. All I have to do is think what I'd do if our roles were reversed to know his next move. It's a thought that makes me pause.

Does that make me as awful as he is?

No, I'm way worse.

"Don't even think about killing me, Dylan. Do you really believe I'd be so dumb that I wouldn't have redundancies in place? A way to distribute the evidence against you if something happens to me?"

That fire in his expression goes out, and I laugh, knowing I've won. I let him go after that, confident I'll never see his miserable face again.

Back in my car, I lean my head against the headrest, feeling the adrenaline from my confrontation with Dylan slowly ebb out of my bloodstream. I let out a shaky chuckle.

First Brad and now Dylan. Jessica's made my life *so* much more interesting.

Soon, I'm back home. I head straight for Jessica's room, making sure my footsteps are silent on the metal rungs of the stairs. I've come here every night since she moved in. It's my ritual now, the last stop before I lie down in my bed and try to find the slumber that so often eludes me. Usually, I sit in the armchair in the corner of the room and watch her sleeping, bathed in the golden glow of the nightlight. I take peace from the soft sounds she makes, how her eyelids flicker as she dreams. One night, she even said my name in her sleep. "West," she said, her voice filled with longing. How pleased I'd been, to know she dreams about me the same way I dream about her.

Tonight, I don't go to the chair. Instead, I kneel by the bedside, next to her head. It's been a monumental evening. I can feel the shift in our dynamic. The deepening of our connection.

Softly, so I don't wake her, I confess all the truths in my heart. "Sometimes I think fate made you just for me. That you're the world's way of making up for every shitty thing that came before. If that's the case, then I'm okay with it. It was worth it, all the pain and suffering, to get you at the end." Gently I brush blonde waves away from her angelic face.

I press a feather-light kiss to her forehead and whisper, "I've fucked hundreds of women, but I've only kissed one."

Then I inject the tracker into her neck.

She's mine now, and I'll never let her get away.

ATTENTION! Want to know what happens the second time West takes Jessica to his "secret" exam room? Spoiler alert! It's spicy! So spicy that this chapter was taken out of the original version. Do you dare to find out? Available exclusively for my newsletter subscribers, sign up NOW to read it. Click the link or QR code below.

https://dashboard.mailerlite.com/forms/179195/149735069602285008/share

Chapter Fourteen

Jessica

The next three months pass like a fever dream. We eat dinner together. Sometimes we read next to each other on the couch. More often than not, we end up in his secret room, where I'm Ms. Jones and he's Dr. West.

The things we do there defy my wildest fantasies. They shatter every boundary I had. In that room, he teaches me to speak the language of my desires.

During the second week of our trips to the room, after his hands have roamed my body, touching everywhere until I'm panting for him, begging for him, he takes a step back and crosses his arms over his chest.

"Tell me what you want, Ms. Jones. Just say it, and I'll do it. You'll find I have no limits. There's nothing I won't do. You want me to spank you, fist you, call you names, I'll do it. You want me to make love to you slow and gentle, like you're made of glass, I'll do that too." He tilts his head, running his eyes over my naked body in a way that makes me feel more seen than I've ever felt before. "All you have to do is tell me what you want."

What do I want?

No one's ever asked me that before.

There are so many options, and I've already learned he's good at all of them—at least the ones we've tried so far. There is one thing I particularly enjoy... My cheeks heat as my gaze drops. In a whisper I say, "I want you to kiss me." I flick my eyes to the space between my legs.

He purses his lips and arches an eyebrow. "I'm sorry." He raises his voice like he's hard of hearing. "What was that? Couldn't quite understand."

Clearing my throat, I try again. "I want you to kiss me down there." I repeat the eye flick, exaggerating it this time.

He's trying not to smile. I can tell from how his lips twitch. "It's funny. I don't remember any location labeled as 'down there' in my anatomy class back in med school."

I huff, understanding now what his game is all about. I'm just as stubborn as he is. I clamp my mouth shut and glare at him. At least I try, but his hand is between my legs, stroking and swirling until my mouth drops open with sharp gasps.

"Use your big-girl words." West smirks at me, annoyingly unruffled.

"I want—I want you to lick my—I don't know. It feels weird to say!" I throw up my hands in exasperation, glad he hasn't bound them for once.

"Let me help you." He's using his professor tone now. "I'll accept the following terms. We can go clinical and call it your vagina, or we can go casual and say pussy or cunt." His fingers are relentless, gliding, sliding, shifting on my core until it's molten, on fire from his touch. He makes it hard to concentrate, but I know him. He's trying to make a point, and I won't get what I want until I learn the lesson.

So bossy.

"Fine," I snap out, irritated. "I want you to lick my pussy. Happy?"

The grin that stretches across his face is wide, radiant. "Delighted," he says. He easily lifts me into his lap and lays down beneath me. Pressing my ass, he inches me up his body.

I wobble, dangerously close to the edge of the examination table, which is really more of a firm, flat bed.

"What're you doing?" I throw my arms out, balancing like I'm walking a tightrope.

"I want you to ride my face," he says huskily, like the idea turns him on just as much as it does me.

"Oh—uh—okay."

I've never done that before.

It takes a minute to get settled with my thighs on each side of his head. I stay upright, suddenly shy. "I'm going to smush you."

He snickers at that, as close to a giggle as I've ever heard from him, and I can't help but grin in response. It's a gift. Every laugh, every smile I coax out of West feels like a victory. Like I've won a fucking gold medal.

"You won't *smush* me, pretty girl." His hands glide from my thighs to my hips and in one swift motion he jerks me down, so I land on his face with the full weight of my body.

"Oh my god, are you okay?" I yell, convinced I broke his nose. He must be fine because he pulls me harder against him and ravages me with his tongue, licking, stroking, and thrusting it against my already wet pussy.

"Shit." I collapse against him, unable to bear my weight as my body succumbs to the pleasure. His hands grip my hips, raising and lowering me so the sensation alternates between more intense to less and back again.

I lose control, grinding against him. I chase the high he offers. It's in me, the orgasm, growing with each brush of his lips and tongue. I'm almost there when he lifts me off him and flips us around so I'm under him.

I cry out in protest, which makes him chuckle, a sinister sound.

"I don't think you've been properly examined yet tonight, Ms. Jones." He yanks me down to the edge of the table and whips out the stirrups.

I'm still whimpering and complaining when he slots my feet into each stirrup and then ties my ankles to the stirrups with leather straps. He's humming cheerily as he binds my wrists above my head, tying them into metal rings that were placed there for just that purpose. I wiggle against the restraints, annoyed and turned on in equal measure.

West pushes the stirrups out, spreading me wide. His back to me, he rummages in one of the cupboards above the sink.

"It's my turn to play," he says when he comes back with silver instruments in each hand. "Hemostats." He holds them up. Clicks them open and closed a few times with a loud ratcheting sound. They look a little like pliers. He points to the middle of one. "This locking mechanism will hold them closed. Don't worry, though. I'll pad them so they won't hurt...not too bad anyway." His eyes glimmer with a sadistic gleam.

Crap.

Fear stirs in my gut, a noxious swirl that mixes with my arousal and—God help me—heightens it. I'm learning I like it, this dangerous collision of emotions, of sensation. Sweet with spicy. Hot with cold. I strain not away from him, like a sensible person would, but toward him.

West sends me a knowing look, like he always knew this darkness was inside me. Like he thinks it's beautiful.

He lectures while he works between my legs. "These outer lips are the labia majora, and the inner, smaller ones are the labia minora." Gently he clamps my folds together in the hemostats.

I moan at the pinch of my tender flesh, at the stretch of it as he bares me to the cool air. I'm a butterfly, spread wide, wings pinned open.

"This will hold everything out of the way, so there's no resistance when I sink into you." He slips the black lab coat from his shoulders and lets it drop to the floor. His pants and underwear follow.

A condom and then he's pushing into me with a sigh, like this is his version of heaven.

"You're perfect, Ms. Jones. A perfect fit," he whispers huskily, his gaze unfocused, his breathing uneven.

He grabs each hemostat and pulls them to the sides. It hurts, a burn that washes up my inner thighs, but it's countered by the stroke of his cock against my G-spot as he thrusts into me. My back bows as I groan, and his voice answers mine with a guttural sound that I've never heard before. It's primal and erotic. Pleasure spirals up into my low belly, tightening it, and then moving to my chest, which heaves.

This must feel good to West too, because soon he's rutting into me like a beast, like he wants to burrow into my body and make it his new home. He glances at the hemostats every few minutes, obviously enjoying the sight of them melded to my skin.

That tingling, tightening tension grows and grows in me. My body pulls together into a ball of concentrated energy. I'm electrons in a cloud moving together until I burst into lightning. I'm a bomb lit by a single match. I'm a swirling storm about to rip apart an unsuspecting village. I'm so small, yet multiplied into infinity when I'm joined with him like this.

We come together, crying out in unison as he slams into me one last time and then freezes with his eyes squeezed shut like he wants to memorize this moment. To hold onto it forever. When he opens his eyes again and looks down at me, I know it. It's there shining and unspoken.

We're in love.

Jessica

The next thing I know, it's Christmas. West gets out suture. We use it to string popcorn that we've popped in the microwave. We loop it over the branches of our tree, which rests against the window. The lights of the Navy Pier shine almost as brightly as the lights on the tree.

Christmas morning, we sit on the floor with our legs crossed to open our gifts. West gives me diamond earrings the size of blueberries. I protest that they're too much, but he just laughs and says there's never going to be any "too much" when it comes to me.

I give him a stethoscope I had custom made, only to be used in our special room. The entire thing is black, even the metal parts, and I had his initials engraved on the back, *A.W.*, in curling cursive script.

When West opens the gift, he stares at it for so long that I start to worry.

"Do you not like it?"

He presses the box to his chest and in a fierce whisper says, "It's perfect." I'm shocked when I see his eyes have a sheen to them, like he's holding back tears. "It's just—it's—no one's given me anything like this before."

"You mean something custom made?"

"I mean a gift, like a real gift." His head droops. "We didn't have money when I was young. Mom said Santa couldn't make it to every single house and that's why he skipped ours. I thought it was because I'd done something bad, something naughty. That it was my fault we had no tree. No presents."

A hush settles between us. This is the first time he's mentioned his childhood or his mother. I've gotten the feeling before that he had it rough growing up. It's in the way he hoards food in the pantry, stocking up on cans of soup that he never eats, and how he takes such painstaking care of his shoes, polishing them himself, so he doesn't have to buy a new pair.

"But you grew up, and I'm sure you got gifts then, right?" I ask, my composure slipping as I wait for his answer. Tears build in the back of my throat.

A shrug. The corners of his mouth pull down. "A bottle of wine from a colleague. Cookies from a patient. Stuff like that. Never something like *this*—with my name on it." He crawls to me, buries his face in the crook of my neck, and whispers, "Thank you." I lift my hands and let my fingers sift slowly through his hair. When he finally pulls away, neither of us mentions the single tear that he leaves behind, but I feel it slide down the skin of my throat.

"Tonight, when I make you come, I'm going to listen to your heart," West says, holding up his gift. "I want to hear what it sounds like."

That's what he does. He listens to my heart as I orgasm.

He says it sounds like a symphony.

Chapter Fifteen

J essica

Spring appears out of nowhere. Petals unfurl, sending their sweet perfume into the air. At school, a sparrow makes its nest outside of my classroom window. The students and I carefully monitor the eggs that lie in their bed of twigs and feathers. Even the hardest of my kids cheer on the day when they hatch and three baby birds emerge, blind and bumbling.

My principal, Kent Wilson, remains an ever-present thorn in my side, a fact that I carefully hide from West. I still haven't forgotten his expression, twisted with rage, when he saw Dylan's hand on my arm at the gala or the fact that Dylan mysteriously disappeared from the hospital after that night. When I asked West if he had anything to do with Dylan's sudden decision to transfer to a hospital in Alabama, he'd spread his hands wide and said innocently, "Who? Me?"

Yeah, right.

I didn't buy that for a second.

If West was incensed by a man touching me once, I can only imagine his response if he knew how Kent breathes down my neck every time we work together. How he comes up with one preposterous excuse after another to keep me on campus. He's always been weird with me, even back when we were in school together, but it's grown worse since he found out I have a boyfriend.

A few months ago, I was at the copy machine, gushing to Julie about West, when Kent barged in. With a stormy expression, he'd interrupted our conversation and told us to get back to class. For a minute, I thought he'd confused us with the students, that's how condescending he sounded.

Now, I clean the top of my desk, neatly stacking papers and logging off my school-issued computer. I stifle a yawn. It's been a long day. West kept me up late last night with his "examination." Then I had a 7:00 a.m. staff meeting, followed by six periods of teaching quadratic equations, material my students can't seem to grasp.

I don't blame them. That shit is hard.

Kent's cologne announces his arrival before I see him. Its musky, pungent smell makes me wrinkle my nose.

"Jessica," he says, sweeping into the room, bringing his stench along with him. "Richardson is sick. I need you to chaperone the dance this Saturday."

"No," I say calmly, not looking up from the drawer while I put away my favorite pen for grading. I worked through lunch to make sure all my papers are done. West is taking me to a bed and breakfast in Traverse City, Michigan, this weekend. It will be our first vacation together. I'm hoping there will be more "bed" than "breakfast."

"No?" Kent sputters. "But we need at least three chaperones to run the dance."

Finally, I look at him, wondering how the star quarterback of our high-school football team turned into this pot-bellied, wispy-haired, pasty-skinned man. When I was a freshman and he was a senior, Kent Wilson had ruled these halls. Many of my cheerleader friends had crushes on him back then, but I had never understood the appeal. He was selfish and mean-spirited, always picking on the smaller, weaker kids. When I think about it, he hasn't changed. Now he has a job where he's allowed to wield the power he always craved.

"Sorry, Wilson," I say, surprised to find I'm not sorry at all. "I have plans with my boyfriend." I've never actually called West my boyfriend in front of him, and I've certainly never heard him call me his girlfriend, but given how I've stopped my New York job searches and my Chicago apartment hunting I figure that must be what we are. We live together, see each other every day, talk and text constantly. And our nighttime activities...well, they require a level of trust that can only be found in a stable relationship. If we aren't the definition of dating, then I don't know what is.

"What about the kids?" Kent whines, wringing his hands together. "You don't want us to have to cancel the dance, do you?"

That's how he used to get me. Where my weakness lies, with "the kids." Kent knows I'd do anything for my students. What he doesn't understand is that finding my voice in the bedroom has spilled into the rest of my life. It's those lessons with West that allow me to speak up now.

"Don't be ridiculous," I snap. The sharpness of my tone makes Kent's eyes widen. He takes a step back as if my words have assaulted him. "You won't cancel the dance. Contact the Parent-Teacher Organization or send out a message to the parents. There are lots of families who will want to help out. I'm sure you can find a couple of dads to come in. Honestly, they'll be more helpful than I would be if you need to break up a fight or separate some couple kissing in the corner."

"Jessica! I can't do that. It has to be you. You're best suited for the job," he says, confirming my suspicion that this is more about him wanting *me* there than him needing a teacher to fill the role.

Monica was right. He really is a little weasel.

I shrug on my jacket and pick up my purse, flinging it over my shoulder. "You know," I tell him, "I was doing some light reading the other day—going through my work contract—and it specifically states that I only have to do a certain number of hours outside of the regular school day." I pause to let that sink in, noting how his face flushes red in anger.

Nonchalantly, I say, "I even took the time to count up the hours I've worked on things like guard duty, field trips, after-school club monitoring, and you'll never guess what I discovered!" Sarcasm leaks into my voice. "Turns out I'm *way* over the limit for those extra hours. I've done more than my fair share, so you'll have to excuse me, but I need to go. Someone is waiting for me."

I don't smile at him or wave like I used to do. I just give Kent a pleasant nod and head to the door, calling over my shoulder, "Have fun at the dance."

I skip outside to the curb, where my boyfriend waits for me in his fancy sports car, ready to whisk me away for a weekend of fun. Although I love my students—

I love West more.

Adam

A few weeks after we get back from our Michigan vacation, a storm hits. It's 4:00 a.m. and I'm in bed reading when my room is suddenly flooded with white light, so bright I squint and raise my hand to block the glare. I look out the window just in time to see a jagged spike of lightning followed by ear-bursting thunder, loud enough to make the windows rattle.

On bare feet, I pad to the security room. Rain like this always puts me on edge—I hate how it makes everything blurry, how it obscures the details so I can't see what's coming at me—but the condo looks fine. Jessica's asleep in her bed, and every other room is empty.

I've just climbed back into my own bed when the lights give a single flicker and then go out. It's pitch black, the kind of darkness you'd see from the inside of a coffin. The entire city must be affected because no light comes in through the window. Navy Pier is nowhere to be seen. It's just...disappeared.

My heart slams in my chest, as my breathing picks up. I flail around, knocking over the crystal bedside lamp. It hits the floor with a loud crash and shatters, tiny shards tinkling as they scatter across the wood floor. Panic sets in.

Jessica.

I need Jessica.

She always makes me feel better.

I yell her name, scream for her, as I fumble with the nightstand drawer. I keep a flashlight there for emergencies like this. The cold metal of it hits my hand and rolls away. I chase it, swearing and yelling. Finally, I get my fingers around it. I click the power button and...nothing. I shake it, hit it with the palm of my hand, and try again, but no luck. It's dead. The batteries must not be working. I should have replaced them months ago.

Fuck. How could I have been so stupid, so careless?

Grasping the covers on my bed, I bring them up to my chest. My eyes blindly search but find nothing. That's when the smell hits me mothballs, old clothing, stale air. I'm in the closet again. I've done something wrong, been a bad boy. Tears spring to my eyes, as terror fogs my brain. I lose grasp of time, of reality.

"Mommy?"

Jessica

West wakes me, bellowing from downstairs, the sound raw and terrified. Dread seeps, curling around my ribs. It chills me to the bone.

"West?" I call out, on my feet before my eyes have fully opened. I stumble to the door and flick the light switch, but nothing happens. Everything is dark, like someone has placed a blindfold over my eyes. I realize what's going on. The power is out. Something I've only guessed at before becomes much more convincing as I hear the sound of a crash downstairs followed by more desperate yelling.

West is scared of the dark.

That's why there are so many nightlights in this condo. That's why he's always looking up to see if it's a full moon, why in Michigan he refused when I suggested a nighttime walk.

I have to get to him. Save him.

Stuttering flashes of lightning make the condo look like a scene from a horror movie as I leap down the spiral stairs, praying I won't slip and break an ankle.

He's stopped shouting. The ominous silence that follows is far worse.

"West!" I yell when I hit the bottom rung. "Where are you?"

No answer.

With my hands out in front of me, I feel along the wall and furniture. The last time I heard him it sounded like he was in his bedroom, so that's where I go.

His door is ajar. Hastily, I shove it all the way open. I'm blind. There's no light at all. Just an inky blackness so thick it's oppressive, suffocating.

"84, 85, 86…"

He's counting.

My blood turns to ice because it's West's voice, but there's a lisp to it, like it's also the voice of a child, a little boy. The fine hairs on the back of my neck rise, and my skin prickles. I get the sense that we're not alone in this room. That the ghosts of his haunted past have risen from whatever dark graves he's buried them in. My imagination slips into overdrive as I feel them crowd me, their skeletal hands reaching, clinging to my nightgown, scraping along my skin. They want to slow me down, to stop me from reaching him.

I won't let them.

"West?" I shuffle forward, so I don't trip on the furniture or the edge of the rug by his bed. I'm a few steps in when something sharp bites my toe. "Ouch!" I hop on one foot, but that was a bad idea because whatever razor-sharp material is on the floor slices into my other, uninjured foot.

"Fuck!" I thump to the floor, landing on my bottom, and pull my stinging feet into my hands. Something warm and wet drips across my palm.

I'm bleeding.

"West! West!" I cry with a sob, pain and fear mixing together.

"93, 94, 95..." There's a vacancy to his voice. It's mechanical, detached, like he's gone somewhere far away.

My fingers probe the soles of my feet and find sharp-edged shards of what must be glass sticking out. I cut my fingers and my palms as I wiggle the larger pieces free from my feet, which are slippery with blood.

"West!" I call out raggedly.

Still nothing but counting, the sound coming from the bed. That must be where he is.

Sweeping my hands in front of me, I brush more broken glass out of my way. Slowly, I clear a path so I can painstakingly crawl forward on my hands and knees. I force myself onward, filled with an urgency to get to him. To wake him from whatever nightmare he's slipped into.

I've just reached the edge of the bed when he says in an eerie high-pitched voice, "Please. I promise I'll be good. Please, please let me out." Those words make me freeze, fear and grief slicing into my soul as sharp as the glass did in my skin. A sick feeling curls in my stomach, like I've swallowed something poisonous.

He goes back to counting. I use those numbers as a beacon to lead me to him.

Finally, I feel the outline of his feet, his legs, his body under the sheets. I trace his form until I get to his face. I take it in both hands.

He keeps counting, low and monotone.

"West!" I shake his head from side to side, squeezing. "West! Wake up!"

Nothing.

My hands find his shoulders. I shake them, but still he doesn't stop. I tug at him, shaking him harder so his head flops. I'm almost at the point where I'm going to slap him awake when abruptly he sits up straight.

Strong hands grasp my wrists and tighten.

"West! It's me," I hiss, worried he's so disoriented that he'll think I'm a stranger and hurt me by accident. He would feel so terrible afterward.

He mumbles a groggy, "Jessica?"

"Yes! It's me. I'm here." He lets go, and I scoot closer. Climbing into his lap, I circle his neck with my arms and pull him to me. Trembling, he burrows into my chest. Still blind, I search with one hand in the darkness until I find his face.

Scratchy, stubbled jaw. Full lips. Sharp nose. His cheeks wet with tears.

"Jess?" He sounds dazed.

I lower my face to his, whispering, "I'm here. I'm here. You're okay. The power went out. That's all. You're safe." My cheek presses to his cheek, then my lips to his lips. I kiss him in the void of light, touch our only working sensation.

At first, his response is sluggish, but then he kisses me back, gasping consuming kisses, like he can't breathe unless he's breathing the same air as I am. I slide down his body until the length of me is molded to him. The pain of my torn-up feet and hands is long forgotten.

"Jess, Jessica, Jess," he chants my name as his hands come to life. They thread into my hair so he can angle me to deepen our kiss. His tongue slips into my mouth as I open to him. His hands roam down to the straps of my nightgown. Without breaking his mouth from mine, he peels it off my shoulders so my breasts are freed.

West rolls and lays me flat on my back. He hovers over me, braced on one arm, while his other hand travels over my jaw, down my collarbone, and onto my breast. I arch into his palm, filled with longing. Spooked by what just happened, I need the physical reassurance of his touch. West trails kisses down my neck and over each peaked nipple. I cry out as he bites down gently.

"Are you real or am I dreaming?" he whispers into my skin.

My hands are in his hair. I tug his head until his mouth comes back up to meet mine. "Real," I whisper back, right before we kiss.

Hands shuffle until we're both naked. West moves between my legs and then pauses. His voice is steadier when he says in a hushed tone, "I don't have a condom...is that...is it okay?"

I want to remind him that he's the one who prescribed the birth control pill I slip onto my tongue every morning, that he's the one who ordered the labs that show I'm clean, but this isn't the time, so instead I reach down and guide him to my entrance. When he slips into me, it's a new kind of high. The sensation of his skin on mine, of how it shifts and glides as he moves is so intensely arousing that I almost come right then.

It's more than the physical, though. It's a deepening of our emotional connection. How we're peeling back parts of ourselves, revealing all the things that were hidden before. All the hurt and pain and grief. It's there between us, and I want to help, to take care of him the way he takes care of his patients, of me.

"Adam," I whisper, my breath catching as he hits a sensitive spot that feels *so* good. "I don't know what happened just now, and you don't have to explain until you're ready, but I need to tell you something."

At the sound of his first name, he slows down, stops, still hard inside me. In the blackness of his room, I can't see his expression, which may be a good thing. I'm not sure I'd have the courage to go on otherwise.

"Adam, I know you don't like the sound of your name. I—"

Hatred and grief curls toxicity into his words as he hisses, "*She* used to say it all the time. I love you, *Adam*. I hate you, *Adam*. You ruined my life, *Adam*. You ungrateful piece of shit, *Adam*—" He cuts off abruptly and draws in a shuddering breath.

Tears spring to my eyes and tumble down my cheeks. I can't fathom it, to be abused like that by your own parent. My house growing up was filled with love, but I'm realizing that his was a horror show beyond anything I'd imagined before. My heart shatters for him.

I cup his cheek, stroking it with my thumb. The way he leans into that caress with a sigh reminds me of when we first met back in my apartment. Of the first disastrous time I kissed him.

I gather my thoughts, wanting to make sure I get this right. "I hope I can help rewrite that part of your story. Maybe sometimes, not all the time, but sometimes I can call you Adam. I can tell you how you're good—"

"No. No, I'm not." He corrects me with so much conviction that it makes me cry harder. I hate her, the woman who broke him like this.

His mother.

"Yes. Yes, you are. You're good and so kind and caring and—" I gulp, choking back my tears so he won't notice I'm crying. I don't want to make this about me. It needs to be about him, about us. "And I love you, Adam. You're everything to me."

A stunned silence, the quiet filled with only the steady drumbeat of our hearts, pressed together.

Then his lips are on mine and he's thrusting deep, making love to me like his life depends on it. The lights come on, blinding in their harshness. There's blood from my cuts everywhere. Smeared across his face and staining his white sheets. We're fucking in it, in my blood, but I barely notice. All I can see is how he stares at me, his gaze adoring, worshipping.

"I love you, Jess. My pretty girl. I've loved you forever, and I'm going to keep on loving you until my bones break and my heart stops. That's the only thing that will ever separate us because I'm never ever leaving you, and you can't leave me either."

My orgasm rips through me as the last of his words fade, but I heard every one of them. "Never." I say the words I know he desperately needs to hear. "I'll never leave you."

"Promise me," he demands as he comes shuddering inside me, and, for the first time, I feel his warmth fill me up and gush down my thighs. "Promise you'll never go."

Meaning it with every fiber of my being, I tell Adam, "I promise."

Chapter Sixteen

Adam

We're at Jessica's school, the one I used to hate. I can't help but laugh at the irony of it. Now I leave work early and rush here, of all places. Of course, I'm not coming for the school or even for the students.

I'm here for *her*.

Jessica.

The woman who loves me, and I love her back.

The spring musical is coming up in one week, but the drama teacher, Mrs. Fletcher, tripped down a flight of stairs and busted her hip. Jessica, being the angel she is, offered to take over as director. This year the musical is *Wicked*, and that's why my condo is now filled with songs about "defying gravity" as Jessica panic crams the lyrics, memorizing them. Rehearsals every night last from the end of school until 9:00, sometimes 10:00 p.m. This means that Jessica spends over fifteen hours a day here on campus.

At first I stayed home, but that's a lot of hours away from my girl. Too many hours. If I want to see her—which I do—it dawned on me that *I* need to come to *her*. It took twenty minutes to drive here and exactly five minutes before she put me to work.

"West," Jessica had called, raising her voice to be heard over the obnoxious squeaking of the cadet band as they warmed up. "Could you help the set design team? They need to move some heavy pieces of furniture."

"Fine," I'd grumbled, not excited to be the servant of some pimply-faced sixteen-year-old. "Moving furniture" quickly turned out to be rearranging a two-dimensional version of the Emerald City, complete with a Yellow Brick Road. In my teenage years, when I was desperate for money, I'd worked every job imaginable, including construction, so on my third trip to rehearsal, when the Yellow Brick Road crumbled for the fifth time and pieces of mortar landed on Jessica's still-healing feet, I'd finally had it. I'd plucked a hammer out of a kid's hand and had barked orders, sending the rest of the kids scrambling.

"You," I'd pointed, "nose-ring girl, get me a measuring tape, and you, redhead with the bad attitude, we need a level. This wall is crooked. That's why it keeps falling over."

The redhead, who I later learned was named Steven, stuck his lower lip out pouting, but he did as I asked. Next thing I know, I'm spending lunch hour in the hospital drawing blueprints for a pulley system that will magically, and safely, hoist the main actress into the air so she can fly on her broomstick. A few days later, forty-eight high schoolers burst into awed applause when it actually works, and the Wicked Witch soars high above their heads.

"Good job, Adam," said Jessica, slipping her hand into mine. It wasn't until hours later, when I was buried inside her, that I realized I hadn't flinched when she'd said my name. I hadn't broken apart, fallen to pieces. For the first time, that name didn't cut—it stitched something back together.

"Thank you," I'd whispered to the heavens as she shattered beneath me, shuddering and moaning. "Thank you for sending her to me." Later, when she drifted off in my arms, in my bed, where she now sleeps every night, I stared at her for over an hour, filled with wonder that someone as miraculous as her was destined for someone as flawed as me.

Now, it's past 10:30 p.m. The students have left. Jessica and I are cleaning up, stacking chairs on top of one another until they make a wobbling tower as tall as my chest.

"They like you," Jessica says after we're done.

"Who?"

That bright laugh of hers. "The kids."

I do a double take, to make sure she's serious. "Really?"

"Yes, really. They look up to you. I can tell. Oh!" Her eyes light up the way they do when she's excited about something. "I know! You should come talk to them!"

I wave at the now-empty stage. "I've been talking to them. Every night for the past week. It's excruciating."

She laughs again. "No, I mean come to my classroom. Tell them about how you came from humble beginnings, just like them, but you made it. Now you're educated and successful. You could be an inspiration to them. Show how they can build a better life."

I snort. "I'm not an inspiration to *anyone*."

She frowns at that, deep creases at the corners of her mouth. "West," she says in a scolding tone, the one that usually makes me relent.

"Okay. Fine." I hold up a hand. "Maybe I'll do it." She's more correct than she'll ever know. I understand *exactly* what it takes to come from this school and end up with a stable life. Still, I hesitate. "Are you sure? I'm so bossy with them, the kids." I haven't bothered to baby any of her students, but I haven't talked down to them either. I've found myself teaching them as I worked beside them. Showing them how to use a plane to shave off curling pieces of wood until it's straight and true.

"Mmm," murmurs Jessica, lifting up on her toes to kiss me, her lips soft. She leaves behind the faint taste of cherry Chapstick. "I personally love it when you take control."

Her words head straight to my dick, which twitches as I visualize all the ways I'd like to control her.

"It's fun when you take charge too," I remind her, thinking of how much more assertive she's become in the bedroom recently. It sparks a feeling of pride in me, to think how over eight months ago she couldn't even say the word "pussy" out loud.

We grin at each other, the connection between us humming and alive.

"Say you'll do it," she says, breaking the silence. "You'll come talk to my classroom. We can schedule it for the first day back after spring break. You said you're off that week."

"Okay, I'll be there."

"Promise?"

"I promise," I say, knowing I'd do anything she asked.

I get a kiss for that, long and lingering.

"Come on." Jessica links her arm in mine. "I need to return the keys for the supply closet to the nurse's office. I promised Chelsea I'd put them back when we were done."

I follow her down corridors I remember all too well. Many times, bruised and bleeding, I walked this same path after being pummeled by school bullies. The nurse's station is just as I last saw it. Two beds, each with a hanging curtain you can pull around for privacy. The drawer where Jessica replaces the keys is the lowest in the desk, which means she has to bend over to reach it. This puts her very fine ass on display. She's wearing leggings, and I can see the outline of her thong. My dick is still awake from earlier. The sight before me makes it even more eager. I move closer so when she stands up and turns I'm right there.

"Oh!" she says, startled. One look at my face, and she knows exactly what's on my mind. She's gotten very good at reading me. I used to think I'd hate to be so transparent, but I find I love it. Love how we can communicate with just a single glance.

Jessica smirks, a sly look in her eyes. She steps into me, rises up, and circles my neck with her arms. When she feels my erection against her stomach, her grin widens. In a low, alluring purr, she says, "Why hello, Dr. West. How lovely to see you here."

Fuck.

She knows *exactly* how to turn me on. I bring my mouth to hers in a hungry kiss. As our lips collide, the air around us shifts. It becomes charged and electric. My palm slides down to grip the ass that started this whole thing. I dig my fingers into it and press her against my length. Jessica moans as I plunder her mouth with my tongue, wishing it was her pussy I was tasting. We're both panting by the time we break apart.

Without letting go of me, Jessica leans back and surveys the room. I can see the idea form in her pretty head. "You know," she begins, "this isn't exactly like your special exam room, but I see a lot of the same equipment…"

I cock my head to the side with an indulgent smile, sure she's not bold enough to finish that thought.

"We could do it here. In the nurse's office."

Damn.

She's always surprising me.

Jessica walks over to a set of shelves. Her back blocks my vision so I can't see what she grabs until she turns around and holds them up. They're tourniquets, the yellow rubber bands that you use to draw blood, the kind I used to bind her to the exam table the first time I fucked her in my secret lair.

"These look awfully familiar," she teases with an impish grin. "Maybe it's my turn to tie *you* up for a change. You did just say how you like it when I take control…" The corners of her delectable mouth rise higher as she lets that sentence dangle between us.

I pause, internally battling with myself. Many times in my past I had no control. The thought of willingly putting myself back in that position sends panic skittering along my nerves, but is it really fair to refuse? I've taken that same control from Jessica many, many times now. I've bound her, blindfolded her, pushed her out of her comfort zone, and she's gone along with everything.

If she can be that brave, maybe I can too?

I shake out my shoulders and soak in the mirth that dances in Jessica's expression. I force myself to smile. "Okay, let's do it."

A few more kisses, and we're both breathless as we undress while stumbling to one of the beds. There's the thump of our shoes coming off, the metal clink of my belt as I unbuckle it, the whisper of fabric on skin when I pull her shirt high over her head, kissing each inch as it's exposed. Soft sighs and warm hands tangle together. At the last minute, I reach out and pull the curtain closed, casting us in shadow.

"This is so naughty," Jessica snickers. "I can't believe we're doing this at school."

I climb on the bed, which is really a stretcher much like the ones we have at the hospital, and lay on my back, shivering as the cool plastic contacts my bare skin. "There should be a handle in the back of this that sits it up. In that position, there's an opening where you can tie the torniquets," I tell Jessica, fully understanding that I'm signing my death certificate.

"Okay." Her golden ponytail bobs as she bends over and adjusts the bed. With her hair up like this, it's hard to find any difference between the girl who once ruled my wet dreams and the woman I've fallen in love with. The truth is that I was obsessed with her then and I'm obsessed with her now, but it's more than that. I trust her, and that's why I don't resist when she ties my hands above my head with efficient, tight knots.

I raise my eyebrows, equal parts surprised and impressed by her handiwork.

She lifts her chin, smug as she says, "I've watched how you do these knots. I'm a quick learner."

"I can see that." I don't bother to hide the pride in my voice.

Jessica dramatically tosses her hair, preening, and I laugh.

I'm naked, tied up, in a place I swore I'd never come back to, and she's making me laugh.

Fuck. I'm so gone for this woman.

Once I've stopped chuckling, I challenge, "Okay, funny girl. You've got me where you want me. Now what?"

She steps back and chews her plump bottom lip as she thinks. "Hmm. Oh! Wait! I've got it." I get a nice glimpse of her naked backside as she ducks past the curtain. There's the banging and clattering of drawers opening and closing and then she's back, holding a thermometer. The old-fashioned kind, long and made of glass with a sliver of mercury gleaming inside. It's a relic, something left over from past generations.

A nervous buzz runs through me. "I don't think I have a fever…"

Mischief sparkles in her eyes. "You are pretty hot, but that's not what I'm going to do with this." Slowly, she approaches the bed with her back straight and her head tall, the very picture of confidence.

I squirm, alarmed. "If you think you're sticking that up my butt, you're crazy."

"That's not my target," she sings out merrily.

When her hand reaches for my dick, I jerk my body away. "Hey! What the hell!"

I never appreciated before how fast her reflexes are. Jessica grabs me and holds on, unwavering, with a determination I've never seen.

"Have you ever heard of urethral sounding? Monica told me about it."

My heart spasms. "Um, I basically invented kinky sex, so yes, I've heard of it, but why the hell were *you two* talking about it?"

"I told you. Monica's crazy. She knows about all that stuff. Have you ever done it?"

I swallow. "No, and I'm not sure I want to."

Jessica lifts a brow. "Are you saying it's okay for you to stick things in me, but not vice versa? That sounds like a big double standard. Besides, Monica said it gives guys an incredible orgasm." Her hand strokes my shaft, making it infinitely more difficult to form a counterargument. "I think you should let me try. If it hurts or sucks, we can stop."

I really want to say no. Tying me up is one thing, but urethral sounding is next-level insanity.

"Don't tell me you're scared," Jessica taunts, fully aware that she's igniting my competitive side.

That's not why I submit, though. It's not because I want to prove a point. It's because I'm loving this new Jessica—the domineering one, the one so comfortable in her own skin.

"Okay," I agree, internally wincing. "Wipe it off with alcohol, though."

"Good idea."

Jessica does as I ask, then approaches me with the now-sanitized thermometer. When she brings it close, I can smell the rubbing alcohol she used, so sharp it stings the back of my nose and throat.

She holds it up. "I put some lube on it too."

With a firm hand, she holds my penis and puts the thermometer into the opening at its tip. I hiss at the burning stretch of it.

"Remember," Jessica says, winking, "the safe word is *cupcake*."

I narrow my eyes at her, and she laughs, then pushes the thermometer farther in. I turn my head, queasy from the sight of it.

"I don't think it's working," I tell her when suddenly it hits me—a burst of pleasure extending from the tip of my penis to the base. It's startling in its intensity. "I—oh. Um. Oh." I can no longer form coherent sentences. Jessica advances the thermometer, and that feeling spreads like wildfire along my shaft, heading straight to my balls. It's such a strong response that I gasp, my eyes rolling back in my head. "Oh, my god. Wow."

"Yeah? It's good?" Jessica asks, sounding delighted.

"It's...weird, but also good. Not quite like anything I've felt before."

With the thermometer all the way in, she begins to move it back and forth. There's a pleasant electric sensation. My cock hardens to the point where it's almost painful, leaking pre-cum. My muscles tense, stomach tightening, as she moves it faster. I want to put my hands on her, to touch her back, so I tug on the restraints, but to no avail. Jessica's knots hold.

My chest heaves, and sweat dots my brow as I concentrate on the strange, yet pleasurable, feeling. Soon a tingling grows at the base of my cock, an orgasm gathering strength. My mouth drops open in shock when Jessica places her lips on the tip of the thermometer and starts to hum. The vibration from her voice travels through my entire dick, the sensation overwhelming.

"Holy shit, I'm going to come," I spit out, practically hyperventilating from the rapture of it.

"Not yet!" Jessica pulls out the thermometer and places it on a table next to the bed while I do my best to hold back my climax. Quickly, she climbs onto my lap, straddling me. Watching me must have aroused her because she's nice and wet as she slides down my length and starts to bounce. I groan at the way she grips me, soft yet firm. As she rides my shaft with her eyes half-lidded, Jessica lifts a lazy hand to her breast and squeezes, teasing and tugging at her nipple as I stare enraptured. The sight of her touching herself is so fucking sexy that the orgasm I just buried rises in me again, tightening my balls.

We both hear it at the same time—a man's voice out in the hallway, right by the door. We freeze mid-thrust. Jessica's arms tighten around my neck as her terror-stricken gaze meets mine.

Shit. Please don't come in here. Please don't come in here.

The door opens with a squeak, and the man's voice gets significantly louder. He's in the room with us. I'm looking into Jessica's eyes, so I see the moment they widen with recognition. Whoever this guy is, she knows him.

I raise my eyebrows questioningly, and she mouths back silently, "My principal. Wilson."

Crap. I've heard her say that name before. Wilson. Her boss. Literally the worst person in the world to catch us in this position. She'd be fired for sure, which I know would kill her. Jessica loves her students like they're her own.

Rapidly, I think through every scenario possible, wanting to be the hero who saves her. Should I go out there and attack the guy? Knock him out so she can escape? No. Too risky. Should I throw something across the room and when he goes to investigate the source of the noise, we sneak out? No. That only works in the movies. What else can I do?

As usual, Jessica reads my mind. She shakes her head at me, pleading silently for us to stay still. She lifts a single finger to her mouth in a "shhh" gesture. I nod back, agreeing with her that our best shot is to stay hidden and hope this guy moves on.

Clutching each other, we watch tense with fear as Wilson steps closer. His shadow slips across the room and under the curtain that separates us. If it had eyes, we'd be finished. He talks loudly, telling someone how he hates the Board of Education and how he thinks they're all a bunch of idiots with their heads stuck up their butts. His voice is high with a whistling, nasal tone. It's vaguely familiar, but I can't place it.

We stay frozen, barely breathing. The curtain twitches as he walks past, yammering on about how whiney and demanding his teachers are and how if they don't raise their test scores this year, he's going to fire them all himself.

That makes Jessica turn five shades of red. She glares at the curtain that separates us.

Finally, Wilson's footsteps grow fainter as he heads toward the door to the parking lot, which is on the other side of the room. As he leaves, the last of his words trail back to us, "Still can't believe I got stuck in this loser school. It's all because of McMillian down on the board. I swear he's got it out for me." The door slams shut behind him, thankfully ending his stream of negativity.

"What a dick!" I say in my quietest voice, unsure how far away her principal is.

"He's an asshole," Jessica hiss-whispers in agreement. Angry blotches still paint her cheeks.

I'd assumed that interruption had ruined our little escapade, but Jessica proves me wrong. She lets out a relieved sigh, then kisses me long and deep. With her mouth on mine, she rises up onto her knees and slams down, taking all my length at once.

"*Fuck*," I gasp, my neck muscles straining. I've spent the last ten minutes stopping myself from coming, but now I let that swirling pleasure work its way back into my system until I'm flooded with it. It only takes a few thrusts before Jessica's cheeks flush pink and her head lolls back. Breathless, she leans her forehead to mine and says, "I'm so close. Come with me, Adam."

She doesn't have to ask twice. I let go with a hushed roar. My cock pumps hard and fast, the most powerful orgasm of my life. Jessica cries out with soft moans as she collapses onto me. She lays there panting, her golden hair spilled across my chest. I let the moment stretch out, not wanting to rush how her breath slows until it matches the steady beats of my heart.

Finally, I can't ignore the tingling pain in my hands or the fact that I'm aching to hold her. Appreciating our role reversal, I press a kiss to the top of her head and murmur, "Pretty girl, I'm about thirty seconds away from losing both of my hands. Can you please untie me before I have to learn how to do everything with my feet?"

Jessica stirs, her nose scrunching as she blinks out of her post-orgasm daze. "What?" she mumbles.

"Not to ruin the mood, but my hands are turning blue," I say with a grin, as I shift beneath her. "I kinda need them—you know, for my job. To do surgery. So untie me."

Jessica blinks at me, her drowsy brain catching up, before an amused smile curls her lips. "You were right earlier. You *are* so bossy."

"And you're so comfortable."

She sits up, smirking as she reaches for the knots. "This is what you get for letting me have full creative freedom."

As soon as my hands are free, I don't hesitate. I wrap my arms around her and pull her down, flipping us over so I can pin her beneath me. "Freedom, huh?" I tease, brushing my lips over hers. "You're lucky I like your wild ideas."

She giggles, her arms looping around my neck. "And you're lucky I didn't tie your feet too."

I tuck my face into Jessica's neck, inhaling her sweet scent. "Let's save that for next time."

She tilts her head back, laughter bubbling up her throat. I want so badly to capture that sound in a bottle, to live in this perfect moment with her forever.

Jessica

As we dress in the nurse's office, I'm still in awe of what we just did. The way West gave himself over to me was one of the most empowering experiences of my life. To be loved like that, trusted like that, especially by *him*, someone who doesn't trust easily, is something pretty special. I sense a shift between us, a deepening of our relationship, a rebalancing of power, and I know West feels it too. His fingers trail over my arm, his hand lingers at the small of my back, and his lips press fleeting kisses to my temple like he can't bear to stop touching me.

I scoop up his car keys and toss them to him. "Let's head home. I'm ready for a bath and bed."

The door that leads to the parking lot bangs open, letting in the sound of honking cars and distant sirens. Immediately, West steps in front of me, like he's a human shield, ready to protect me from any threat.

The intruder barrels into the room, out of breath and wild-eyed. It's Kent Wilson. When he sees us, he jerks to a stop and puts his hand on his chest like he's having a heart attack. "Jesus! What're you doing here, Jessica?"

"The spring musical, remember?"

"Oh, yeah." Kent runs his eyes over me, such a common occurrence that I barely notice it, although I hope he misses my crazy post-sex hair.

"When's the show start?" he asks.

It's an effort, but I hold back my sigh of annoyance. He's the principal—he should know this. "Tomorrow is opening night."

Kent's gaze shifts to West, and the room seems to freeze.

West stiffens next to me, his shoulders tight and squared. The color drains from his face. I glance between the two men, confused.

What the hell?

"This is Adam West," I tell Kent. "He's been helping me out with the musical."

"Adam, this is Kent, my principal...," I trail off, baffled by the obvious tension in the room.

In strained voice, West says, "I thought your boss was named Wilson."

"Yeah, Kent Wilson. We mostly call each other by last names around here."

My gaze bounces back and forth between the two men, who look like they're locked in a staring contest.

Kent breaks first, with a disbelieving shake of his head. "Adam *fucking* West. It *is* you, isn't it?"

West flinches next to me.

"I'm sorry," I ask, baffled. "Do you two know each other?"

Kent barks out a laugh. "Are you serious, Jess? You don't remember this little twerp?"

I glance around the room, wondering who he's talking about. Surely it can't be 6'3" West with his chiseled body and model good looks. "Who?"

Kent's laughter turns cold. His gaze slides to West. "This kid. I used to beat him up all the time. Such a weak little cunt. He never lifted a hand to stop me."

West doesn't respond. He just stares at Kent stonily with his jaw tight.

"Remember, Jess? He was a senior, in the same grade as me." There's pure spite in the glare Kent sends West. "Fucker kept ruining the curve in every class I had with him. It's *his* fault my grade-point average fell. I missed a football scholarship in Florida because of this asshole." He takes a threatening step toward West, but I move forward to block him.

"Stop it, Kent." I put a hand on his chest, so he can't come closer. "I don't know what this is about, but leave him alone."

Kent gapes at me, then flicks a look to West and back. "Wait...wait a second. Don't tell me you two are together?" His voice pitches louder with disbelief. "No fucking way. *You?* With *him?*"

I pull myself tall and let the pride I feel for West flow into my words. "He's my boyfriend. The one I told you about."

Kent points with his mouth hanging open. "*This* nerd loser? Is *your* boyfriend?"

I nod and say, "Yes, but I think you've mistaken him for someone else. West didn't go to school with us."

Malice dripping from his words, Kent leans around me. "Tell her, Adam. Tell her how I used to fuck you up."

Silence from West. The first tendril of doubt takes root in my mind.

My chest tightens as I turn to West, my voice barely above a whisper, and ask, "West?"

It's like watching a balloon deflate. West's shoulders bow, and his frame sags like the weight of this moment is crushing him. His mouth moves, silently counting. 1, 2, 3, 4. When he gets to 5, his mumble is so quiet that I strain to hear. "It's true."

My heart stutters. "What?"

Louder this time, but still not meeting my eyes, West says, "I graduated from here."

My stomach lurches, my world tilts dangerously like the ground opened beneath me and I just tumbled into a new reality. One where West isn't who I thought he was, who he *said* he was.

"You knew me? Knew who I was?"

West doesn't answer, his silence speaking louder than words ever could. Minutes ago, I felt like I was in a dream, but it turns out this is a nightmare.

Adam

Jessica stares at me, her brow knit together with a pleading look like she's begging me to say it isn't true.

I can't, though. I can't lie to her. Not anymore.

"I knew."

I see the second it happens, when the betrayal hits. Rose blooms on her cheeks, such a pretty sight for such an ugly moment.

Kent gasps dramatically. "What?! You didn't know?" He lets out a sharp, braying laugh that echoes in the small room. He bends over, his hands on his knees, laughing so hard he wheezes. "He didn't tell you, Jessica? This *boyfriend* you've been bragging about for months?"

My fists clench so tightly that my nails dig into my palms. Of all people—why does *he* have to be Jessica's boss? Kent, my high-school tormentor. My bully. The urge to shut him up is almost impossible to resist. It would be so easy to give him back all the pain and misery he gave me, but magnified by ten.

I can't, though.

Not here. Not now.

Because if I do, Jessica might pay the price. Her reputation, her job, the students she loves so much—one wrong move, and I could ruin it all for her. I grit my teeth and swallow the anger, letting it simmer beneath the surface.

"Jess," I say with quiet desperation, begging her to look at me. "Let's go. We can talk about this at home."

"Home?! Oh my god, don't tell me you *live* together?" Kent howls, every bit the smug prick he was back in high school. "This keeps getting better."

Her jaw working, Jessica ignores both Kent and me, but she's holding back tears. I can see how she swallows them down.

I run a hand through my hair and steady my voice to say, "Come on. Let's go." I place a gentle hand on her upper arm.

She rips away from my grasp and hisses, "Don't touch me!"

Panic thumps its wings in my chest. I'm losing her, right before my eyes. I'm losing the only person I care about in this entire godforsaken world.

Kent, ever the opportunist, smirks at her. "Don't worry, Jess. You can always come home with me."

God help me, I'm going to kill him.

Jessica curls her lip, disgust written across her face, and answers with an icy, "No thanks."

"Your loss, babe," Kent shoots back, shrugging as if he didn't just pour gasoline on an already raging fire.

Jessica doesn't spare him another glance. She turns her focus entirely on me—her eyes filled with anger, betrayal, and something far worse: heartbreak.

Jessica

I don't talk to West on the drive home. God knows, he tries. He explains, cajoles, argues, and eventually begs, but I don't hear any of it. I've tuned him out. Instead, I'm listening to my own internal dialogue, which repeats like a mantra.

Stupid, dumb Jessica. So naïve.

Barely holding onto my sanity, I grip the door handle so hard my knuckles ache and take in one shuddering breath after another.

Should've known better. Can't trust him...or anyone.

No parents. No love. No family.

That's my destiny.

The minute we enter the condo, West moves toward me, but I hold up my hand. "Just...just leave me alone. I need to think. To process." I can't stand to look at him right now. "I'm sleeping up in my old room. Please, don't follow."

His face falls. A little part of me wants to go to him, to reassure him everything will be okay, but the louder part of me is still reeling. Without waiting for his answer, I wind up the spiral stairs, dragging my feet like I'm going to my execution.

My bed is just as I left it, neatly made with the nightlight shining beside it. I don't bother turning on any other lamps. The covers are smooth and cool as I climb in and pull them over me. Once I'm lying down, all the questions I've been holding back come flooding in.

Why didn't he tell me?

How could he have lied for so long?

Was this entire thing a setup? Did he plan to lure me here to his home, into his arms, or was it a series of coincidences that spiraled out of control?

The clock ticks away the hours as I toss and turn. Anxiety and insecurity gnaw at my insides, leaving me hollow. My mind replays the look on Kent's face, his malicious glee as he exposed West's secret. I see West's pale expression, the truth unraveling in his silence.

By 4:30 a.m., I've had enough. Frustration boils over, and I fling the covers aside.

The condo is silent when I wander downstairs. The door to West's room is partly opened, which is how he always leaves it. I've learned he hates to be in a closed room, although he's never explained why. Chalk it up to one more secret he hides from me.

I peek through the crack in the door and see he's asleep. The top of his dark hair sticks out from twisted and tangled blankets. Looks like he had a restless night as well. One muscled arm extends to the empty side of the bed where I usually sleep, like he's reaching for me...but I'm not there.

The sight sends a pang through my heart.

For a minute, I think about going to him, crawling into bed so he can cover me with kisses, so he can soothe me, but I resist. The sting of his betrayal is too sharp.

I turn away, heading for the kitchen. *Coffee*, I decide. Something to occupy my hands, my mind, since I'm not going back to sleep anytime soon. As I pass the door to his private examination room, I notice it's open. He never locks it anymore.

Nostalgia tugs at me, begs me to enter.

The lights are bright when I hit the switch, making me blink. I go to the exam table, where West has tested me, taught me, loved me in ways I never would have imagined, and trail my fingers along its surface. I'm not sure if I'll ever lie here again.

My tears fall silently, splattering like raindrops on the upholstered surface.

The security monitors catch my eye, their screens glowing faintly in the corner. They're always on, showing every angle of the condo. Wanting to get a closer look at the place I once called home, I sink into the padded chair, the leather creaking under me, and lean forward.

The keyboard offers five options:

Play. Stop. Rewind. Fast forward. Search.

I press rewind, sending the footage spinning back in a blur of motion. Images fly by—West pacing at the bottom of the stairs, glancing up toward my room. I slow down and watch as he takes a step forward, then retreats, repeating the motion like a man at war with himself. The timestamp says this was earlier tonight. At a slower pace, I fast forward. Hours pass, and he doesn't leave that spot. At 3:00 a.m., he finally gives up and trudges to his room, collapsing onto the bed fully dressed.

This isn't the comfort I was looking for.

With a sigh, I rewind further, going back days, weeks, until I find a memory. West and I are on the couch, with the fireplace casting a golden light over us. I'm laughing, holding up my romance book, teasing him about a ridiculous sex scene.

"There's no way," a giggling, blissfully ignorant, past version of me says. "No one can do it in that position."

Dramatically, West tosses his own book over his shoulder. "Sounds like a challenge."

He pulls me into his arms, his laughter infectious. We tumble onto the couch, the memory glowing with the warmth of love and lust and everything we used to be.

How I wish we could go back to being those people.

Eyes blurry, I rewind again.

This time, it's my bedroom. It must be late because the cameras are in night vision mode, which paints the scene in muted tones. I'm asleep, my hands tucked under my cheek. Movement catches my eye, and I see him—West. He's sitting in the armchair, watching me.

What?

I advance through every night that follows, and it's like one of those nature shows where a time-lapse movie shows a flower transform from a bud into a full-blown blossom. Every night he sits in that chair like a guardian angel and watches me sleep, but over weeks and months, he evolves. First, he moves closer. A few weeks later, he tucks the covers around me before he leaves. Soon, he brushes hair from my face, and by the end he presses a kiss to his fingers and transfers it to my forehead. It's like I'm witnessing the slow progression of his love for me, the dismantling of his walls.

For the first time, I think maybe we can make it through this. I'm sure if we talk about it in the morning, he'll have a good explanation. Judging from what Kent said, West was a very different person in high school. He must have been ashamed. That's probably why he hid that he recognized me. If I put myself in his shoes, it all starts to make sense. He was embarrassed and wanted us to have a fresh start. It's almost romantic when I think about it. Maybe he's had feelings for me all these years. He saw his one opportunity with me and didn't want to pollute it with the old image of himself.

We can do this, I think.

We can move past the lies and make it work.

I hit play on one final clip, the night of the gala. West kneels beside my bed, whispering words I strain to hear.

"Sometimes I think fate made you just for me," he murmurs. "That you're the world's way of making up for every shitty thing that came before. If that's the case, then I'm okay with it. It was worth it, all the pain and suffering, to get you at the end." He tenderly brushes my hair away from my face and gently kisses my forehead.

My hand rises to clutch my chest as I stifle a sob. It's the sweetest, most impassioned speech I've ever heard. Emotion swells in my chest, overwhelming joy to know he loves me so deeply.

On the screen he whispers, "I've fucked hundreds of women, but I've only ever kissed one."

Something silver and sharp flashes in his hand.

Time stretches out—freezes.

I watch with mounting horror as West stabs a needle into my neck.

My hand flies to the spot, and sure enough. There it is. A tiny, hard object embedded under my skin.

What the fuck?

Chapter Seventeen

Adam

She's gone.

The realization slams into me the moment I wake, and the world tilts off its axis. The condo is too quiet, too still. There's an emptiness I can sense without even leaving the bedroom. My pulse surges as I bolt upright. My gaze darts around and finds nothing. I was asleep for less than an hour. How could this have happened?

Maybe it's a mistake. Maybe I'm overreacting, and I'll find her upstairs, safely tucked away where she belongs.

I stagger out of bed, my voice hoarse and breaking as I call her name.

"Jessica?"

Only silence answers back, deafening in its loudness.

"Jessica!"

Room by room, I tear through the condo, my heart a drumbeat of panic. Each empty space is a mocking reminder of her absence, each unanswered shout a knife twisting deeper into my chest.

She's not in her room. I search her closet and the downstairs bathroom where she once left her butterfly necklace on the counter.

Nothing.

Her things—every trace of her—is gone as if she never existed. It's like she was a dream, a figment of my overactive imagination.

That can't be true, right?

She was *real*. I held her. Loved her.

Then I see it.

I've just entered my lair, where the security cameras and my special exam table reside. My throat goes dry when I look at the monitors. Every single one of them displays the same haunting image.

She wanted me to see this. For me to *know*.

On the screens, frozen in damning clarity, is the moment I slid the needle into her neck and placed the tracker under her skin.

My pulse roars in my ears.

She found out.

I run a shaking hand through my hair, my mind a storm of disbelief and fury. Doesn't she understand? I had to do it. I was protecting her. Keeping her safe.

Keeping her *mine*.

I'd been so sure we'd work this out. She just needed time, space to cool off and see reason. I thought she'd realize what I already know—that we're meant for each other. Soulmates. Bound by something greater than logic.

But now... Now, she wants to escape me.

A dark, hollow ache spreads through my chest, twisting into something sharper, something hungrier. My jaw tightens, and I clench my fists until my nails dig into my palms, drawing blood.

Jessica saved me. Before her, I was too broken, too damaged, to find happiness, but like a miracle she reentered my life. She brought light into my darkness. She healed me, showed me there's beauty, love, and trust in the world—even for someone like me. She proved there are things worth fighting for.

After all that, she thinks she can just walk away? That she can leave me behind?

Never.

I take a slow, steadying breath, my panic cooling into a deadly resolve. I've faced impossible odds before and crushed them. I've bent the world to my will when it refused to yield. And I'll do it again.

For her. For us.

Because Jessica is *mine*.

I'll track her down, no matter where she hides, no matter how far she runs. I'll bring her back, even if she's kicking and screaming. She belongs with me.

And nothing—*nothing*—will stop me from bringing her home.

Jessica

He comes to the opening night of the musical. Of course, he knew I'd be at the sold-out theater. The sight of West—calm, unbothered, like he belongs here—makes me want to scream.

How *dare* he?

The *nerve*!

I should call the police, but I don't. It's the same problem I had when Brad tried to break down my door. I can't afford the negative attention. Can't risk a scandal, not with my job.

West is gone by the time the students take their last bows and the curtain falls, but when I walk to the car Monica lent me, I swear I feel his eyes on me.

The next morning he's outside my favorite coffee shop, then by the yoga studio, and finally by the grocery store. He's stalking me, always close enough to see but too far to confront. This goes on for two more days. West in the distance. I ignore him, hating the way my skin heats under his burning gaze.

On the third day, when he loiters outside Monica's apartment, where I'm temporarily staying, I lose it.

"Leave me alone!" I scream across the street at him. "Dylan was right. You're a lunatic." Angry tears sting the back of my throat as I fumble in my purse. The Ziploc bag I pull out has a shiny metal object in it. It's tiny, the size of a grain of rice.

"Recognize this!" I screech, waving the bag in the air. "It's the tracker they had to dig out of me." Dried blood still clings to the tracker. *My* blood. "The one you put in while I was sleeping, you fucking pyscho."

He barely raises his voice, but still I hear him over the noise of the city—as clear as if he were standing next to me. "I may be a psycho, but I'm *your* psycho, Jess. If I'm crazy, it's because you make me that way."

My harsh bark of laughter has nothing to do with humor. "Says every abuser."

I spin on my heel and stomp into the building, grateful that Monica makes enough money to live in an apartment building with a doorman, Dimitri. We've already given him strict instructions to not let West inside.

The next day West waits three cars down from Monica's luxury sedan.

"Don't you have a job to go to?" I snap when I see him.

His answer is calm, breezy. "Ten years with no time off. I've got *lots* of vacation days stored up."

My hands ball into fists as I resist the urge to punch him. "This is how you're spending them? Stalking me?"

A half shrug, the motion leisurely. "I'll retire if I have to. Make this my full-time job."

Anger surges through me. "You're wasting your time. I *hate* you."

"You know what they say about love and hate." He pauses, waiting for me to ask what, but I refuse to give him that satisfaction. My silence doesn't seem to perturb West, though. He sends me a lazy smile. "Two sides of the same coin, Jessica. Love and hate."

"Well, I flipped the coin, and it landed on hate, so fuck you." I hurry to the car.

He follows, calling, "You know you still care about me."

At the last second, I wheel around to face West and hiss, "I hate that I care. If it would burn you out of my veins, I'd set myself on fire."

I fling myself inside the car and slam the door, but not before I hear him call, "You're adorable when you're angry."

He's laughing as I drive past with my middle finger raised.

It's a week into spring break, and still West follows me. He comes closer now and tries to get me to speak with him, but I won't. I pretend like I'm deaf to him, like he's invisible, even though my breath stutters every time he's near.

How does he know where I am? I've changed my routine. Driven miles out of my way. Tried every trick I know to lose him, to disappear, but inevitably I look up and there he is—lounging, staring, waiting. His hungry gray eyes fixed on me like he'll never look away.

Like he'll never stop wanting me.

Adam

It's 11:00 p.m. Dimitri snores softly beside me, the sound like a small boat sputtering in the open sea. His head is slumped forward, his chin on his chest, one hand clutching the vodka bottle I brought for him. It's half-empty now—he'd polished it off mumbling about how much he hates the old lady in 13C.

Turns out Dimitri has a drinking problem. A little fact I uncovered over the past week while I carefully wormed my way into his confidence, supplying him with his favorite poison so I can hang around the security office of Monica's building without raising suspicion. Tonight, I needed him incapacitated, and he delivered.

His snores cut off abruptly, and I freeze, heart pounding.

A choked inhale, and then he's snoring again. Thank God, he's still out cold. His chest rises and falls in an uneven rhythm. The bottle teeters precariously in his grasp. I gently pry it from his grip and place it on the table.

Perfect.

The faint hum of the tracker app on my phone pulls me back to the task at hand. Jessica thinks she's so clever for finding the tracker I implanted in her neck. She doesn't know there's another one hidden in the diamond earrings I gave her for Christmas.

They always say two trackers are better than one…or wait—maybe *I'm* the only one who says that?

Hmm.

Either way, the earring tracker was a brilliant idea. I can keep an eye on her like a guardian angel, or in my case a guardian devil. Not only does this tracker show Jessica's location, but it contains a microphone. I can hear everything—her conversations, her surroundings.

The catch? I have to stay within range for it to work.

That's why Dimitri had to go down tonight. With him snoring away, I've claimed his jacket, with the security company's logo stitched on the back, and stationed myself at the desk. If any tenants wander through, all they'll see is a new doorman eager to help.

I've even figured out where to put packages and how to contact maintenance. Not that it matters. At this hour, the building is silent. Most of the residents are older and have long since gone to bed.

Movement flickers outside the wide front window, catching my attention. It's Brad, the junkie from Jessica's old apartment building. The one who tried to break down her door, so I had to break his face. He's barely recognizable now, with unkempt hair and eyes wild enough to rival a feral raccoon. Not that he was ever a picture of stability, but this?

This is next-level tragic.

I've been keeping tabs on him, so I already knew his rich family cut him off. I figured that might be his wake-up call, but nope, he's only spiraled further. Evicted from the building he shared with Jessica, now he's here, lurking like a Z-grade villain who hasn't realized he's only supposed to be a one-scene side character.

I swear, Jessica attracts trouble like a magnet. First me, now Brad. What is it about her? Her beauty? Her innocence? Honestly, it's a little insulting. *I* put in the work—learning her routines, syncing my schedule with hers, and, of course, monitoring her emails. It's called commitment. Brad, meanwhile, just stumbles back into her life uninvited, no finesse, no strategy. It's amateur hour, and I'm offended by the association.

I'll have to deal with him at some point...preferably before he escalates his creepy lurking into *actual* danger. Not because I'm worried about competition, but because *I* am the gold standard in this obsessive dynamic. If anyone's going to be the shadow in her life, it's me. Not him.

That's a problem for later. Right now, my focus is where it belongs: Jessica. I pull up the app on my phone, the familiar hiss of static crackling before the microphone connects. The first sound I hear guts me.

Jessica. Crying.

Muffled, shuddering sobs, like her face is shoved into a pillow to stifle the sound. My entire body tenses, a knot of despair tightening in my chest. Unable to bear it, I half rise from my chair, ready to sprint up twenty-seven flights of stairs, break down Monica's door, and take her in my arms.

I sit back down when I hear Monica's groggy voice. "Jess? What's wrong?"

At least she isn't alone.

I've never met Monica, though Jessica had planned to introduce us before...well, before the tracker debacle. Still, from what I've overheard through the earrings, I like her. She's feisty and clearly loyal to Jessica.

Jessica sniffles, her voice trembling. "I didn't mean to wake you. Sorry."

"I wasn't asleep yet," Monica replies gently. "What's going on? Why are you crying—again? Scratch that. It's West, isn't it? Are you missing him?"

Miss me. Please God, say you miss me.

I hold my breath, leaning closer to the phone.

"N-no," Jessica stammers, and I hear the lie in her voice. It wavers, breaking at the edges. "It's...I got some news today. I was going to tell you at dinner, but then I decided to think on it."

"What news?" Monica presses.

Jessica hesitates. "Remember that job I applied for in New York? The first one?"

"The one near Sarah's apartment?"

"Yeah." Jessica sighs. "The one I really wanted."

"What about it? I thought they already rejected you," Monica asks cautiously, like she doesn't want to dig up old wounds that might make Jessica even sadder.

"They did," Jessica says, exhaling shakily. "Months ago. But today the administrator called. The woman they hired, an internal candidate, her husband's job got transferred to California. She had to back out, and I'm next in line."

"You got the job?" Monica doesn't sound any more excited about this idea than I am.

Go, Monica. Talk Jess out of it!

Jessica's voice cracks. "They want me to start in two weeks."

Too soon.

My stomach drops, and panic spreads, burning like a firestorm through my chest. Two weeks? How am I supposed to fix this mess in two weeks?

A pause, which I guess means Monica is gathering her thoughts. When she talks again, her voice rings with false enthusiasm. "That's great, right? You wanted to go to New York? To be with Sarah?"

Jessica cries harder, not bothering to hide it now. There's rustling sounds, and when Monica speaks again her voice is louder, like she's moved closer to comfort Jessica.

"Hey, Jess. Shh. It'll be okay."

"Nothing's okay," Jessica chokes out. "You're right. I should be happy. This is exactly what I wanted. But *he's* ruined it."

"Who?" asks Monica. "West?"

I perk up at the mention of my name and press the phone closer to my ear, praying no one comes downstairs right now.

"I—I should be excited, ready to go," Jessica says, her voice breaking, "but you know what my first thought was? When they told me?"

"What?" Monica asks.

"I thought about *him*. How would I see him if I'm in New York? How would we work things out if I'm so far away?"

A flicker of warmth sparks in my chest. *She still cares about me,* I think with a smile.

Jessica gets louder, anger vibrating in her words. "Can you believe that, Monica? That I'd let *him*—that asshole—invade my thoughts? He put a tracker in me, for God's sake!"

Not smiling now.

The warmth vanishes, replaced by a cold, sinking weight.

Monica's voice is soft, hesitant. "Maybe it means something? That you thought of him?"

"It means he's brainwashed me into thinking he's human when he's not. He's a *monster*."

My grip on the phone tightens at her words.

Am I selfish, obsessive, possessive? Yes.

Am I irrevocably fucked-up from my past? Also, yes.

Am I a monster?

Ten months ago, I would've agreed with her. I'd have worn the label proudly. But not anymore. Not since meeting Jessica. Loving her. She taught me that I do have a soul, one that's shredding itself apart at the thought of her moving to New York.

Their conversation fades into background noise. I can't focus. My mind is already spinning, frantically crafting a plan to reclaim her love.

To make sure Jessica stays *mine*.

Jessica

Monica convinces me to go out for drinks. She says I only have one week of break left, and I should live it up. That the only way to get over West is to move on. Go out and flirt. Remind myself that there are other men in the world.

I have no desire to move on. No motivation to let another man into the space West left vacant, but I go along with her plan. She's been wonderful, letting me sleep on her couch and mope. I owe her since I've ruined her crazy active love—or should I say lust—life. The least I can do is go out with her.

The bar downtown is dark and loud, full of bodies crammed together on a Friday night. We take our place at a table in the corner, falling easily into our pre-West routine. Within minutes, a couple of guys approach and offer to buy us drinks. We accept. They sit down and talk to us. The man I speak with is named Mike. With brown hair and light brown eyes, he seems like a nice guy. We laugh over shared trash TV shows that we like and commiserate over the state of the environment. When I ask if he likes to read and he says no, I try to ignore the jolt of disappointment, the comparison to West that springs immediately to my mind, but it's hard.

I find that my gaze drifts over Mike's head, searching for dark hair and piercing gray eyes. It gets so bad that at one point Mike asks if I'm expecting someone. I flush, choking on my sip of wine, and sputter my denial. The night wears on. Mike and his friend leave, only to be replaced by another pair of men and then another.

Monica goes to the bar and gets waylaid by a tall, handsome, blond man, just her type, while I'm left alone to fend off several men who approach with cheesy pick-up lines. Already tipsy and on a fast train to drunk, I decline. I have a feeling that if I let myself get wasted tonight, it'll end up with me crying on some man's shoulder about West and how much I miss him. That wouldn't be fair to anyone, so when 1:00 a.m. hits and the room has a shiny, spinning haze to it, I decide to call it quits. Weaving slightly, I make my way to Monica, who's now licking her way up the blond dude's neck with complete disregard for the astonished stares around her.

"Monica," I say when I reach her, followed by a louder, "Monica! Get your tongue out of his ear."

She disengages herself from the man and swings her gaze my way. "What? Are you okay, Jess?"

"Fine. I want to go home, though. Don't worry. I can walk by myself."

She squints at me like she's trying to separate out exactly who I am. Drunk Monica is just as formidable as sober Monica. I brace myself to argue, determined she won't ruin her night because of me.

"I'll come too. I don't want you to go alone." She casts a look filled with longing at the blondie, who stares at her enraptured, like she's a goddess brought to life.

I roll my eyes, used to Monica's effect on men. Poor bastard. She'll sleep with him tonight and then never see him again. Even fresh off my disaster with West, I'd love to see Monica finally settle down with someone. She says that's never going to happen. That she's not the monogamous type. I disagree. After all, she's been my faithful best friend for over fifteen years.

"It's okay," I reassure her—desperate to be gone, far away from here. "It's only two blocks to your place. I can make it home myself."

The blond guy caresses her arm and kisses her neck. Monica's eyes drift closed, and a pleased smile curls her lips. "Are you sure?" she mumbles, her breath hitching as he sucks on her earlobe.

Watching Monica only makes me miss West more, so I reassure her that I'll be fine and beat a hasty retreat to the door.

Once I'm outside, a warm spring breeze lifts the hair off my face. I let out a relieved sigh and raise my arms to let it wash over me, drying the sweat from being in that packed bar. The scent of flowers drifts over from a planter by the door, carried on the wind. The noise of the city hums around me. Laughter drifts out from the open door, a car drives by with its bass blasting, and in the distance someone plays a saxophone, the timbre mournful. I absorb the sounds, the breeze, the sweet scent. The familiarity of it all soothes me, draining the tension that's been building all night.

"God, you're beautiful," says an all-too-familiar voice from the shadows.

My heart falters, fumbles. I gasp and spin around to see West leaning against the wall of the bar, over by the alley. He's stunning, wearing neatly pressed slacks and a blue button-down. His dark hair is swept back from his face. His cheeks are hollowed, like he's lost weight. His eyes are locked on me, his mouth twisted with melancholy and longing.

"You're like an angel, an apparition with your arms up and your head back. I thought for a minute you were going to cast a spell, to call down the moon or the stars to do your bidding."

I pause, wondering what's got into him. It's not like West to wax poetic.

He continues in that same wistful, melodic way, "Do you know what it was like? Standing out here watching all those men court you? Fawn over you while you smiled up at them? Can you possibly understand what torture that was? How much it *hurt*?"

Something feral slides into his tone, and the first stirrings of fear rise from the deepest recesses of my brain. The parts that used to run from the wildebeests, the saber-toothed tiger.

"You were watching me?" I ask shakily, already knowing the answer.

He pushes off the wall and stalks my way. "I'm *always* watching you, Jessica."

Those words should be a red flag. They should make me reach for the pepper spray in my purse. But they don't.

Instead, they make my breath quicken and my body heat.

He's reached me now. He holds his hand out to me, his eyes mesmerizing, his scent intoxicating. "Come with me, pretty girl. I need to talk to you."

Wine swirls through my bloodstream, lowering my inhibitions. I let him lead me to the alley like a lamb to slaughter. The moment we're cloaked in the shadows, he backs me up against the rough brick wall. The cool surface presses into my spine as his body closes in, warm and solid, a cage I don't have the strength, or maybe the will, to escape.

"Jess, Jessica. I miss you so much," he whispers huskily in my ear.

There's the hint of alcohol on his breath, something smokey like whiskey or bourbon. Fear trickles down my spine. West rarely drinks. He hates to lose control.

"Have—have you been drinking?" I ask.

A sigh whispers over my skin. "This is what you do to me. You drive me to this." His lips are inches from my neck. Suddenly they're on me, warm and consuming. He kisses down my shoulder and over my collarbone. My body arches toward him, and I moan.

We shouldn't... is what my rational mind says, but my body gives it a big fuck you and acts on its own accord. My hands rise and tangle in his hair. Temporarily insane, I pull his mouth up to mine and kiss him. He responds instantly, shifting himself so he's between my legs, his erection pressed to my core. West licks into my mouth with greedy open kisses. We're hasty and clumsy, frantic to get closer. Teeth clash, and our noses collide.

"Please, Jess," West says into my mouth. "Please come home."

"That's not my home." My heart pounds in my ears as his hands roam my body, running over my shoulders, my breasts. "I'm angry at you," I gasp as he reaches into my shirt and runs a finger over my pebbled nipple. "You tricked me, lied to me." My sanity frays with each touch. I reach deep inside, try to hold onto my fury. Without conviction, I tell him, "I hate you."

"Be mad at me, hate me. I don't care." His fingers trail down my ribs. "Hate me at breakfast, hate me while you sleep next to me, hate me when I'm deep inside you making you scream. You can hate me all you want, just do it at home. Please. *Come home.*"

He unbuttons my pants, pulls down my zipper. I'm paralyzed with desire, unable to stop him.

"Do you want me to beg? Is that what you want? To be on my knees for you?" Shocked, I watch as West slides to the ground, taking my pants down with him. He looks up at me, an expression of pure devotion on his handsome face. "I'll bow to you, worship you."

He leans forward and licks between my legs. His tongue expertly lands on my sensitive clit, and I moan so loudly it bounces off the buildings around us. West takes the sound for the encouragement it is. He pulls my legs wider and places his head between my already-wet thighs. His hands reach around to grip my ass as he licks the length of my slit, concentrating extra-long on the front. He sucks on my clit, licks it, and sucks again.

My hands drop to twist into his hair as I guide him to the place that feels the best. I half-scream in pleasure as he draws my clit between his teeth and bites down gently at the same time that he slips two fingers into me. He's moving, using his fingers to pump into me and his tongue to lap at my clit. I breathe in ragged gasps and groans, my pelvis rocking madly to the fast pace he sets.

A tiny part of my mind warns that this is stupid. We're in an alley next to a popular bar. I'm naked from the waist down. West is kneeling with his nice slacks on the dirty, trash-strewn ground. Anyone could walk by and see us. We should stop. We're being completely idiotic.

That's what I think, but my body doesn't care. It's missed him, my beautiful broken boy. Missed his company, his touch. I come alive when he's with me, like I've been living underwater, drowning, the entire time we were apart, and now I can finally breathe.

He's moving faster, using his entire mouth to rub against me. His tongue probes into my opening, joining with his fingers. My orgasm is a tsunami that washes over my body from head to toe. I scream as I come, a guttural sob of ecstasy. My hands grip West so hard, I'm sure I pull out some hair. Aftershocks rack my body, almost as intense as my orgasm.

West rises and tugs up my underwear, followed by my pants. He kisses me open-mouthed so I can taste myself. The salty earthiness of my essence is all over his tongue.

He grips my shoulders and looks me in the eyes. "I love you, Jessica. I'll love you forever. Please, I'm begging you, don't move to New York."

My addled brain takes a few minutes to process his words. "New York?"

I see the second he realizes his mistake. His eyes widen, and his nostrils flare.

My hands regain their strength. I push him away, needing space to figure out what he just said.

"How do you know about New York? I only told Monica, and she wouldn't tell you."

West reaches out to me. "Uh—you must have mentioned it to me. That's how I know."

Thinking hard, I shake my head slowly. "No. I never said anything about it to you or to anyone besides Monica." A sharp inhalation. My mouth falls open.

"Are you—did you—are you *spying* on me? *Again?* After everything? That's the only way you could have known about that job offer."

"What!? No—no—I, um. You told me."

"I did *not*! I never mentioned it." I step away from him until my back bangs against the wall. "Tell me how you know!" I demand. "Did you monitor my emails? Bug my phone? What is it?"

"No. No. I didn't." West looks me straight in the face and lies to me. I'm certain of it. He's lying. There's no other way he could have known.

Does he think I'm stupid?

Does he have zero respect for me?

He frames my face with his large hands and moves in to kiss me. Right before his lips meet mine, I say it.

"*Cupcake.*"

He reels back like I punched him, his face pale, horror-stricken.

"Cupcake?" he repeats hoarsely.

I'm crying, tears streaming down my face, as our reality punches me in the gut. I can't trust him. That's why I said it—the safe word. I didn't say it when he was taking my body, but I say it now, when he's taking my heart, ripping it out with his deceit and treachery.

"Cupcake!" I scream at him. He recoils at the word like it's a physical thing, a sword, a knife, a bullet.

"Cupcake. Stay away from me, Adam. We're through. I mean it. I'm done." I gather my unbuttoned pants in one hand. "You've lied to me for the last time. I never want to see you ever again."

Sobbing, unable to breathe, I shove past him and run. The word tears from my throat one last time, a final good-bye.

"*Cupcake!*"

Chapter Eighteen

Adam

She finally did it.

There's a roaring in my head, like all the cruel and hurtful words that have ever been said to me are being repeated now but not whispered or spoken softly. No. They're screamed, every one of them shouted simultaneously in a symphony of torment. My mother's voice is loudest.

Piece of shit.

Ruined my life.

Who could ever love you?

Of all the terrible words I've heard in my life, including the ones my mother spoke, none can compare to this.

None of them matter.

Except this word.

Cupcake.

The worst of them all because…it's not just a word.

It's the end.

Jessica

Saturday—no West.
Sunday—no West.
Monday—no West.
Tuesday—no West
Wednesday, Thursday, Friday, Saturday, Sunday—no West.
He's not here.
Not watching. Not spying.
Not laughing.
Not kissing me until I see stars.
Just...gone.
This is what I asked for, so why am I so fucking miserable?

Chapter Nineteen

J essica

"What do'ya mean you're leaving?" asks Milo in the front of the classroom. His bewildered expression punches a hole in my chest.

Kieke won't look at me. She stares out of the window and dashes tears away with an angry swipe.

Ari, usually so sweet and mild-natured, glares at me, his thick brows slashing downward. "I don't get it. You always say how important we are to you, but now you're leaving? There's only two months left before summer. Can't you at least finish out the year?"

Nick and Cheri hold hands, like they need each other's support to weather this storm, but, then again, they're always holding hands. I've had to tell them to stop nearly every day since they started going out. Today, I don't have the heart to separate them.

I scrub my hands over my face, already exhausted, and it's only 9:00 a.m.

Kent Wilson hadn't been any better than these kids when I handed in my resignation earlier this morning. He'd basically had the same reaction.

"*No*. Take it back." He'd slapped the paperwork onto his desk and shoved it toward me, like he was rejecting it. "Why would you quit? Your parents taught at this school."

"Because the school in New York offered me the assistant principal position," I explained patiently. "You know, the job I applied for here but didn't get?"

Red climbed his neck. "Listen, Jessica, I have a lot of clout with the school board. I'm sure they'll promote you if I say the word. You don't need to leave."

Stubbornly, I set my jaw. "*Yes*, I do. I've giving you my two-week notice." I push my resignation back to him. "I read my contract and that's what's required."

"What're we supposed to do?" Kent exclaims with his hands in the air.

I anticipated this question. "I think you should have Julie take over my classroom. If you combine her period three and four Spanish, she should have time. She's been wanting to move out of the language department."

At least my friend Julie will get something good out of this mess. She hates teaching Spanish, but Kent forced her into it when another teacher left partway through last year.

Kind of like what I'm doing now...

"Is this because of that boyfriend? Adam?"

"No." I lifted my chin and lied, proud that my voice remained steady. "I need a change of pace, that's all, and I want to be closer to my cousin, Sarah."

Kent had tried to argue, but he finally surrendered when I showed him the terms of my contract. I'd had Monica read through it, just to double-check that I could leave with such short notice. When she confirmed that two weeks were acceptable, Monica said she was happy for me, but her voice had caught on the end of the sentence and I saw the tears in her eyes just before she walked away.

Tears like the ones Beck now sheds. "Who's going to help me prepare for the National Science Fair, Ms. Jones?" He sniffles, not caring that Adrian in the back row is laughing at him. "You're the only one who knows how Newton's third principle affects the thermodynamics of jet propulsion."

I'm sure no one else in the classroom followed what he just said, but I understand it perfectly, a fact that makes me pause because he's right. No other teacher on campus can teach math at his accelerated level. I remind myself to talk to Kent about Beck before I leave. Maybe he can take online calculus and have it count for high-school credit?

I'm thinking that plan through, worrying about Beck's future, when I hear the door creak open behind me. Instantly, the students fall silent.

Twenty-eight teenagers.

Not a single word.

Curious, I turn.

West.

He strides through the doorway, all sharp angles and quiet intensity.

"Wow," Kensie Hamilton in the back of the room whispers as he passes her.

"Totally," Samantha Baker agrees.

I freeze for a second, stunned by this sudden collision of my worlds, then I spring into action. I intercept West in the center of the classroom.

"What are you doing here?" I demand. My fists balled on my hips, I strive to contain my anger at his invasion. No need to make a scene. I don't want the kids' last memory to be me yelling at my sociopath ex-boyfriend. Some of my ire fades when I see how gaunt West has gotten, how dark circles rim his eyes like poorly drawn eyeliner.

He easily sidesteps me with a curt, "Teacher invited me. Said I'm supposed to be inspirational."

I hurry to catch up with his long legs. "I didn't think you'd show up," I hiss at him, making sure to say it quietly, so the students won't hear. He's reached my desk. "Go home, West."

Flat gray eyes shift my way, cold on the surface but with wild emotions swirling underneath.

"Not much of a home recently," he says, the implication obvious.

For the hundredth time today, guilt floods through me.

No, I tell myself. *Don't let him into your head. This is all his fault. Not yours.*

My desk is front and center, the best spot for keeping an eye on the students. I stand next to it while West settles on its edge with his long legs stretched out before him. Even stressed, he's still handsome. A brown leather belt cinches his slim waist, and his crisp white shirt accentuates his broad shoulders. I can't help but drink in the sight of him, like I've been stranded in the Sahara Desert for years, dying of thirst.

"Hi, everyone." He raises his voice so it's loud and clear. "Can you hear me okay? Even in the back?"

The kids nod in response, silent and respectful.

"My name is Adam, and I'm a doctor."

I jolt, a reflexive startle. He *never* says his first name.

He continues, "I'm here to talk to you about your future."

The kids exchange glances, some skeptical, some intrigued.

"Our future?" Beck's head swivels between West and me, trying to read the situation. His forehead puckers with concern, and I'm reminded that his parents went through a nasty divorce last year. I smooth the tension off my face, not wanting to trigger his anxiety.

"That's right. After I talk to you today, I want each of you to deeply examine your life." West makes deliberate eye contact with each kid, one by one. "Figure out where you are now and where you want to end up. You're all unfinished books. Your pages are blank. Write whatever story you want. For me, my goal was to go away to college, then to medical school. You may wish for something totally different, and that's okay. Just be realistic about the amount of work involved and, if it's worth it, put in that effort."

A low groan from the back of the room, probably Nick. He hates it when he thinks someone is talking down to him. My theory is confirmed when his voice, squeaky from puberty, comes from behind me. "If this is one of those 'you can be anything you can dream of' speeches, you're talking to the wrong people, mister. Most of us won't ever leave this neighborhood."

West sizes up Nick, taking in how he holds Cheri's hand like she's the only thing keeping him steady. "You must be Nick, right? And that's your girlfriend, Cheri?"

I suck in a breath, impressed he remembered.

"Yeah, how'd you know?" Nick's eyes narrow with suspicion as he grips Cheri's hand tighter.

"Your teacher told me."

Great, now the entire class stares at me, trying to figure out my connection with West. I don't talk too much about my personal life, but I'd mentioned my boyfriend a couple of times. The girls catch on first. I can see it as they put two and two together. My private life just became front-page news.

Ari pipes up with, "What would someone like *you* know about getting out of here?" He makes a point of staring at West's expensive watch.

West is unfazed by the antagonism in Ari's question. Leisurely, he crosses one ankle over the other. "I know because I *was* you. I came from this school, graduated a few years ahead of Ms. Jones."

His eyes roam the room, lingering on the security bars that cover the windows. A muscle ticks in his jaw. "Didn't think I'd ever leave this neighborhood. Hell, I didn't think I'd survive it."

Now he's got their attention...and mine too.

"You lived here, big deal." Nick curls his upper lip. "Doubt you had to deal with the shit we've had to go through."

"Nick!" I reprimand him sharply. "Language!"

He drops his tough-guy act. "Sorry, Ms. Jones."

"No. It's okay. I get it," West tells Nick, then lifts his gaze to include the rest of the room. "I'd be suspicious too, if I were you. But I'm telling the truth. Not only did I go here, I came from a pretty crappy situation." West pauses and swallows hard, then drags in a deep breath like he's gathering his strength. I've never seen him apprehensive before, but he is now. Whatever he's about to say, it's going to cost him.

"You see, I was raised by a single mom. She was…troubled. Some days, she was the best mom in the world. She'd smother me with kisses, buy me toys, and make pancakes for dinner just because I asked." His lips press together. "But then there were the other days."

A slow blink, like he's bracing himself.

"She could be abusive. When I made her mad, she had a special punishment. She'd lock me in the hall closet. If I cried, she'd say, 'Why are you making such a fuss? It was only for a minute.'"

His voice shifts on the last part, mimicking her tone—high, dismissive, almost amused. My stomach churns uneasily. Nausea rises up the back of my throat.

"I was terrified of that closet." He stares at the floor for a second before looking up again. "It smelled like mold and mothballs, and when she shut the door the darkness swallowed me whole. I'd lose track of time in there. So I started counting. Just to have something to hold on to."

Horror pierces through me at those words. *Oh, God*. That's why he does it. That's why he always counts when he's stressed or scared.

West lets out a tight breath, shaking his head. "As I got older, I'd count just to see if she was right. If it really was a minute. Sometimes, I'd get to ten and she'd let me out. Other times, I'd hit a hundred. A thousand. Ten thousand. I'd count until I lost my voice, and still, the door wouldn't open…"

Kieke, my most empathetic student, clutches her chest. "She left you in there?"

West nods once. "It was the worst kind of punishment. Not because of the dark, or the cold, or the way the walls felt like they were pressing in. It was because when she finally let me out, she'd act like nothing had happened. Like I was crazy for being afraid." His voice tightens, and he swallows hard. "That kind of thing…it messes with your head."

I take a subconscious step toward him, then stop myself. It's quiet in the classroom. I hear every inhalation and exhalation of my students. Even Nick, perpetually unimpressed, appears shaken.

West blows his breath out slowly. There's tension in his shoulders, the weight of the story pressing down on him. "They took me away when I was twelve." His eyes flick to me. "A teacher saw the bruises and called child protective services. It took two grown men to drag me away." His voice tightens, becomes raspy with old pain. "I knew what would happen. She killed herself that same night."

A choked noise comes from one of the girls. My hands clench and unclench.

"She always said I was the only thing worth living for," he adds, his voice barely above a whisper.

West blinks hard, like he's waking up from a nightmare. "It wasn't until I went to medical school that I realized my mom was bipolar—that's why she swung so high and low." His shoulders bow under the weight of his sorrow. "If she'd been diagnosed and treated, everything could have been different—for both her and me." He sighs, a deep guilt-filled sound.

A few of the kids, mostly girls, cry openly now. I cry with them. A hushed sob rushes out of me as my world shifts. I see a new West standing there, the man but also the boy. Abused and alone. I barely have time to process that contrast before he starts talking again. He's going faster now, like the quicker he gets out this poison the less likely it is to kill him.

"After that, I bounced from one foster home to another—some worse than living with my mom. I was a mess, angry and reckless. I ran away constantly, living on the streets, stealing to survive, fighting. No matter how far I ran, I always got caught and ended up back in the system."

Silent tears track down my cheeks. I grasp the edge of the desk to stop myself from embracing him. I haven't forgotten what he's done, how angry I am, but even with that weighing me down, there's the urge to comfort West as well. To help him battle against the darkness his mother and foster families planted deep in his soul.

"The cycle kept repeating, interrupted only when I landed in the hospital. Stitches from a fight. Pneumonia because a foster parent refused to turn on the heat in winter."

"That's how it is," interjects Nick. "Some foster families, they don't care, at least the ones I've been with."

He and West share a look of understanding, like they're the only ones who get it. Like they've seen the same things, been to the same places.

Puzzle pieces click into place. Things that didn't make sense before, such as Nick's prickliness, his suspicion of authority figures. This must be where it all comes from.

West continues his story. "Those hospital stays were the only time I felt safe. It was clean and warm there. People were nice to me, fed me. It was always bright—no shadows creeping in, nothing to fear. That was when I decided to become a doctor."

He grimaces. "It was hard, though. I had almost no education. My life had been too unstable. Eventually, I applied for emancipation, got it, and moved here because it was the only place I could afford. I stopped fighting. Poured everything into my studies. A scholarship was my only shot at college, and I wasn't going to waste it.

"In the end, I made it. I'm a doctor now. I have a nice home, a car. I never go hungry. No one can take away what I've built." He shrugs like that's it—he's run out of things to say.

Kenzie raises her hand. West gives her a nod.

"So you're happy?" she asks. "You got everything you wanted?"

West's gaze lands on me, clouded with despair and longing. "Not everything…and I wouldn't say I'm happy. Not exactly. I'm comfortable, which is all I ever hoped for, but happy? No. I was for a while. I met a woman." He looks straight at me as he says the next part, like we're having a private conversation with no one else in the room. The intensity of his gaze makes my heart skip a beat. I'd almost forgotten how much I like having his eyes on me.

"She was someone I'd dreamed about for years." He gets a distant look, and I wonder if he's picturing it—young me. The one who walked these same halls. "The crazy thing is that the reality of her was even better than my imagination. She made me happy, so much that I didn't know what to do. How to act. No one taught me how to love someone the right way. I lost her."

These kids aren't dumb. Cheri glances at me first, then Kieke, Beck, and Ari. They hesitate, unsure how to handle this situation. One by one they turn to me, understanding I'm the woman he's referring to. I feel their judgment against me. Their sympathy for him. It makes me want to defend myself, to explain all the mistakes, the bad things West has done.

"Ms. Jones," Kenzie whispers at my elbow. She flicks her eyes to West. "Put the dude out of his misery."

"Yeah, Ms. Jones," Cheri says, her eyes wet from crying. "Give him another chance."

More voices join the chorus. Their words crash over me, but it's West's eyes that deliver the final blow. That deep, aching longing. The raw, unguarded way he watches me. Like I'm the last bit of light in his world.

God help me, I feel it.

The part of me that still loves him. The part that remembers the way he used to whisper my name like a prayer, how he held me as if I was something sacred. The way he let me into his world, little by little. I see now how hard that must have been.

But love isn't always enough.

Does his past justify his mistakes? Does it erase the lies? The betrayal?

I swallow, my voice quieter than I intend. "West?"

He straightens slightly, waiting. Something flickers in his gaze—hope or maybe relief that I'm willing to talk at all.

My mind wars with my heart.

Can I do it? Give him another chance?

I square my shoulders. Take in a steadying breath.

"Can I see you in the hallway, please?"

West hesitates, searching my face. With a single nod, he rises from my desk.

As he follows me out the door, twenty-eight pairs of eyes track us, the weight of their hope pressing down on me.

But this isn't their story.

It's mine. I get to figure out how it ends.

Jessica

Together, West and I step out into the hallway, right outside my door. There's a window so I can make sure no one's goofing off. I left Nick in charge, a move that had shocked the entire class but surprised Nick most of all.

"Me?" He pointed at himself. "You want *me* to make sure everyone behaves? Not Beck or even Ari?"

I nodded, confident in my decision. Now that I understood more about his background, I wanted to give him a chance. To prove to himself—and to me—that he could be responsible.

West clears his throat, drawing my attention back to him.

"What happened to all the lockers?" he asks, nodding toward the scuffed hallway walls. Where once there were rows of metal doors, there are now only remnants—chips, divots, the ghosts of old flyers and posters once stapled in place.

"Got rid of them. Too many kids hiding drugs or weapons." I scan the space, a dull ache of nostalgia creeping in. "It looks kinda empty now, doesn't it? Different from when we went here. My locker was just over there." I point across the way.

"I know." He shoves his hands in his pants pockets. "Mine was six down from yours."

"It was?" My mouth falls open, and guilt buzzes through me like a swarm of angry bees. "I'm so sorry. I feel terrible that I don't remember you."

He shrugs, but the downturn of his mouth tells me that, even though he wants to deny it, it hurts his feelings. That I never saw him back then. "It's okay. I mostly hid when you were around."

"But you saw *me*?" I ask, not understanding how he could know me so well from those days, yet I have zero recollection of him.

"I watched you," West admits. His gaze goes soft, unfocused, like he's looking backward into our shared past. "You had a mirror on the inside of your locker, the magnetic kind. Pink with purple hearts around the edges. After lunch, you'd always get out this little red jar of lip gloss and put it on. *Cherry*. I could smell it from where I hid around the corner. You'd rub your lips together until they were shiny and then smile at yourself in the mirror, as if you liked the person staring back at you."

He lets out a sigh filled with melancholy. "I couldn't imagine it, liking myself. I was so filled with anger and self-loathing. Looking at you gave me hope that maybe someday I could look in a mirror and not hate my own reflection. That was when I fell in love with you. I was seventeen."

He reaches into his pocket and pulls out something small, holding it between his fingers. A penny, old and dented.

"Here," he says, offering it to me. "You dropped this."

My brows knit together as I extend my hand. He presses the coin into my palm, and I bring it closer, confused about why he's bringing this up now. "When?"

"My last day of high school. You were getting into a car full of your friends, and it fell out of your purse. I ran over to grab it, thinking, *finally,* an excuse to talk to you. But by the time I stood up, all I got was a face full of exhaust. You were already gone."

The breath leaves my lungs in a rush. My gaze snaps to his. "You *kept* it?"

"All this time."

I flip the penny over. It's just as worn on the other side, so faded you can't even read the year it was made. "But you moved. College. Med school—"

"It moved with me."

My fingers curl around the coin, pressing it to my chest. He kept this tiny, insignificant thing. Carried it with him for years. A reminder of me, of a moment I never even knew existed.

"I'm sorry I didn't tell you the truth, that I knew you from when we were young." West's gaze drifts over the hallway. The scuffed floor. The dinged, dingy walls. "This place wasn't kind to me. I was beaten here. Humiliated. Bullied. It made me feel ashamed. I didn't want you to see me like that." He swallows. "I worried if you knew, you'd look at me differently. That it would make you turn away and I couldn't stand for that to happen." His eyes find mine again. Steady. Pleading. "I wanted—I want *you* to want *me*. I still do."

I draw in a slow breath and just *look* at him.

At the boy who once loved me from the shadows.

At the man who broke me.

At the man who, despite it all, still owns a part of me.

"You said something in there," I finally say, my voice quiet. "About not knowing how to love someone the right way."

West nods slowly.

"Love isn't about getting it right all the time," I continue. "But it is about trust. And when you broke mine...you didn't just hurt me, Adam. You made me question everything. Myself. Us. What we were."

He flinches, like the words land deeper than he expected. "I know," he murmurs. "This is the part where I'm supposed to throw myself at your feet, beg for forgiveness, promise to change, to be a better man. But Jessica, I love you too much to do that. You want trust? You want no more lies?"

I nod.

"The truth is, I won't change." He barks out a harsh, sorrow-filled laugh. "Believe me, I've tried."

His gaze flicks to my ears. "The earrings you're wearing, the ones I got you for Christmas, they have trackers in them. I can see where you are, hear what you say."

My breath escapes me. My hands fly to my ears, touch the cold, sharp-edged gemstones. So that's how he always knew where to show up.

He watches my reaction with no change in his expression. "I'm going to need you to leave them in, and if you take them out, I'll find another way to follow you because I won't leave you, ever. I used to think I had no heart, but that's not the case. I do have one, but it's in *your* chest. You hold my heart. You're out there walking around, getting into danger, being reckless with *my* heart. I can't tolerate the thought of something bad happening to you. The only thing that makes it bearable is always knowing where you are, that you're safe. It's the only thing that brings me peace."

I digest that information, appalled and yet somehow moved. Now that I know more about his past, it makes a painful kind of sense. He's never been loved. Not by his mother. Not by anyone who was supposed to protect him. His adult relationships have only been sexual—no attachment, no real connection.

This man, this poor scarred man, has been alone his entire life.

It's a thought that breaks my heart, rips it into tiny shreds.

I see now how loving me scares him. He's afraid he'll lose the only person who truly cares for him. Afraid he'll fail me the same way he thinks he failed his mother—when he couldn't keep her safe. Couldn't save her.

And this? The tracking, the control—it's not about ownership. It's *fear*. His desperate way of holding on to the one thing in his life that feels real.

I don't know what to do with that.

Do I give up my privacy to ease his anxiety?

Is that a fair trade?

West doesn't give me a chance to think it through. His voice, raw with emotion, pulls me back. "You ruined me, Jessica. When you were sixteen with cherry lip gloss. It wasn't your intention, your fault, I get that, but that's what happened. No one will ever compare to you. And now that I've had you, loved you, my obsession has only grown. You're mine forever."

Mine. Forever.

I swallow hard, those words settling somewhere deep in my chest, lodging themselves against my ribs.

"I hope you'll be with me willingly, as my girlfriend and someday my wife." His eyes darken, become stormy. "If you won't, I still refuse to leave. I'll be outside every door, every window. I'll follow you across the world if I have to. I can be the villain in your story. The stalker. The maniac. Or I can be the hero. The man who stands by your side through any storm. Either way, I'm with you. Always."

He sucks in a deep breath, as if all that talking has taken the wind out of him. He meets my eyes, holding me rooted in place, and says, "*That's* the truth."

The bell rings.

Doors are flung open, and students spill out into the hall. A sea of chatting, laughing, frowning, stressed, rushing humanity fills in the gap between West and me, forcing us apart until we're two separate islands. My next class walks by, heading into my room with a litany of, "Hi, Ms. Jones," "Hey, Ms. Jones," "I forgot my homework again, Ms. Jones."

West watches me, unblinking, with his arms across his chest, like he needs an answer immediately, but I can't give him that. Not yet. I need to prepare for this next class, to think things through.

The hallway begins to empty, each student finding their place, leaving empty candy wrappers and dropped homework assignments on the floor.

"I—I've got to go," I stammer, aware that West won't like this. He's a man who needs resolution as quickly as possible, but I don't want to answer in haste.

This is too important.

My happiness, my entire future, hangs in the balance.

His jaw tightens, but he gives a curt nod.

"I'll call you later. I promise." I turn my back on the storm clouds in his eyes and walk away.

Adam

The fireplace is lit, flames dancing with each other. Usually I find its warmth comforting, but tonight it mocks me. The fire hisses, crackles like it's laughing at me. It seems to say, "You lost her, you idiot. Today you told her everything, let her see how ugly you are on the inside. You think anyone can love you after that? *You pathetic piece of shit.*"

I wince. That last part—I recognize that voice.

Mom, on her worst days.

The memory of her saying those words makes my stomach swirl with fear and loathing. She'll never leave me, not really. I've carried her voice like a curse, every cruel word etched into the marrow of my bones. But when Jessica was here, it got quieter.

Jessica.

Jessica who I had, who loved me.

Jessica who I lied to, who I lost.

I wonder what she's doing now? Probably registering with the witness protection agency. Changing her name, dying her hair, anything to shake me off her trail. It won't work, though. I meant what I said in the hallway. I'll follow her to the ends of the earth.

There's a click from the doorway. I turn just as she steps in. Rosy-cheeked, pale hair glowing, reflecting the flames. Such a fucking vision that I almost buckle to my knees.

"Jess." Wonder bleeds into my voice.

She stares at the floor. Awkwardly standing in the doorway like she needs permission to enter what I already think of as her home.

"You didn't change the door lock," she says quietly. "My thumbprint still works."

My chest aches. I make my voice as soft and nonthreatening as possible. She's like a butterfly perched on the edge of a flower. A strong breeze might send her fluttering away.

"I'll never change it. You're always welcome here. Come in." I beckon, waving her toward where I sit on the couch, where we've read together, made love.

She approaches, moving so slowly it's torture. She trails her fingers along the kitchen counter, meanders over to the bookcase, pauses to look out the window. I want to scream, to run to her, but I don't. To calm myself, I breathe in through my nose and out through my mouth, hoping this is her stalling, her hesitating so she can make the right decision.

Finally, she stops a few feet away. Out of arm's reach. She eyes me. "I—I wasn't sure if I was going to come."

"Me either," I answer honestly.

My fingers flex against my thighs, aching for her warmth, her weight. I'm clenching each muscle. That's how much effort it takes to stop myself from grabbing her, dragging her to me, but if I move too soon, I'll ruin this.

She looks at the fire, silent for a long pensive moment. I'm sure then that she's come to tell me good-bye. My stomach clenches. I brace for her to break the news and run to the door.

When she finally speaks, her voice is soft. "I've been thinking a lot about love. About how it's not until you love someone that you find out who you really are. When you love someone, they test you, stretch the fabric of your morals, redefine your self-worth. Love transforms. Sometimes it brings out your best, or it can make you become smaller, a worse version of yourself."

I squeeze my eyes shut, not wanting to watch when she walks away. "Is that what you think I've done to you? Forced you to be smaller? To fit into the boundaries of what I want? I know I'm not the fairytale ending you probably dreamed about."

I dare to open my eyes to see her looking at me with her face drawn, serious. She takes a step closer. A single step, but it feels like an ocean of divide has been reduced to a trickle of a stream. One that we can cross to reach each other. Hope flickers to life in me, a fragile flame.

Her voice steady, Jessica says, "That's the thing. With you, I've never felt more alive. You've made me bigger, braver, than I ever thought I could be. You taught me the power of my own voice—how to speak up, to demand what I want."

"Isn't that a good thing?"

"It is…but then you lied to me. You violated my trust. You could have just asked me where I was going, where I would be. You didn't have to take information I would have freely given. I told you trust is important to me. My parents, they were good to each other, never lied to each other. I want a love like that."

The sting of shame is tempered by the knowledge that I would make the same decision again and again. I need to know everything about her. To protect her and to love her are the same thing in my mind, inexorably bound together.

Still, she has a point. "Maybe I'm the one who needs to work on trust. Trusting you to be okay without me being so overbearing. It's just—that's nearly impossible for me."

"I know. I understand you better now. About why you're that way." She blinks, her eyes suddenly filling with tears, which makes it twice as hard not to reach for her. I tuck my hands under my thighs to hold them in place, a last-ditch effort to keep control.

"I think I've been selfish," she whispers as the first tear breaks free and slides down her porcelain cheek.

Fuck this.

I'm not going to sit here and let my girl cry.

I surge to my feet, closing the distance. My hands find her waist, drawing her against me, grounding her in my hold. "What are you talking about?" I tenderly wipe the tear away before it has a chance to hit the ground. "You're the least selfish person I've ever met."

"No." She shudders as more tears fall. "I've been so busy thinking about what *I* need that I forgot *you* have needs too."

I murmur soothing noises and stroke her hair, so soft and smooth. My lips brush her forehead. "I don't need anything. Just you, Jess. All I want is you."

"No, that's not true. You need the same things I do. Trust, but also acceptance."

"Acceptance?" I ask, confused because who could ever accept someone like me? Tolerate me, that's the best I can hope for.

Jessica tilts her face to mine, searching for my understanding. Her hands raise and cup my face. "I see you, Adam. *All* of you, and I accept you. Your flaws, your fears, your need for control."

Her words strike deep, crumbling walls I've spent a lifetime building.

She pulls herself tall and with a note of challenge asks, "You want to track me?"

I nod. Swallow past the lump that's grown in my throat.

Her chin lifts. She stands there, so brave. "Then go ahead. Track me. Follow me. The only thing you'll see is me coming home to you. Every day. Every night. I'll come back to you."

For a moment, I think I must have heard her wrong. I wait for the catch. There has to be one. A second shoe, waiting to drop. But all I see is Jessica, steady and unflinching. That's when it hits me. She's not leaving. Not running away. Not abandoning me. She knows who I am, what I've done—and still she loves me. The breath leaves my lungs. I've spent my life being too much, too broken, too wrong. But this woman, this incredible woman, chooses me anyway.

My love. My pretty girl.

Her unconditional love—it brings me to my knees. There's nothing I wouldn't do for her. No length I wouldn't go to in order to keep her safe and happy.

I have no words, so I let my body do the talking. I kiss her, my mouth crashing into hers like a man starved. Hungrily, greedily, I drink down her gasps, her moans as she melts into me. Seeking the warmth of her flesh, my fingers slide under her shirt and slip up to her ribcage, then around her back where I flick her bra open with a single twist. I can't get her naked quick enough, and Jessica is just as desperate. We're clawing at each other, tripping over discarded pants and shoes. Until, finally, she stands dressed only in the glow of the flames.

So beautiful.

Gently, I lower her to the floor in front of the fireplace and cover her body with mine. I trail kisses down her slender neck to her breast. Her nipple stiffens as I run my tongue over it, flicking it and biting gently.

"Adam," she breathes out, arching under me, and I don't mind it, the sound of my name. I might even love it, as long as she's the one saying it. "Need you, please." She opens her legs for me, and I slide between them with reverence, like they're the gateway to heaven.

She's soaked with need, making it easy to push into her with one smooth thrust. I go deep as we both cry out in pleasure.

Her fingernails scrape down my back, run over each muscle, trace each contour, while she brings her lips to mine. I plunge my tongue into her along with my cock, and it's fucking perfect. She's perfect. With the next thrust, I grind my pelvis into her, let it stimulate her clit. She wraps her legs around my back, hooks her ankles together, and matches each of my movements with her own.

She's warm and wet. We move faster, consumed with need for each other. When her moans reach a fever pitch, I reach between us and rub her hard. She comes like a freight train, loud and thunderous, screaming my name...my first name. Her pussy clenches down, pulses, draws me deeper. My balls tighten, and electricity zings along my spine down to the base. One last thrust as she whimpers her submission. I let go and pump into her. Hard and hot. Jessica's coming again. Her second orgasm crests with mine, peaks into the sublime, and together we fall.

Later, when I've pulled a blanket over us and we lie together, with her head on my chest, I thread my fingers through her hair.

"You can still say cupcake, you know," I whisper huskily. "I'm not going to stop pushing you, at least in the bedroom...or exam room, Ms. Jones."

She chuckles, her breath warm on my chest. "I wouldn't expect anything less, *Dr. West*."

My breathing quickens. *Fuck*, I love it when she says my name like that.

"We'll keep cupcake for Ms. Jones and Dr. West," she murmurs. Then, softer, more hesitantly, "But no more cupcake for Adam and Jessica."

My pulse slows. A thick, heavy beat. I wait for her to continue, sensing this is something important.

Her throat moves as she swallows, and her voice is quiet but firm. "When we started, *cupcake* was a way to keep things separate. A boundary. A safety net. But I don't want that between us anymore. Not you and me. Not Adam and Jessica."

She searches my face, like she's making sure I understand. "In real life, we're equal. Both of us deserve to have our needs met. We don't need a safe word to protect ourselves from each other. We don't need an escape hatch." She inhales sharply, like she's steadying herself, then continues, "I trust you. I know you'll stop if I ask, that you'll never hurt me in a way I don't want."

The breath stalls in my chest.

I hadn't realized how much I needed to hear those words until she spoke them.

She's not afraid of me.

Not of my control, my possessiveness, my need to keep her, own her, protect her.

And even though I don't deserve it, she *trusts* me.

I tip her chin up, forcing her to meet my eyes, as I answer, my voice rough with emotion, "No more of anything that stands between us. No more barriers, no more walls. Just you and me." I pause, letting the words settle between us before I say, with finality— "Adam and Jessica."

"Are you scared?" she asks, her green eyes wide.

It only takes a second to answer because the truth is obvious to me. "I know fear. I've lived it, breathed it. I think there's always been a part of me stuck in that closet, no matter how old I grew. Until you, Jessica. You opened the door and set me free." I brush a kiss to her temple, letting my lips linger against her skin. "So, no. I'm not afraid. Not even a little."

She exhales a soft laugh. Curling closer, she presses her heart against mine. "Good. I'm not either."

The firelight paints her bare skin golden, and for a moment, I just look at her—breathless, overwhelmed that she's here. That she's *mine*. I take her mouth in a kiss, slow and reverent, pouring everything I feel into it. Then I hold her tight, like she might disappear if I let go. But she won't. Not anymore.

Because she chose me.

And I'll spend the rest of my life proving she made the right decision.

Chapter Twenty

Adam
Six Months Later

The wine cork opens with a satisfying *pop*.

"All right, you two. This is the last bottle. After this, I'm cutting you off." I pour a generous amount into Jessica's long-stemmed glass and then Monica's. I walk away, shaking my head as they giggle like schoolgirls. Three bottles in, and they're deep in some whispered conversation, Jessica's blonde head tipped close to Monica's dark brunette. I don't know what they're talking about, but, given the bright red on Jessica's cheeks and how she keeps dramatically fanning herself, I'm probably better off not knowing.

Monica is the raunchiest woman I've ever met. When she and Jessica start discussing the more scandalous scenes from their favorite romance novels, they make *me* blush. *Me*—a man with a dedicated sex room in his house—these two put me to shame. Not that I'm complaining. I've had the pleasure of reenacting some of those scenes with Jessica—with spectacular results.

As I make my way back to them, I overhear Monica saying, "I'm telling you, Jessica. It's creepy."

"What's creepy?" I ask, settling on the arm of the couch, right next to Jessica.

"That homeless guy." Monica takes a swallow of wine, then places her glass on the end table with a clink.

My body goes rigid. "What guy?"

"It's nothing. Monica's overreacting." Jessica waves her hands like she can erase the entire conversation.

"Not so fast. What guy?" I ask Monica, knowing I won't get the truth out of Jessica. She's as danger-prone as ever and just as oblivious to a threat. The best proof of that is the fact that she lives with *me*.

Monica leans forward, propping her elbow on her knee. "There's this homeless guy who follows Jessica around. He was outside the restaurant when we had lunch together last week, outside my condo when she came to dinner the week before, and just now, when I walked in, I saw him here, lurking around the corner."

"Old guy? Young guy?" I ask between clenched teeth, already suspecting her answer.

Monica tilts her head, thinking. "It's kind of hard to tell with the beard and dirty, long hair, but young, I think. All I know is he has crazy eyes."

"I'm sure he's just down on his luck," Jessica interjects.

"You've seen him too?" I work to keep my tone even, to not interrogate her. Instead, I ground myself by touching Jessica's earrings, the diamond studs I gave her for Christmas. She still wears them, knowing I can track her with them. It's her way of humoring me, and *God*, I love her for that.

Jessica shrugs. "Sometimes. Once he rode the bus at the same time as me, but he didn't get off at my stop."

I swear under my breath.

Fucking Brad.

Knowing how protective I get, Jessica is quick to reassure me. "I'm sure he's harmless. I feel bad for him, poor guy. You don't have to worry, Adam."

My grip on my wine glass tightens. "I'm not worried, Jess." I press a kiss to the top of her head. "You know I'll always keep you safe."

She casts a wary glance my way, probably hearing the threat in that statement.

"Did you tell Monica about Paris?" Quickly, I change the topic, not wanting her to dwell on Brad and his craziness.

"Oh!" Jessica bounces excitedly. "You know how I've aways wanted to travel! We got reservations at this incredible restaurant. It has the most beautiful view of the Eiffel Tower. Just a couple more weeks, and we'll be walking along the Seine, looking at the river." She beams at me, reaching over to squeeze my hand, her enthusiasm infectious. I grin back, knowing I've never smiled as much in my life as I have since she walked into my office for that first examination. The moment that set everything in motion.

Monica nibbles on a piece of cheese. "What made you guys pick Paris, anyway?"

"I owe Jessica some new underwear," I smirk and send Jessica a wink. "I keep tearing them off her."

"Adam!" Jessica exclaims, blushing the most delicious shade of pink.

The breath gets knocked out of me when, laughing, she jabs her elbow into my ribs. "Don't tell all our secrets, Marshmallow," Jessica whispers teasingly with a grin.

Most people would be shocked to hear about torn panties, but not Monica. She brightens and pokes Jessica in the shoulder with a red-tipped fingernail. "You didn't tell me that part! Jessica Joy Jones, you've been holding out!"

Jessica just laughs, making Monica giggle too. I bask in it, the sound of happiness, the sense of home. It's hard to remember how cold and lonely my condo used to be before Jessica filled it with light.

Later, when Jessica excuses herself to use the bathroom, I take a seat next to Monica.

"We're still on, right?" I whisper, eyeing the hallway to make sure Jessica doesn't catch us.

"Yeah, next Tuesday? Noon?" Monica confirms in the same hushed tone.

"Thanks for helping. I'm in over my head when it comes to looking for a ring." My palms have begun to sweat. It happens every time I think about my plan to propose in front of the Eiffel Tower. I'm going to put the ring on top of a cupcake, an inside joke just for the two of us.

Monica waves a hand. "*Please*. Jessica's been telling me about her dream ring for years. Don't worry. I've got you."

"Thanks, Moni—" I startle at a loud knocking on my door.

When I open it, Parker comes bursting in, talking a mile a minute, which isn't unusual for him. What is unusual is the distressed twist of his mouth and how his perfectly styled hair is mussed, like he's been running his hand through it.

"Adam!" he says in a loud, booming voice, and I flinch. I still don't like anyone but Jessica calling me by that name. "You have to help. I'm in trouble with a capital M."

"What're you talking about?" I step aside so he can enter.

"I just got served with a malpractice lawsuit." He throws his hands up. "*Me!* Can you believe it? Who would sue *me*?"

I roll my eyes. Parker has lots of reasons to be confident. He's smart, a brilliant surgeon, a YouTube sensation, and—much to my annoyance—Jessica has confirmed he's good-looking.

Although, when she saw my wounded pride, she quickly amended that statement by saying, "He's not as handsome as you, Adam. Not by a long shot."

Yeah, right.

I know a pity compliment when I hear it.

Even with all those things going for him, Parker's level of self-love is through the roof—sometimes a little too much.

He groans. "Now I have to get a lawyer. You know how much I *hate* those self-important, soul-sucking leeches. God! I can't believe this."

We've wandered into the living room. Monica rises from the couch and turns to face us.

Parker slams to a halt, his wide blue eyes fixed on her. I wait for him to make one of his witty comments, but for once in his life, the man is speechless.

There's a strange tension in the air, an electric crackling.

It's...odd.

"Um." My gaze bounces between the two of them. Parker is staring with his mouth open, and Monica has crossed her arms over her chest and is glaring daggers at him.

This is awkward.

"Monica, this is my colleague—"

"Best friend," Parker interrupts.

"Whatever," I continue. "This is Parker, who's a surgeon at my hospital. Parker, this is Jessica's friend, Monica. She's a lawyer."

Her mouth in a tight flat line, Monica angrily growls, "Yeah, you know...a lawyer. One of those *self-important, soul-sucking leeches* you were just talking about."

Parker's eyes widen even further. He stumbles toward her, which she matches by moving backward.

"Will you do it?" he asks eagerly.

Her brows knit together in confusion. "Do what?"

"Take my case? Will you represent me?"

And just like that I know—

This is going to be a disaster.

(To be continued in the next *Deeply Desired* novel.)

Epilogue

Chicago Tribune, page 9
Homeless Man Found Dead

Authorities discovered a homeless man dead in Lincoln Park last Tuesday. They've identified him as Bradley Wagner of the Chicago area. The exact cause of death is unknown, but locals report the man has a long history of drug and alcohol abuse. The family has declined an autopsy.

The End

***

Thank You for Reading!

Dear Reader,

Can I ask for a HUGE favor? If you enjoyed this book, would you take a quick moment to leave a review?

I know your time is precious, but your words have an incredible impact. Reviews help other readers decide if this book is worth picking up—but they do more than that—they also tell retailers like Amazon to show it to more people, keeping stories like this alive and thriving. Every review, no matter how short, makes a real difference.

YOUR reviews help small indie authors like me compete with big publishers. If you love supporting authors who pour their hearts into their stories, this is one of the easiest and most meaningful ways to do it. Plus it's FREE! The only cost is a few minutes of your time— even a sentence or two on Amazon or Goodreads is a huge help.

Beyond that, I genuinely want to hear from you! What did you love? What made you stay up way too late flipping pages? Your feedback helps me craft even better books—the kind YOU want to read. I read every single review, and I appreciate you more than I can say.

Your review isn't just a favor—it's helping keep books like this alive.

From the bottom of my heart, THANK YOU.

XOXO, Lexi

Click link or scan QR code to review!
https://a.co/d/cdG4Tvd

***

BONUS: FREE first chapter of *Paging Dr. Hart* by Dr. Melissa Dymond.

Have you read this swoony bestselling medical romance with suspense yet?

Available on Amazon and at most major booksellers. FREE to read on Kindle Unlimited.

Get it now! https://a.co/d/4KDi2bz

Loving him might give her a heart attack.

Chapter 1
Present
Columbus, Ohio

Everyone's staring at me when I get the first mysterious text message. Because of course that's when it would happen. Not when I'm home alone or in my car or studying at the library.

Nope.

It has to be right then, when I'm about to start my presentation. The Mercy Hospital medical staff gathers in our auditorium every day at 8:00 a.m. for our morning educational conference. We take turns giving lectures about interesting cases, using them to teach the medical students and younger residents about disease processes and how to treat them.

Today it's my turn—my very first time. I'm not nervous, though. I mean, sure, my mouth is the Sahara Desert and my heart has crawled up into my throat, but I'm fine. *Totally fine.* At least that's what I tell myself as I gaze out into the sea of doctors. They look back with expressions that range from vague interest to frank boredom.

"Ladies and gentlemen," I begin. Heads swing my way, and conversation hushes. I've set my phone to silent. It sits on the podium, next to my laptop. I take a deep breath, about to continue my lecture, when the phone screen flashes and the phone vibrates so hard it skitters across the wooden surface. The noise startles me. I jolt and drop the microphone, which falls to the ground and lets out a squeal of feedback, like it's crying about its rough treatment.

Shit.

Heat warms my cheeks. I let out a shaky, apologetic smile. The audience stares back, waiting for me to get on with the show. While I'm on my hands and knees, fetching the microphone, I wonder who the message could be from. Hardly anyone ever calls or texts me. The phone is still vibrating rhythmically when I stand. Acutely aware of the crowd, I peer at the tiny screen. The text is from an unfamiliar number, but the image is all-too-familiar. It's a photo of the iconic Las Vegas sign. The one you see when you first drive into town, right before you reach the southern end of the neon-lit Strip.

"Welcome to fabulous Las Vegas, Nevada," it proclaims in bold, blood-red letters.

That's . . . odd.

I grew up in Las Vegas, but everyone I knew there is long gone. I scroll down. There's no message, no name. Nothing to explain who sent the picture or why. A chill shivers through me, the icy fingers of the past walking down my spine. I inhale a shaky breath and glance around, searching the shadows of the room, but find them empty. Nothing lurking. Still, foreboding settles low in my stomach, weighing me down.

With the audience watching, I can't react, so I carefully school my features. I need to nail this lecture. Hopefully, if I do well, it'll win me the Resident of the Month award. I've wanted that certificate, with its shiny gold seal, since I first started working here three years ago. It's physical proof that I've transformed. More importantly, I need it for the $1,000 bonus that comes along with it. I'll give this same presentation at a medical conference in a couple of months. It's an honor to speak there, one not usually given to residents. The money will let me stay at the swanky hotel at Disney World, where the conference is being held, instead of a cheap motel 30 miles down the road.

Another glance at the text stirs dark memories, which I bury. With a sigh, I set the phone aside, refusing to think of it again. It's time to focus. Luckily, or rather unluckily, I'm good at compartmentalizing.

I've had *lots* of practice.

"A 56-year-old male presents to the emergency department with blood in his urine," I begin. Methodically clicking through my slides one-by-one, I outline how the patient was diagnosed with renal cancer. A CAT scan appears on the screen. With my pointer, I demonstrate how cancerous tendrils extend from the kidney and worm their way up into the biggest vein in the body, the inferior vena cava.

"For renal cancer," I explain, "we use tumor staging to help define the extent of disease and prognosis. Because the tumor extends outside the kidney, this patient is stage T3c." A click later shows photos from the surgery when the kidney was removed. Nearing the end of my talk, I discuss the patient's treatment and what imaging we will use for follow-up. This man will get repeat CAT scans every six months to make sure he remains cancer-free.

I pause to catch my breath, since I've been talking nonstop, and survey the audience. Everyone's still alert, and most are paying attention, which is all I can ask for. These early-morning presentations are often dry. Even I've had to fight to stay awake in this dark room when it was someone else up here lecturing.

"I'd like to open the floor to questions now," I say. There are a few raised hands from the crowd, asking about the man's long-term chance of reoccurrence and treatment options, which I answer easily. Relief floods through me. The finish line is in sight. There've been no technical difficulties. I haven't stuttered or said anything embarrassing. I give myself a mental pat on the back and prepare to end the presentation.

That's when a hand shoots up into the air.

It's a man, about my age, with ruffled brown hair, dark straight brows, and a square jaw. He sits next to Dr. Washburn, my residency director and boss. There's something mesmerizing about him. Something difficult to define but makes it hard to look away. It's partly his eyes, which are stunning, an unusually light color, warm amber like a glass of whiskey when the sunlight filters through it.

I've never seen him before.

I'd remember a face like that.

I nod politely. "You have a question?"

The man's voice is deep, carrying easily through the auditorium. "Yes. It's about the tumor staging. You said it was stage T3c?"

"That's correct." I frown, wondering where he's going with this.

"I think it's actually T3b. T3c is when the cancer is in the inferior vena cava but goes *above* the diaphragm. T3b is when it stays *below* the diaphragm. In those images you showed, the tumor was below."

Flustered, my normally orderly mind reels.

"Um—give me a minute." Time stretches out as I frantically search through the notebook where I wrote my research to prepare for this lecture.

Someone in the crowd coughs. Chairs squeak as people shift. The projector overhead whirs, its fan turning on. My breath comes in brief spurts. Hands shaking, I flip through the pages.

Where is it? Where is it?

Ah. It's there in my handwriting.

T3b.

The handsome stranger is right.

Crap. There goes my award.

Heat rushes up my neck to splash across my cheeks. Humiliation gives way to fury. I'm mad at myself for making the error, but I'm also angry at *him*. Why would he correct me in front of everyone? Who even does that? I should have known. No man can be that pretty without also being cruel. Every eye is trained on me, waiting to see how I'll respond.

I swallow around the boulder in my throat. "It is T3b. I must have typed it wrong. I apologize."

"No problem," he says graciously.

Now, I hate him. First for pointing out my mistake and second for acting like it's not a big deal.

To me, it's a *very* big deal indeed . . .

Available on Amazon and at most major book sellers. FREE to read on Kindle Unlimited!

Get it now! https://a.co/d/4KDi2bz

***

Also by Melissa Dymond/Lexi Davis

- *Holiday Star*- a celebrity holiday romance https://a.co/d/53YUnxd

- *Holiday Wedding*- a holiday romance with suspense https://a.co/d/39b6gyh

- *Paging Dr. Hart*- a medical romance with suspense https://a.co/d/bvCcctp

- *Hold Me For Now*- a spicy dark romance novella https://a.co/d/6CDvmQh

***

Do you like games?

Me too!

There are 4 superhero names/references in this book.

Some are obvious and some are more subtle.

Can you find one or more of them?

Email me if you do at authorlexidavis@yahoo.com!

I have special prizes that I'm ONLY sharing with winners of this challenge, so email me your answer, and if you get it right, I'll send you a prize.

Let's play!

Chapter Twenty-One

Acknowledgments

A cknowledgments

Hello, Dear Reader,

The most important person I want to thank is YOU. There would be no book without you. Please know how much I appreciate you taking a chance on an indie author like me. Thanks also to those of you who leave a review, post on social media, reach out with an email or a DM, and recommend my books to your friends and family. Those extra steps make all the difference.

If I can be known for one thing as an author, it's that I write for you, my readers. It's your happiness I'm after. The ability to entertain you. Make you laugh, cry, or swoon. That's what I want, and I'll do anything to make sure you're smiling by the time you read the words "The End."

I'm fortunate that I have a talented team who help make this book a hundred times better. Thank you to my editor Lura Dymond. I couldn't do this without you.

Thank you to my personal assistant, Hayley Faryna, who has completely transformed my Instagram page into something gorgeous. Beyond that, she beta reads, strategizes, and occasionally talks me off a ledge. Thanks to Maude Levesque, who also helps with social media and is just about the nicest person ever. Mikala Beers is another social media genius and Sara Usera is a huge help with advertising.

Thanks to my beta readers: Diza Parker, Jane Litherland, Aubrie Lane, Celina Lyles. Your insight helped make this book better.

Thanks to book communities on social media, especially Bookstagram, BookTok, and BookTube. I love connecting with readers there! @authorlexidavis

**She came in for a routine checkup.
She left with a prescription for trouble.**

Jessica never expected her annual exam to change everything. But the moment she steps into Dr. Adam West's office, the air between them crackles with unspoken tension, awakening forbidden desires she's never dared to explore.

He should keep his distance. She should walk away.

But when her safety is threatened, West's protectiveness crosses a line—he demands she move into his luxurious penthouse. There's something about him—something dark, something that calls to her in ways she doesn't understand—that makes her agree.

Under his roof, boundaries blur and rules shatter. Late-night conversations turn into whispered confessions. Their fiery, physical connection transforms into something far more dangerous: trust.

But the closer they get, the more Jessica realizes—West was never a stranger. And she was never just another patient.

Now, she's tangled in a web of obsession and desire, where love and control blur.

When West's past and present collide, one question remains:

Will love save them... or ruin them both?

Deeply Examined is a **dark, forbidden** medical romance featuring a possessive, **morally gray** doctor and the **sunshine heroine** who challenges him. Prepare for **forced proximity, sharp banter, sizzling chemistry, emotional twists,** and **a love as dangerous as it is undeniable.** If you crave **grumpy vs. sunshine, touch her and ***,** and **high-stakes storytelling,** this one's for you. Expect spice—both in and out of the exam room. This dark romance ends with a **guaranteed HEA,** but be warned: it's **not for the faint of heart** and includes an extensive list of trigger warnings. Intended for mature audiences only.

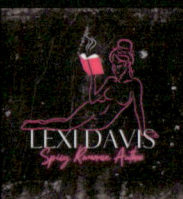

ABOUT THE AUTHOR

LEXI DAVIS loves long walks on the beach, drinking iced mochas, and writing smut. She believes in the ultimate power of love to heal and transform. She hopes her books bring joy to her readers and allow them to escape one page at a time.

ISBN 979-8-9925298-2-1

www.ingramcontent.com/pod-product-compliance
Lightning Source LLC
LaVergne TN
LVHW010319070526
838199LV00065B/5605